TRIALS

THE OMEGA SUPERHERO BOOK 2

DARIUS BRASHER

D1564590

To everyone who keeps going and doesn't quit.

1

Two of the five bank robbers had their guns aimed at my head. One held a pistol, the other a sawed-off shotgun. I stood facing the two masked men with my hands over my head.

I calmly said to them, "You fellas don't know it yet, but you're having a really bad day."

Robber and victim alike looked at me in disbelief. My fellow customers and the bank employees lay cowering on the floor. The three remaining masked robbers had their guns pointed at the prostrated people.

"This dude's crazy," the robber with the shotgun said. The shotgun shook a little. The man's eyes were wild behind his mask. He sounded young. Late teens, early twenties, tops. Around my age.

"Boy, I ain't gonna tell you again—get your narrow ass on the floor," the robber with the pistol said to me. He waved his gun menacingly.

"Here's a counter-proposal," I said. "You five drop your weapons, run out of here, and we'll all forget this unpleasantness ever happened."

"How about I drop you instead?" Pistol said.

"As appealing as your offer is, I must decline."

Pistol shook his head in disbelief.

"There's always some jackass who wants to play the hero," he said. "Well, I warned you."

Pistol pulled the trigger. The blast of the gun echoed off the bank's high ceiling. Some of the people on the floor screamed.

Pistol was a good shot. The bullet rocketed toward the center of my forehead.

It stopped in mid-air, an inch from my skull. The bullet hovered there, spinning like a top.

There was dead silence in the bank for a moment. Shock was in the eyes of both the robbers and the victims.

"Fuuuuuck!" Pistol said, drawing the word out in disgust. "He's one of those Metahuman freaks."

"If by 'Metahuman freak' you mean Hero, then yeah, that's me. 'That is I,' if you're a grammar snob," I said. Actually, I was merely a Hero's Apprentice. I hadn't passed the Trials and gotten my Hero's license yet, but Pistol didn't need to know all that. "And guess what that makes you? If you were gonna say 'screwed,' then you guessed right. If you were gonna say 'clichéd,' that's a good guess too. Who tries to rob a bank in person anymore? Ever heard of computer hacking? Which one of you is Bonnie, and which one is Clyde?"

Pistol wasn't as impressed by my spiel as I was.

He yelled, "Let him have it!"

All the robbers' guns turned on me. They fired almost simultaneously. It was like watching a firing squad. Unfortunately, I was on the receiving end of this one.

The sound of the multiple guns firing was deafening, like standing in the middle of a Fourth of July fireworks display. The sound swallowed the shrieks of the victims on the floor.

When the crooks stopped firing, the silence seemed equally

deafening by contrast. The robbers undoubtedly expected me to be lying on the floor, dead or dying.

I was not.

"Holy shit!" one of the robbers exclaimed.

I still stood, completely unharmed by the bullets and the shotgun pellets. The projectiles hung in the air, suspended around me in my invisible force field, like metal flies trapped in amber. I felt a rush of adrenaline. Winston Churchill had been right: There was nothing so exhilarating as to be shot at without result.

Jaws dropped as people stared at me. From their perspective, it probably looked like I was surrounded by a tiny asteroid field. Unlike the first bullet Pistol had shot which was still spinning only an inch from my head, the other bits of ammunition ranged from a foot to a foot and a half away from me. I had been showing off a little when I had let the first bullet from Pistol get so close. When stopping multiple projectiles, I hadn't wanted to cut it as close. If I had messed up and let myself get shot to pieces trying to show off again, Myth and Smoke, my fellow Hero Apprentices, would visit my grave to alternate between grieving for and making fun of me.

My raised hands, now clenched tight, burned the way they always did when I exerted my telekinetic powers. I used a tiny bit of my focus to use my powers to pull my hoodie's hood up over my head to help protect my identity. The robbers had already disabled the bank's cameras, but I wanted to make it harder for the people in the bank to remember me. I didn't have my mask and costume on as I hadn't expected to use my powers in a routine trip to the bank. Lesson learned. Maybe I needed to start taking my mask to the bathroom, too.

"Wow," I said, still in a calm voice as the bullets and pellets hovered around me, "every single one of you missed. From close-range, too. What are the odds? They really don't make robbers like they used to." I shook my head in sham sorrow. "I'll bet I'm a better shot than you guys. It would be hard not to be. Let's find out."

I concentrated, exerting my will. I flung my hands wide open, releasing the kinetic energy I had stored from stopping the bullets and pellets.

The hovering projectiles shot out from around me like shrapnel from an exploding grenade. They made a slight whistling sound through the air. They rocketed toward the five robbers, striking every one of them.

The robbers howled and cursed in pain. Three fell over. Despite the fact they were yelling bloody murder, I had been careful to hit them all in non-vital areas. I was trying to hurt them, not kill them. I wouldn't have shot them at all if one of them hadn't backhanded an obviously pregnant lady earlier when she had not hit the floor quickly enough to suit him. That had pissed me off.

I had already frozen the triggers of the men's guns to prevent them from firing more and maybe hurting one of the customers or employees. Now, I used my telekinesis to rip the guns from the men's hands. I floated them overhead, out of reach.

I picked the bleeding men up, holding them inches off the ground. Confused cries mingled with pained ones. They windmilled their legs and feet, but they couldn't budge an iota from where they hovered. They reminded me of Wile E. Coyote trying to run in midair after chasing the Road Runner off the edge of a cliff.

With flicks of my wrist, I sent the hovering men flying through the air. They all slammed back-first against the far wall. They cried out again in pain. Their feet still dangled off the ground. Despite their struggling against the force of my powers, I kept the men pinned to the wall like dead roaches in an entomologist's collection. Still using my powers, I ripped their ski masks off. Two whites, one black, one Asian, one Hispanic. It was the United Nations of douchebaggery. Their faces were contorted with pain.

Except for Pistol's, that is. He glared at me with hate in his eyes.

"I'll get you for this you little piece of sh—" Pistol's voice became an angry mumble when I forced his mouth shut with my powers. That little trick would come in handy if I ever had potty-mouthed children.

"Who knows how to handle a gun?" I said to the frightened people still on the floor.

No one responded. They just looked at the men dangling against the wall and back at me like I was some sort of wizard who might turn everyone into frogs. I suppressed a sigh. Though I was accustomed to being around Metas, not everyone had seen Metahuman powers in operation close-up. I probably scared these people as much as the robbers had. I wished I had my costume and cape on. People knew a cape usually signified a Hero.

I said, "Come on, speak up. I have the situation under control. No one's going to hurt you."

"I'm ex-military," someone said. It was the pregnant woman the robber had slapped. She struggled to her feet. Though otherwise slender, she looked like she was smuggling a beach ball under her smock. If she hadn't been pregnant, she would barely be a hundred pounds dripping wet. Ex-military, huh? It further proved you couldn't judge a book by its cover.

"Keep these knuckleheads covered until the police arrive," I said to her, floating one of the robber's pistols into her hands. She moved the gun's slide back slightly and checked the chamber for a bullet like a pro. Adopting a shooter's stance and holding it in both hands, she pointed the gun at the robber in the middle of my wall of Dillinger wannabes.

Emboldened—or maybe shamed—by the pregnant woman's example, a few other people got up and said they knew how to handle firearms. I dropped guns into their hands as well. The bank guard, whom the robbers had disarmed when they first came in, was the fourth person to get up and be given a gun. A portly man wearing a manager's tag on his blazer looked at the guard with obvious disgust. Though clairvoyance wasn't in my power set, it wasn't hard to guess the guard wouldn't have a job by the close of business.

By now, everyone was back on his feet.

"I don't know how to thank you, young man," the bank manager said. His fleshy face was flush from fright and excitement. "The police should be on their way. I hit the silent alarm before these thugs dragged me from my desk."

As if on cue, I heard sirens in the distance.

"Oh my God, you were amazing," cooed a blonde girl around my age. She flung herself into my arms. She pawed me like I was a rock star and she was a groupie. I let her, even though I needed to get out of here before the police showed up.

You are amazing too, I wanted to say to the girl. She was very attractive. Despite my powers, I was still a 20-year-old guy. It was hard to say no to a hot blonde when she wanted a hug.

Come to think of it, it was hard to say no to a hot anything. Even Metahumans were only human.

I had noticed the blonde before, when she had come into the bank after me. Like clairvoyance, detecting hot girls was not one of my superpowers, but it may as well have been since I was so good at it. This one was chattering a mile a minute.

"What's your name? Are you famous? Can I get your autograph? How about a selfie? Can you fly? Shoot lasers out of your eyes? What other cool stuff can you do?" she gushed breathlessly.

"Uh, my name's not important," I said, suddenly embarrassed by the barrage of questions, not to mention the softness of the girl's well-developed body pressing against me. "I'm just glad everyone's okay and that I was here to help." I could have told her my code name, Kinetic, or my real name, Theodore Conley, but I didn't want to blow my secret identity. I wasn't in costume, after all. The first rule of having a secret identity was to not talk about your secret identity.

Reluctantly, I gently untangled myself from the girl. I needed to get out of here. As an unlicensed Hero's Apprentice, it was illegal for me to use my powers unless I was under the direct supervision of Amazing Man, my Hero sponsor. An exception to that general rule was an imminent threat to public safety. An attempted bank robbery probably counted as such a threat, but I had no interest in arguing the intricacies of the Hero Act of 1945 with the cops. They might arrest me along with the robbers and let the lawyers sort it all out later. I had already been to jail once for unauthorized use of my powers some time ago when I used them to defeat Iceburn, the superpowered assassin who had been hired to kill me.

I didn't want to repeat my jailbird experience. As Myth was fond of saying, I was too pretty to go back to jail. If I did, I would wind up being someone's girlfriend, Myth had predicted. He had used a stronger word than "girlfriend," though.

I released my hold on the men pinned to the wall. Three collapsed onto the floor; the other two were able to remain on their feet. The people with the guns had them covered.

With the scent of the blonde's perfume on me, I strode to the bank's revolving glass door. A chorus of "thank you"s followed in my wake.

I hadn't gotten out fast enough. Flashing police lights greeted me as soon as I was outside. The street was lined with the red, white, and blue cars of the District of Columbia

Metropolitan Police. Multiple guns pointed at me. As Yogi Berra said, it was déjà vu all over again.

"Put your hands up where we can see them," came the voice of one of the cops.

"Sure thing, officer," I said, raising my hands yet again. Arms up, arms down, arms up, arms down. Who knew a trip to the bank would give me this kind of upper body workout?

I sprang into the air, using my powers to rapidly rise high over the heads of the assembled police. Their shouts receded below me. In seconds, the cops were mere specks below. No one shot at me. It was good to see that these cops didn't have itchy trigger fingers.

I looked down at the landscape below. South of me, I spotted the Washington Monument, the tallest structure in the District of Columbia. I had taken the subway to Chinatown to go to my bank rather than flying there, so I didn't know how to get home by air without using a landmark to orient me.

I shot off in a northwestern direction, toward Amazing Man's mansion in Chevy Chase, Maryland where I lived with him, Myth, and Smoke. I would have to do my banking later. The Old Man—that was what we Apprentices called Amazing Man, but never to his face—was a very wealthy man, and he paid his Apprentices a hefty salary. Thanks to that, and the fact I didn't have any living expenses to speak of as Amazing Man also provided room and board, I had more money in the bank than any 20-year-old farmer's son had any business having. In all honesty, we Apprentices should have been paying Amazing Man rather than the other way around. We had learned so much about being a Hero from him in the two years we had been his Apprentices.

As I flew homeward, I thought about how I had handled things in the bank.

Not bad for a South Carolina farm boy, I thought with satisfaction.

I was pretty pleased with myself. I had foiled the robbery, disarmed the robbers, all but gift-wrapped them for the cops, and had a pretty girl call me amazing, all without anyone getting hurt. Anyone except the robbers, that is. That jackass really shouldn't have slapped that pregnant lady.

Before I had become the Old Man's Apprentice, there was no way I would have handled the situation in the bank so easily. The Old Man himself couldn't have done a better job, I thought. Plus, I had done it with style. I thought that Bonnie and Clyde remark in particular had been a good one. It sounded like something Myth would have said. Maybe he was rubbing off on me. Though I never would have said this to his face, I could think of few better people to be influenced by.

This year's Hero Trials were scheduled to begin in a little over six months, and its application deadline was rapidly approaching. Though the Old Man hadn't yet said he would certify us Apprentices to apply to stand for the Trials, we hoped he would. The way I felt right now, I just knew the Trials would be a walk in the park. I'd have my Hero's license and be a full-fledged Hero in no time.

I felt twenty feet tall and covered in hair. There was nobody's butt I couldn't kick. I felt like I could single-handedly take on the Sentinels, the world's preeminent Hero team. To make it a fair fight, I'd even give them the first punch.

Then, something that had been nagging at the edge of my conscious mind pierced my cockiness. My hoodie felt slightly heavier than it should. As I continued flying, I reached into its left pocket. Something was inside. I pulled it out. I looked at a round, metal, brass-colored ball that was about half the size of a cue ball and a lot lighter.

Where in the world did this come from? I thought. I brought the ball up to my face to look at it more closely. I had never seen it before, nor did I know what it was.

Then I thought of how the blonde girl in the bank had so aggressively put her hands all over me.

Right as I thought that, the ball flashed, turning an incandescent white.

It exploded in my face.

2

Only two things kept me from getting my fool head blown off. The first was the fact I always raised my personal force field when I flew to keep from hitting birds, bugs, and other debris while I was in flight. The field I normally used when I flew was permeable to air so I would not suffocate.

The second thing that kept me from doing a Headless Horseman impersonation was the flash of light from the ball before it exploded. I wish I could say I was smart enough to have deliberately made my force field air-impermeable before the explosion, but I can't. The explosion happened too fast for me to consciously react to it. Rather, me making my force field air-impermeable in reaction to the light flash was entirely unconscious, a muscle memory reaction thanks to countless hours of Heroic training.

Even so, enough heat and force from the blast made it through my shield to sear my face before I made the shield air-impermeable. It felt like my head and upper body were plunged into lava. I almost blacked out. My control of my powers faded. I felt myself dropping out of the air like a shot duck.

Fortunately, muscle memory kicked in again. My barely conscious mind raised my personal shield again mere moments before I slammed into a tree branch. I crashed through it like a missile. Splinters went flying. I bounced off of and crashed through more branches as I descended.

I slammed to a stop when I finally hit the ground. Everything hurt. It felt like a giant had flung me to the ground, and then had stomped on me. I tasted blood. At some point I had bitten down hard on my tongue.

Flat on my back, I moaned in pain. Through bleary, half-shut eyes, I saw that I was surrounded by trees. I felt grass and damp dirt under me. Had I fallen into Rock Creek Park? That was the only place I knew in D.C. that had this kind of greenery. My eyelids felt droopy. Rock Creek Park was as good a place as any to take a nap.

Darkness closed in around the edges of my vision like a camera shutter. I fumbled for the specially-made watch on my wrist. The Old Man made us Apprentices wear it when we weren't in costume. With unsteady fingers, I flipped up the watch face. I managed to hit the tiny panic button mounted inside.

So much for being ready to take on the Sentinels, I thought hazily. *I got duped by a mere girl. She probably isn't even a natural blonde.*

That was my last thought. Then the darkness constricted around my eyes and swallowed me whole.

WHEN I FINALLY PRIED MY EYES OPEN, I LOOKED UP AT THE concerned face of Isaac Geere, one of my best friends. His code name was Myth. He was a light-skinned black guy a couple of years older than I. There was a jagged scar on his forehead that was a lighter color than the rest of his skin. It was a relic of a fight we had with Iceburn when Isaac and I had gone through Hero Academy together.

"That tears it," I said as I looked at Isaac. "I've died and gone to Hell." My mouth didn't quite feel like it was a part of me, as if it were operated by a ventriloquist. Plus, something was wrong with my voice or my hearing. My voice sounded like a whisper, as if uttered from far away.

Isaac's face parted into a grin.

"You're not dead," he said. "We're stuck with you for a while longer, I'm afraid. A shame. I had called dibs on your room."

I turned my head a little to look around. I lay in bed, but not the one in my room. I was in the infirmary in the Old Man's mansion. While the mansion was the Old Man's house, it also doubled as his lair and base of Heroic operations. A fully equipped, state-of-the-art infirmary was but one of the many things the mansion concealed behind its sprawling red brick facade.

I was in pain, but it was as if I stood outside my body experiencing it secondhand. Being in pain and alive was better than being in no pain and dead, however.

See there, Blondie? I thought triumphantly. *It takes more than a planted bomb to keep a good man down.*

No, wait—I was in fact lying down. Foiled again!

Darn you Blondie! I thought. If she were here, I would have shaken my fist at her. Assuming I could raise my fist, which I couldn't seem to do right now. It didn't matter. I was beyond caring. I felt like giggling.

Whatever pain meds they had me on, they were good ones.

Isaac and I were not alone. My other best friend Neha Thakore, known as the Apprentice Hero Smoke, was here. She was twenty-one and had a lithe, athletic body. Thanks to her Indian ancestry, she had olive skin and black hair. I happily knew from personal experience that silky black hair wasn't just on her head. Her hair was so shiny, it was the color of wet road tar. I had told her that once post-coitus, as the ancient Romans might have said. Those naughty dead devils. Neha had not taken my pillow talk road tar observation as the compliment I had meant it as.

Neha got out of the chair she was in and approached me. I thought she was going to hug me. Thinking of Blondie, I flinched mentally. Once bitten, twice shy. But, despite my recent experience with Blondie, I'd let Neha hug me. Neha and I had been doing a lot more than just hugging awhile now, anyway. I'd risk a hug from her.

Instead, Neha punched me in the thigh.

"Ow!" I said, though the punch hadn't hurt. I barely felt it. I wondered if street dealers knew about the drugs I must have been on. "Can't you see I'm on my deathbed?"

"You're not dying. Don't be a baby. If you hadn't hit your panic button you might've bled to death in the woods, though," Neha said. "Besides, your legs aren't injured at all. I wish I could say the same about the rest of you. You're lucky I don't punch you again. You scared us half to death. You should've seen the way you looked when the Old Man flew you back here. You were a mess."

"How long have I been unconscious?"

"Two and a half days."

Two and a half days? I would have thought it was more like two and a half hours.

"What in the world happened to you, anyway?" Neha asked. "After the Old Man brought you here, he sent me and Isaac to where he found you to investigate the scene. We found fragments from an explosive there."

I opened my mouth to tell them when Isaac held up a hand.

"Hold that thought. There's no point in you telling the story multiple times," Isaac said. He went over to the intercom mounted in the wall and hit a button on it. "I've got an update on Sleeping Beauty. With the bandages on his face, he isn't too beautiful. He isn't sleeping anymore, either," he said into the intercom. He winked at me.

"Be right there," came the voice of Amazing Man.

While we waited for Amazing Man to arrive, I had Isaac give me a hand mirror. As my arms still didn't seem to work correctly, I levitated the mirror in front of myself with my telekinetic powers. At least they worked.

From the neck up, I looked like a badly wrapped mummy. Long white bandages were on my neck and face. Where my skin was exposed, it alternated between being dark red and white and blistered. My eyebrows were gone, as were most of my eyelashes. Much of my brown hair was gone. The patches that remained looked like they had been singed in a fire. The whites of my eyes were no longer so; they were tinted red. Both eyes were swollen.

I never thought of myself as handsome. Looking like this, I didn't have to worry about anybody else thinking I was, either.

"Too bad Halloween's not approaching. I could license my likeness and make a killing on Halloween costumes," I said. Though I looked a mess, I didn't seem to care much. In fact, it was an effort to keep myself from laughing.

"It was much worse when the Old Man first brought you in. You were near death," Neha said. "After leaving you here in the care of the doctor on staff, he flew across the country to fetch Doc Hippoc." Doctor Hippocrates was a Hero, and had been the chief physician at Hero Academy when Neha, Isaac, and I were there. One of his Metahuman powers was the ability to augment and speed up the body's ability to heal itself. Doc Hippoc's powers had saved Isaac's life after Iceburn collapsed a building on top of us. "It's because of Doc Hippoc that you're not either dead or disfigured."

"I'm not disfigured, huh? Are your eyes working? I'm not going to win any beauty pageants looking like this. Unless my competitors are zombies. And I can't lift my arms. See?" I tried to raise them. Nothing happened. "Worst magic trick ever." That struck me as the funniest thing I had ever heard. I giggled like a schoolgirl.

"Dude, you look much better now than you did a few days ago," Isaac said. "You had third degree burns on your face and neck. Your skin was literally charred. You looked like a burnt marshmallow."

"Marshmallow? Is that some sort of racial crack?" Despite looking like I had escaped from a house fire, I felt frisky. I wondered if I could start taking all the time the drugs they had me on. Sobriety was overrated.

"Yes," Isaac said with a grin.

"As for your arms," Neha said, ignoring our banter—she did that a lot—"Doc Hippoc has you on a mild paralytic to keep you from moving around too much as your body finishes healing itself. Your torso got burned too, but not quite as badly as your face. You did suffer some nerve damage there, though. You also suffered some vision and hearing loss, but Doc said he repaired most of it and the rest would come with time. Since he said you'd be screaming your head off without it, he's also got you on pain meds. Something in the morphine family." Whatever it was, I highly recommended it. "Other than maybe some discoloration on your face and left hand, Doc says you should be as good as new in a few more days."

Despite looking like something undead, I felt fine already. I wanted to pull Neha into bed with me and show her how fine I felt. But it would be weird to do it in front of Isaac.

"No, no, no," I said to Neha, shaking my head at her, "not in front of the children."

Neha and Isaac looked at each other, puzzled. Their reaction to what I had said was not only the funniest thing I had ever seen, but the funniest thing I could imagine ever seeing. I started laughing so hard my chest hurt.

"I gotta get Doc Hippoc to give me some of those drugs," Isaac said to Neha. That just made me laugh harder.

I was still tittering when the Old Man came in. To be honest, just thinking of the word "tittering" made me start laughing out loud again.

The Old Man looked at me with quizzical steel-gray eyes. "I see the medication Hippocrates has you on is doing its job," he said.

The Old Man's real name was Raymond Ajax. As Raymond Ajax, the Old Man had made a killing buying, restructuring, and selling chemical and engineering companies, which was how he had been able to retire early and devote his efforts full-time to being a Hero. The Old Man was one of the greatest living Heroes, and I was proud to be one of his Apprentices. When we were in public and in costume, we Apprentices called him Amazing Man; when in public and out of costume, we called him Mr. Ajax; when it was just the three of us, he was the Old Man. We never called him Raymond. It would have been like walking up to the U.S. President, slapping her on the bottom, and saying "Nice tush, toots!" It was unthinkable.

The Old Man was dressed in a plain white tee shirt and gray sweatpants with a MIT logo on it. The Old Man had gotten one of his several degrees from the Massachusetts Institute of Technology. He had gotten his insanely ripped body from being a super strong Meta and decades of weight training. My arms couldn't even budge the electromagnetic weights he worked out with; it was a struggle moving them even with my powers. The

Old Man had gotten his white hair from being old enough to be my grandfather, though he was fond of saying, normally after one of us had done something stupid, that his hair had been jet black until he had started training Apprentices.

The Old Man was tall, taller even than Myth who was a couple of inches taller than I. Even casually dressed, he dominated the room the way a movie star dominates a scene. His muscles rippled under his shirt as he picked up a chair and put it next to my bed. He sat down, straddling the chair.

"All right," he said, "now that you're awake, tell us what happened."

So, I did. Along with telling them all about the attempted bank robbery, I also gave them a precise description of the girl who I suspected had planted the explosive on me. Eyewitness accounts from laymen tended to be shockingly inaccurate. I had read a bunch of studies on the subject during my training, so I knew that better than most. I was not a layman, though. If I missed any of the important details of what that blonde looked like, it was not for lack of undergoing rigorous observational training during my Heroic studies. I only left out that she had smelled like strawberries and that I had snuck a peek down her blouse. Neither fact seemed relevant, but both would make Isaac make fun of me.

As I spoke of the woman, Isaac rapidly made a sketch of whom I described. Isaac had become quite the artist. He normally used his artistic abilities to draw, paint, and sculpt various mythological creatures. Doing so helped him more effectively transform into them with his Metahuman powers.

After I made him adjust the nose and the bustline—in Isaac's initial rendering, the former had been too big and the latter too small—Isaac's sketch looked exactly the way I remembered Blondie.

Isaac handed the sketch to the Old Man. He looked at it

carefully.

"I begin to see why you would let this woman close enough to touch you," he said. If I hadn't been so doped up, I would have been embarrassed. "I can't say she looks familiar. The fragments from the explosive Isaac and Neha found haven't led to any clues. I'll check with the bank to see if they have a camera that wasn't disabled by the robbers. Maybe the bank captured footage of her. If not, I'll run Isaac's sketch through the Heroes' Guild's databases and see if I can identify her. I'll also check with the D.C. Metropolitan Police. They can ask the robbers they took into custody if the woman was working with them."

The Old Man sighed noisily. "If only a big-time Hero such as myself had some eager, well-trained Apprentices who could do this kind of grunt work for him." He looked at Isaac and Neha pointedly.

"He's speaking of himself in the third person again," Neha said to Isaac.

"I told you buying him that 'World's Greatest Hero' mug for his birthday was a mistake. He's gone and let it go to his head," Isaac said to her.

Isaac took his sketch back from the Old Man. Neha patted me on the leg with a smile before turning to walk out of the infirmary. Isaac followed her, but not before blowing me a kiss with a grin.

The Old Man turned his attention back to me once they were gone.

"Now that we have some privacy, I want to talk to you alone about what happened at the bank," he said.

Despite having landed flat on my back in the infirmary, I was still pretty pleased with how I had handled things at the bank. The Old Man probably wanted to single me out for special praise; he didn't want to do it in front of Neha and Isaac so as not to play favorites. I had my modest yet Heroic "aww, shucks, it was nothing" speech all ready.

What the Old Man said instead sobered me up some despite the narcotic glow I luxuriated in.

He said, "Theo, I'm concerned you don't have what it takes to be a Hero."

3

"Now don't get me wrong," the Old Man said, "you work hard. You never would have made it through Hero Academy if you weren't capable of hard work. You're smart, you're eager to learn, you enjoy helping people. On top of all that, you're an Omega-level Metahuman. You have the potential to be one of the most powerful people in the world. You've barely begun to scratch the surface of what you have the genetic capacity to do. Just as your powers first manifested when you were under stress, I suspect your Omega-level potential will show itself in times of great stress."

The Old Man shook his head.

"On paper, you're exactly the kind of person who should become a licensed Hero. The problem is you lack a certain something. Worldliness? Savagery? Toughness? You're just too nice, too accommodating? All of the above?" The Old Man shook his head again. "If it weren't for the fact I can fly as fast as I can and was able to both retrieve you and bring Doctor Hippocrates to you before it was too late, you'd be dead right now. If you become a full-fledged Hero, you won't have me or anyone else around to be your guardian angel. You'll have to rely solely on yourself and your instincts to keep you from getting seriously injured or killed. More importantly, the people around you will have to rely on you to keep them from getting injured or killed.

"The woman who slipped that bomb into your hoodie? You shouldn't have let her anywhere near you. She could have been with the bank robbers. She could be one of those anti-Meta activists we see more and more these days itching for a chance to have one less Metahuman in the world. For all we know, she works for whomever hired Iceburn to kill you. You know we never figured out who it is. He's still out there somewhere, probably still gunning for you for reasons we can only guess at. When you used your powers in that bank, you were a target: not only for the bank robbers, but for anyone who has a beef with Metahumans in general and with you specifically. But instead of keeping that fact at the forefront of your mind, you let some stranger in a volatile situation come up and hug you. Why? Because she looked harmless? Because she was cute? Because you're too nice to tell her no? I can't imagine Neha or Isaac letting that girl get close. They have a ruthlessness you simply don't. Sure, Isaac hides his under a layer of jokes and silliness, but it's there, like an iron fist gloved in velvet.

"And what happened in the bank is not an isolated incident. I've been watching how you conduct yourself as an Apprentice with some concern for a while now. What happened with the blonde girl is just the latest in a series of red flags."

My heart beat faster as the Old Man spoke. The worst of it was, I realized he was right—neither Neha nor Isaac would have made the mistake I had. Despite being doped to the gills, I felt like crying.

How I felt must have been evident on my face. The Old Man let out a long breath.

"I'm not saying all this to hurt your feelings or to upset you. I love you, Isaac, and Neha like you are the children I never had. You're a great guy, and I'm proud to know you. Your parents did a fantastic job raising you. I wish I had known them too. They succeeded in producing a very nice young man. And that's the problem—I fear you're *too* nice. Too nice for the task of being a Hero, maybe. You were literally an altar boy in the Catholic Church for how many years? Three?"

It was four, but I didn't trust myself to correct him without starting to cry. The Old Man didn't seem to expect an answer since he kept talking. "That kind of indoctrination is not easily shed. Hell, some of it shouldn't be shed. A lot of what the Catholic Church and other churches teach is a sound way to live in a civilized society. In a civilized society, it's hard to go wrong with the Golden Rule: Do unto others as you would have them do unto you. But Heroes don't live in a civilized society. We live in a world of often savage, godlike beings, some of whom are as likely to incinerate you as they are to look at you. Hell, some of them incinerate you *by* looking at you. In our world, we often have to do unto others before they can do unto us. My job is not to make sure you're nice. My job is to make sure you're a tough sonofabitch who can stand up against all the forces of evil and chaos in the world without getting yourself or someone else killed.

"There's a saying almost as old as the Hero Act: Good men don't make great Heroes. I'm not saying nice guys finish last, but nice Heroes do tend to wind up dead. Assuming they get to be Heroes in the first place. After all, the Trials have a high mortality rate. That is as it should be. It is better to find out that a potential Hero doesn't have what it takes in the Trials than to find out in the real world when the lives of countless others are at stake."

The Old Man finally paused. It took me a moment to find my

voice. I felt like my entire world—everything I had worked so hard for the past few years—was crumbling around me.

"Are you saying you're not going to let me stand for this year's Trials?" I finally managed to get out. I wouldn't be allowed to participate in the Trials without the Old Man's recommendation.

The Old Man let out another long breath.

"No. No, I'm not saying that. I didn't say anything before now about whether I would let you and the others stand for the Trials because I was concerned about you and what we've been discussing. I'll let you stand for the upcoming Trials. There's not much more I can teach you. The thing I fear you lack isn't something that can be taught, anyway—you either have it, or you don't. You've become proficient enough in the use of your powers that engaging in the Trials won't be an automatic death sentence for you. You might even be able to pass them and get your Hero's license. What worries me is if you continue the way you have, doing things like you did in the bank, you won't have a long life as a Hero. You've seen the statistics. You know we Heroes tend to not have long lifespans. Old Heroes like me are the exception to the rule. What we do is too dangerous for most of us to live long enough to retire to our rocking chairs and die peacefully in our sleep.

"Plus, I fear it will be a blow to Isaac's and Neha's morale if I don't let you stand for the Trials with them. The three of you are thick as thieves. You and Neha especially. I know you two are sleeping together. Don't look shocked. This is a big house, but it's not that big. I'm old, but I'm not blind; I'd have to be blind to not notice how one of you is always sneaking into or out of the other's bedroom in the middle of the night. I didn't say anything before because you're both adults and your nocturnal activities didn't seem to adversely impact your training.

"So yes, I'll let you stand for the Trials along with the

others. But, in light of my concerns, I'd ask you to think long and hard about if you really want to become a Hero. You're young, healthy, and smart. With all that and the discipline your Heroic training has instilled in you, the whole world is your oyster. You can do anything with your life. You could buy your father's farm back and take up farming again. Lord knows the world is not lacking in mouths to feed. If that doesn't suit you, you can start some other business. I know you have a bunch of money saved up that can be your initial capital. Plus, I'll help you with seed money. Or, you could go back to college, finish your degree, and then maybe follow that up with grad school. You could become a teacher, a doctor, a lawyer, an engineer, any number of things that don't involve you getting punched in the face by supervillains. Find a nice, normal girl to settle down with and have a bunch of babies and a good, long life."

I was completely taken aback by what the Old Man was telling me.

"But you're the one who talked me into training to be a Hero in the first place," I sputtered. "You said it was too dangerous for me and those around me for an Omega-level Meta to wander around the world untrained. Now that I've worked my butt off to get to where I am, you're telling me to not become a Hero?"

"I'm not telling you to not become a Hero. I'm telling you to think long and hard about whether it's something you really want as I have concerns you're not entirely suited for it. As for what I said when we first met, I said it was dangerous for an Omega-level Meta to be untrained because there are people in the world who would either view you as a threat or try to exploit you. Now, you're trained and have control over your powers. If you decide to have a normal life and someone like Iceburn comes along again and attacks you, you now would be able to take care of the threat. Even though you're not supposed to use your powers as an unlicensed Meta, the law carves out an exception for that when you're acting in self-defense."

The Old Man abruptly stood.

"Maybe I should have waited until you fully recovered to spring all this on you. But, you know how I feel about these situations: if there's something unpleasant to do, it's best to do it immediately. It hurts more to pull a bandage off slowly than it does to rip it off all at once. Besides, Hippocrates tells me you need to stay in bed here in the infirmary a few more days to fully recover. While you're here, think about what I've said. Let me know what you decide to do."

The Old Man walked out of the infirmary. I stared at his retreating back in shock, hurt, and disbelief.

The Old Man didn't think I was good enough to be a Hero. No, quite the opposite, actually. He thought I was *too* good to be a Hero. That I wasn't tough enough. That I wasn't ruthless enough. Isaac and Neha were, but I wasn't.

I chewed on that. After a while, despite the drugs I was on, I felt my initial hurt turn into anger.

Well, screw that! Like Isaac and Neha, hadn't I worked my fingers to the bone to graduate from Hero Academy? Hadn't I worked just as hard as they at being a Hero's Apprentice? Yeah, maybe I hadn't graduated at the top of our Academy class the way they had, but I hadn't graduated at the bottom. Besides, what did class standing matter anyway? Robert E. Lee had graduated second in his West Point class; Ulysses S. Grant had graduated in the bottom half of his. And yet, during the U.S. Civil War, Grant was the one who gave Lee a thorough shellacking where it counted, on the battlefield.

Hadn't I been the one to single-handedly foil that bank robbery in Chinatown? I had shot the robbers with their own bullets, for chrissakes. Wasn't I the one who misled the Old Man and my friends so I could alone take down Iceburn, the assassin to the Metahuman stars? Wasn't I the one who had avenged my father by crippling Iceburn?

On the other hand, wasn't I also the one who lay flat on his back because I had stupidly let Blondie get too close to me? I was also the guy who, when he saw Iceburn floating over my Dad's burning mobile home, naively assumed Iceburn was a Hero and asked him for help. I was the guy who had let Iceburn blindside me the last time I had fought him because I was too busy chatting with an old lady whose tire I had stopped to change. I was the guy who, just a month or so ago, had let himself get sucker-punched by a Little Person because I had discounted him as a potential threat. It turned out he was a Rogue—a person who used his powers illegally under the Hero Act, and therefore a supervillain—known as Mighty Mini. He had punched me right through a brick wall. If I hadn't had my force field up, the Old Man and my fellow Apprentices would have had to collect my remains with an eyedropper and tweezers.

The more I thought about it, the more I realized there had been threats I had discounted and opportunities to end fights I had missed while I was an Apprentice because I did tend to see the best in people. I did tend to give people the benefit of the doubt. I did tend to take people at face-value. The problem was, there were some people who did not have anything good in them to see; there were people who did not deserve the benefit of the doubt. I knew that intellectually, but I hadn't seemed to absorb that fact in my gut so that I operated on that assumption as a matter of course when I was out in the field.

Maybe, just maybe, you could take the boy out of the Catholic Church and off the small Southern farm, but you couldn't take the church or the farm out of the boy.

As I continued to recuperate over the next few days, all I did was think about what the Old Man had said to me. All that thinking time made me drag out and take a hard look at why I wanted to become a Hero.

Initially, when I first discovered my powers, I had no interest in using them or in becoming a Hero. It was too scary and too dangerous, I had thought. Well, I had certainly been right about it being scary and dangerous: the fact I lay partially immobilized in the infirmary was ample proof of that. But then, Iceburn had attacked me and killed Dad. I had been powerless to stop him. That was when I realized I needed training to track Iceburn down and avenge my father. I had defeated Iceburn, but I still needed to figure out who had hired him so I could bring them to justice for all the deaths Iceburn caused while trying to get at me. But in the process of training and defeating Iceburn, I realized I wanted to become a Hero not merely to seek vengeance, but also because the people I loved and admired—the Old Man, Neha, Isaac, and the other Metas I had met at the Academy—were either Heroes or on the path to become Heroes. Metas like Isaac and Neha were my family. They were the only family I had since both my parents were dead and I had no siblings.

And, even though being a Hero was dangerous, it was often fun too. Heck, maybe it was fun *because* of the danger. I had gone rock climbing with Isaac and Neha a couple of times, and I couldn't imagine it would've been any fun at all if we had been merely a couple of feet off the ground instead of high up on the face of a cliff. Maybe, like rock climbing, the danger inherent in being a Hero was what made it fun.

Plus, I got to help people as a Hero. Helping people as a Hero's Apprentice had brought me a joy far exceeding what I ever would have expected. Wasn't it Dickens who had said "No one is useless in this world who lightens the burdens of another"?

Was seeking justice for my Dad, helping people, and having a place where I belonged enough of a justification for continuing to risk my neck and become a Hero? If the Old Man was right and my lack of ruthlessness might put others in danger, were my desires enough of a justification for me to risk the necks of the members of the public I was supposed to protect?

The Old Man was right—it was a big world out there. If I chose to not be a Hero, I could do just about anything. The world could be my oyster. I had money saved up, more money than I ever would have imagined having just a few years ago. Plus the Old Man said he would loan or give me more if I needed it. Even more important than having money, my Heroic training had taught me I could do anything I set my mind to if I worked at it. I had learned there were two keys to success: setting a goal, and then working like a dog to achieve it. If there was one thing I had learned about myself during Hero training, it was that I was capable of hard work, more so than I ever would have imagined back when I lived on Dad's farm. And I had worked plenty hard there.

Plus, I could count on one hand the girls I had kissed. I could count on one finger the girls I had slept with. I had plenty of fingers and toes left, so there was a lot of catching up to do. Before I had started my Heroic training, my lack of success with girls had been because I was poor, I dressed like a homeless person, and I lacked confidence. Especially because I lacked confidence. Well, that and the fact I had looked like an anemic string bean. Girls tended to not get all dewy-eyed over guys who could fit into their clothes with plenty of room to spare.

Now I was far more confident. And, while I certainly didn't have the Old Man's physique, I now was bigger and stronger than I had ever been in my life. I had accomplished that by eating like a hog trying to put on muscle mass and by working out like my life depended on it because, often, it would.

Now that I was a richer, stronger, and more confident version of my old self, I could catch up on lost time with girls if I stopped trying to become a Hero. Almost every time I was around a group of people, I saw so many pretty girls I felt like a hungry man at an all-you-can-eat buffet. The problem was being an Apprentice was a jealous mistress who had me on a strict diet; I barely had time to look at all the delectables at the buffet, much less put them on my plate. If I stopped my Heroic training, I could date around for a while, and sow my pent-up wild oats. Well, the ones Neha and I hadn't already sown together. I was a healthy 20-year-old man; I had plenty of unsown oats left. Then, once I had gotten tired of single life, I could settle down with a nice girl, someone who would be the kind of mother my Mom had been to me before she passed away from cancer. I definitely wanted kids. I dreamed of one day passing on many of the life lessons my Dad had passed on to me.

It all boiled down to a simple question:

What did I really want?

Did I want a normal and safe life? Or, the dangerous and exciting life of a Hero? Then again, how safe was a normal life anyway? No one got out of life alive. Life was a fatal condition.

While I wrestled with those thoughts as I healed, the words from Robert Frost's poem *The Road Not Taken* kept coming to mind:

> *Two roads diverged in a yellow wood,*
> *And sorry I could not travel both,*
> *And be one traveler, long I stood*
> *And looked down one as far as I could*
> *To where it bent in the undergrowth....*

SHORTLY AFTER THE DOCTORS PRONOUNCED ME WELL ENOUGH TO

leave the infirmary, I went in search of the Old Man. Other than having to wear sunglasses in bright sunlight until my vision returned to normal and a slight ringing in my ears, I felt fine. Other than a bit of skin discoloration on my face, I looked fine.

I found the Old Man sitting behind the desk of his office. He looked up when I knocked on his open door.

"You're up and around again," he said, looking pleased.

"I am." I stood in front of his desk. "I've given a lot of thought about what you said earlier. About how you don't know if I have what it takes to be a Hero."

"Good."

"You understand that I have nothing but respect for you and your opinion, and that I appreciate everything you've done for me and taught me. You're a father figure to me."

"I appreciate you saying that."

"So I've come to tell you what I think about your concerns."

"Well?"

"Well, my father was killed by a supervillain when I was seventeen. I watched his body burn. Then I beat the crap out of the man who had done that to him. My mother was killed by brain cancer when I was twelve. While I watched her slowly waste away for years, I learned to sew, cook, clean, and take care of the house. At first, I did it so Mom wouldn't have to. Later, I did it because she couldn't. I cleaned her, too, when her rotting brain made her lose control of her bladder and bowels. I did all that while going to school full-time and while helping Dad in the fields.

"And you say I'm not tough enough to become a Hero?"

I paused. I jabbed a finger at him.

"Well, I say fuck you. I will become a Hero. Or die trying."

I turned around and walked out. I didn't slam the door behind me.

But I wanted to.

4

The same day I told the Old Man I would continue to try to become a Hero, he told us Apprentices he would permit us to participate in this year's Trials.

Isaac and Neha were excited. I wasn't at all. Thanks to my earlier conversation with the Old Man, I knew he had planned to certify their entries into the Trials and that I was the reason he had not already told them. I felt like the red-headed stepchild who was only getting a Christmas present because his more favored siblings had gotten some and it would've been rude to not give him one too.

"Why so glum, chum?" Isaac asked as he, Neha, and I rehydrated after a hard workout late that afternoon. We were supposed to go out on patrol with the Old Man tonight. Normally I looked forward to patrol as it made me feel like a full-fledged Hero. Today I dreaded it. Isaac said, "We're going to compete in the Trials. We've been working toward this moment for years. You'd think you'd be thrilled. Instead, you look like someone drowned your puppy."

"I'm just tired. Being laid up in the infirmary must've really taken the starch out of me," I lied. Though this was my first workout since the bank robbery, physically I felt fine. Tired from the workout, but fine. Emotionally was a different story. But, I had no intention of sharing what the Old Man and I had discussed. I was both embarrassed by and ashamed of the fact the Old Man did not believe in me.

"Well, perk up. Soon, we'll be fully licensed Heroes." Isaac smiled. "Or at least I'll be. You two I'm not too sure about. But don't worry: if you flunk the Trials, I'll take you on as my Apprentices until you can take a stab at the Trials again the following year. Assuming I let you take them, that is. You might be too busy scrubbing my floors. An important licensed Hero like I'll be can't be expected to clean his own floors. It's undignified."

"You'd better get used to the notion of pushing a mop," Neha said to him, "because that'll be what you'll have to do for a living once you blow the Trials. You're liable to blow them so badly, they won't even let you take them again."

"Nuh uh," Isaac said.

"Yeah huh," Neha retorted. They grinned at one another. Their playful bickering made me feel a little better. Despite the fact the Old Man had doubts about me, I still would get the chance to stand for the Trials with my best friends. It really was a dream come true, if not the perfect dream I expected since becoming an Apprentice.

Life had taught me a dream coming true was usually when the real work began. Over the next few weeks, I discovered entering the Trials was no different.

Applying for the Trials was not like applying to enter Hero Academy. The Academy was required by law to accept any applicant who passed a background check and the mental and physical exams. The people who couldn't cut the mustard were weeded out once they were in the Academy. With the Trials, the weeding out process began immediately. The Heroes' Guild, which ran the Trials, was looking for a reason to not let you compete in them. Only the best and the brightest were allowed a shot at getting their Hero's license. You could take the Trials only three times. After a third failure to pass them, you were barred from taking them again and barred from ever getting a Hero's license.

The first thing we had to do was fill out the application we downloaded from the website of the Department of Metahuman Affairs. The application was the length of a long-winded novella. In addition to answering the type of questions any job applicant would have to—your social security number, your present and last addresses, character references, that sort of thing—the application asked a bunch of questions that seemed like a combination of an intelligence test, a psychological profile, a doctor's office questionnaire, and an overly personal survey written by a nosy neighbor. The application stated in big bold letters at the beginning that the questions were to be answered honestly, in my own handwriting, and without collaborating with anyone else.

Since I had worked too hard to get tripped up by an application, I answered every question by myself and as completely and honestly as I could. Having to answer the questions about my sexual history was an especially tough pill to swallow. That was mainly because, if my sexual history were published, it wouldn't be long enough to be a book. It would be a pamphlet.

Oh, who the heck did I think I was kidding? It would be a line on a business card.

The application's last question read simply, "Is there anything about you that has not been covered by the previous questions?" The devil in me wanted to answer, "I like big butts and I cannot lie." Though the statement was true, I didn't include it. There was a difference between being honest and oversharing.

The application took me two solid days of writing to complete. My mind felt like a wrung-out sponge by the time I finished. The unlucky soul who had to read it would know me as well as I knew myself, and maybe a little bit better. I wondered if that person would also think I was too soft to be a Hero. Apparently there was a lot of that kind of thinking going around.

At the very end of the application were several waivers I had to sign. In addition to giving the Guild the right to examine my life like a boy pouring over his first girlie magazine—my wording, not the Guild's—I had to, as one waiver put it, "release, hold harmless, and indemnify the Heroes' Guild from any and all liability from your participation in the Hero Trials, including, but not limited to, severe bodily injury, maiming, and death."

I must admit the "severe bodily injury, maiming, and death" part gave me pause.

Maybe being a farmer isn't such a bad life after all, I found myself thinking.

I pushed that cowardly thought to the side and hastily signed the bodily injury waiver before I could change my mind.

The application had to be certified by an already-licensed Hero who could attest to the applicant's training and good character. The Old Man was, of course, the one who performed that certification for us three Apprentices. He signed the certification at the end of my application with big, sloping lettering. It reminded me a little of John Hancock's signature on the Declaration of Independence. Then he poured a bit of red wax onto the certification. He pressed the front of a huge gold ring he had taken out of his office safe into it. When he pulled the ring away, the imprint of a masked man's face was left behind.

"You'll get one of these if you pass the Trials," he said of the ring as he put it back into the safe. I thanked him for the certification and left. Though the Old Man hadn't treated me any differently than he always had since our conversation about his concerns, my feelings were still a little raw. I had a hard time making small talk with him.

The completed applications had to be hand-delivered to a Metahuman Registration Center by the Metas who filled them out. So, Isaac, Neha, and I made an appointment at the nearest one and drove over there early one morning. It was located on Massachusetts Avenue in D.C. on Embassy Row, the informal name of the part of town that housed a concentration of embassies and other diplomatic buildings. The registration center was in an imposing, white brick building that had once been the Embassy of Peru. Peru no longer had an embassy in the United States. The U.S. had revoked Peru's diplomatic recognition almost twenty years ago when the supervillain Puma had seized power there.

Once at the registration center, the three of us were taken into separate rooms by technicians who all had the same bored expression on their faces. Mine attached what looked to be electronic thimbles to several of my fingers.

"What are these?" I asked the technician.

"Lie detectors," he said. He handed me my Trials application and picked up a computer tablet.

"Aren't lie detectors unreliable?" I asked. "That's why courts won't allow their results to be admitted into evidence." Though I probably didn't know enough to pass the Bar, the law had been one of my main subjects of study during my Heroic training.

"These detectors were designed by Mechano himself," the tech said. Mechano was the mechanical genius and Hero who was a member of the Sentinels. "If you tell me so much as a white lie, it'll show up here," he said, indicating his computer tablet.

The technician then had me read aloud my answers to several of the application's questions. He stared at his computer tablet as I read. The answers he had me read seemed to be at random, but maybe there was some sort of rhyme or reason I couldn't discern behind the answers he picked. Now I was glad I hadn't added the line about liking big butts.

"All your answers are truthful," the technician said after about an hour and a half of me reading.

"What would happen if they hadn't been?" I asked, curious.

"You'd be barred forever from standing for the Trials and becoming a Hero," he said as he removed the lie detectors from my fingers. "The Guild's philosophy is that if you can't be trusted to answer an application honestly, you can't be trusted to be a Hero."

Forever barred? Yikes! I was suddenly glad I had resisted the urge to fudge the truth when the application had asked me what I thought my greatest weaknesses were. "Caring too much and working too hard," was what I had almost written before coming to my senses and instead putting down what I really thought.

"How many people lie on their applications?" I asked.

"More than you would think. Too many people write what they think the Guild wants to hear rather than what is actually true."

I stood up and handed the man my application back. "What happens next?"

"I'll forward your application to a panel of handwriting experts who'll analyze it for any red flags. If they clear it, it will then be forwarded to the Trials Application Committee. They'll coordinate your background investigation and physical and psychological exams."

I soon found out that "coordinate" meant going over my background, body, and mental state with a fine-tooth comb. I had thought I had been examined thoroughly when I had been admitted to the Academy, but it was nothing compared to the examination I got now.

Two doctors and three nurses wound up examining me like I was a thoroughbred racehorse they were contemplating buying but who they suspected had a well-hidden ailment. I whinnied when one of the doctors had a probe up an orifice I had hoped to never have a probe in.

"Did you say something, young man?" the doctor asked.

"No sir. Just horsing around." There was no longer any doubt: spending so much time with Isaac had definitely rubbed off on me.

"Well don't," the doctor said disapprovingly.

"Yes sir."

In addition to the physical, they took scans of my eyes, prints of my hands and feet, and impressions of my teeth. Once the world's most thorough examination was finally over, the doctors pronounced me "as healthy as a horse." It took a real effort to not laugh out loud at his word choice. The doctor who had told me to stop fooling around eyed me with suspicion.

After I was declared physically fit, one of the nurses gave me multiple shots that she said were vaccines.

"But I was already fully vaccinated as a kid," I protested as she jabbed me over and over like she was a busty sewing machine. The needles she used on me were big and fat, like normal needles on steroids. They distracted me from the fact the nurse was not only busty but cute, and not much older than I. I felt like the nurse was turning me into a human colander. Despite having fought criminals, supervillains, and natural disasters during my training so far, I had not lost my dislike of needles. If a Rogue named Needle Man ever went on a rampage, they'd have to find a sap not named Theo Conley to combat him.

"You weren't vaccinated as a child against the kinds of pathogens you might face in the Trials," the nurse said as she stabbed me again. It was all I could do to not yelp in pain. My head was already averted to not watch the needles go in. If I fainted while getting vaccinated, surely they wouldn't let me stand for the Trials. Heck, maybe these *were* the Trials. *Let's see how many needle jabs this dude can stand before he passes out or punches the nurse,* some fiendish test-maker might have thought. "These vaccines are for the various forms of exobiology you might encounter," the nurse added.

Surprised, my head snapped around in time to see another needle sink into my arm. I got lightheaded. I tried to stave the feeling off by focusing on what the nurse had said.

"Exobiology?" I repeated, shocked. "As in extraterrestrial life?"

The nurse's face dimpled into a smile.

"You're cute and you read? That's quite a combination," she said.

I was stunned into silence. I now barely noticed the continuing needle jabs. No one had called me cute in . . . well, come to think of it, no one had ever called me cute. If I had known all I had to do to get girls' attention was to train night and day to be a Hero, I would have pretended I had superpowers and signed up for the process the day I hit puberty.

In addition to all the physical stuff, I also had to have daylong sessions with two separate psychologists. The first I just had a casual, free-wheeling conversation with. It was like chatting with an old friend. Or at least I thought it was casual and free-wheeling at the time. That night I realized she had managed to get me to talk about every major event in my life, how I felt about it, and what I would do differently, all without me realizing it. I told her things I had never shared with another human, not even Isaac and Neha. I think it was her kind eyes and her approachable manner. I felt like I'd been duped. If there wasn't a blues song entitled *Never Trust a Pantsuited Woman with Kind Eyes,* there should have been.

I went to the second psychologist the day after the first one with my guard up, determined to not reveal too much this time. That was probably why I, when that psychologist showed me what seemed like the ten thousandth inkblot and asked me what it resembled, instead of saying what it looked like—a spider—I said "It looks exactly the way a psychologist would look if a psychologist looked like something else."

I regretted the words as soon as they were out of my mouth. The psychologist frowned slightly and wrote furiously in his notepad. I feared he was writing, "The applicant has a smart mouth and is an obvious arachnophobe. I recommend he be barred from the Trials." Or, maybe he was simply jotting down a few items he had left off his grocery list. I envied the Metas with super vision.

My background also got a thorough examination. All the people I had listed on my application as extended family members, acquaintances, and character references were interviewed by Guild investigators. The interviewees were told I had applied for a job with the federal government that required secret clearance to avoid compromising my secret identity as a Hero-in-training. Even so, I got a call from my freshman English professor I had put down as a reference.

"Are you in trouble, Theo?" Dr. Rich asked after telling me government agents had asked him a slew of questions about me.

"Honestly, I don't know yet," I said, thinking about the Trials' high mortality rate. "Time will tell."

After a few months of my body, mind, and life being examined under a microscope, I was declared fit to stand for the Trials. Neha and Isaac were too. Neha in particular had been worried about the background investigation since her father was the notorious supervillain Doctor Alchemy.

As I read the letter from the Heroes' Guild telling me my

application to stand for the Trials had been accepted, I could not help but focus on two statistics noted by the letter:

The Trials had an eighty-six percent failure rate.

They had a twenty-two percent fatality rate.

So, it was more than likely that I wouldn't pass and get my Hero's license. And, there was an over one in five chance that I would die trying.

I really didn't like those odds.

The letter from the Guild started with the word "Congratulations!"

There was a good chance "Condolences" was more like it.

5

The Old Man saw me, Isaac, and Neha off the morning we headed to the Trials. We Apprentices were dressed in brand-new costumes that were pre-Trials gifts from the Old Man. I was very pleased with mine. I looked like an actual Hero in it. It made me so confident, I was starting to feel like the Trials would be a snap despite the concerns the Old Man had expressed to me and the Trial's passage and death rates.

"I want each of you to know that I'm very proud of you," the Old Man said. Though he wasn't leaving the mansion, for the solemnity of the occasion of us leaving he wore his chrome blue and silver costume and matching blue domino mask. His costume was tight, hugging his muscles like a second skin. He also had on his white cape. The cape was bordered with blue and black. The black on the cape matched the black accents on his costume. The cape was worn asymmetrically over the Old Man's right shoulder.

Even after seeing the Old Man in costume more times than I could count, seeing him in costume this morning was still inspirational. When most people heard the word "superhero," they

42

thought of someone who looked like Amazing Man. I knew I did. We Apprentices ourselves looked pretty snazzy in our new costumes, though. Maybe one day, when someone thought "superhero," they'd think of us.

"With that said, I've had four Apprentices over the years other than you three. Each of my previous Apprentices passed the Trials on their first try. I will be most displeased if one of you breaks my perfect record." The Old Man's eyes twinkled behind his mask. "If you do, I'll add a dunce cap to your new costumes."

Isaac looked at me and Neha and said, "So not only do we have to avoid the all too real possibility of being killed or maimed, but we also have to buck the odds and pass the Trials on the very first try." Isaac rolled his eyes. "Fantastic! I'm not feeling any pressure at all. This'll be a walk in the park. Perhaps we'll bring peace to the Middle East once we're done."

"Let's knock the Middle East out right after lunch," Neha said. "I promised the United Nations we'd solve world hunger tonight."

"I wish you had said something earlier," I added. "I told the freedom fighters in Peru we'd fly down there tonight and depose Puma." I shook my head. "So much to do in too little time. We need to hire a social secretary to coordinate everything."

The Old Man grinned at us.

"I don't know how I didn't notice I've housed the Three Stooges all this time." Then the Old Man sobered. "I want all of you to keep your eyes peeled for any new threats to Theo. We still don't know who hired Iceburn to kill him. We also had no luck in tracking down the blonde woman who slipped that explosive into his pocket. Someone might still be gunning for him."

"I don't need babysitting. I can take care of myself," I protested, still smarting over the doubts the Old Man had expressed about me.

"No one's saying you're a baby," Neha said. "We're friends. Friends look out for one another."

"And it's a good thing you're not a baby, Theo, cause I don't know nuthin' 'bout birthin' babies," Isaac said in a spot-on impersonation of Butterfly McQueen from *Gone With The Wind*. If it hadn't been for my Apprenticeship with the Old Man, I probably never would have seen that movie or a bunch of other classics. The Old Man had made us watch them because, as he had said, "There's more to being a Hero than merely punching people in the face. You've got to understand the culture you're operating in. Movies are a part of that." Isaac had wanted to add *Deep Throat* to the list of classic movies we watched, but the Old Man had vetoed that one.

The Old Man shook hands with each of us solemnly and wished us luck. I felt a lump in my throat as we walked out the front door of the mansion. I was so grateful for everything the Old Man had done for me that I was almost sorry I had cursed at him earlier.

Almost.

The three of us stood in the front yard and looked back at the mansion that had been our home for the past two years. Even if we did not pass the Trials, none of us would return to be the Old Man's Apprentices. As he had already told us, he had taught us everything he could. Now it was up to us.

"My god, are you crying?" Isaac said to Neha. He sounded shocked. Sure enough, her cheeks were wet. I was as shocked as Isaac sounded. Of the three of us, Neha was by far the least emotional. She normally was about as sentimental as a cat.

"I'm not crying," she insisted, angrily wiping her cheeks with the back of her hand. "There's something in my eye, is all."

"Yeah, tears," Isaac said. He easily dodged the punch she launched at his chest. It was merely a feint; Neha's kick hit his right thigh with a solid whack.

"You should stay behind," Neha said to him. "If you'll fall for that, you're not ready for the Trials yet."

"I saw the kick coming. I could've dodged it if I wanted to. I just thought you needed more practice kicking, is all. Besides, it didn't even hurt. You kick like a girl." Despite his words, Isaac seemed to favor the leg Neha had kicked.

"That's because I *am* a girl. And if you learned to kick harder, you could kick like a girl too. If I remember correctly, my girlish kick landed you flat on your back the last time we sparred together."

"It was a lucky hit. Even a broken clock is right twice a day."

"We should get going guys," I said, trying to change the subject. I kind of wanted to start crying myself. I was used to Isaac and Neha's non-stop bickering. It was strangely comforting. It was the sound of home, like the snoring of your dog. Leaving the Old Man's mansion was the end of an era for all of us.

I pulled my new mask out of a pouch on my belt. This mask was larger than the old one from my Academy days. It covered more of the area around my eyes than my old one. I affixed it to my face. It was held there by a technology that had been explained to me, but I barely understood. I also did not understand how the tech built into it subtly altered the contours of my face so that I would not be recognizable as Theodore Conley. I just knew it did.

The greenish-black color of the mask complemented the colors of the rest of my costume. The top was a dark green. It looked like it was covered by tiny fish scales. That was where the resemblance to fish scales ended. Fish scales could not stop a bullet, but the scales that composed my costume could. The part of my costume that covered my legs was made of the same material, though it was black instead of green. My red cape, the one signifying I was a graduate of Hero Academy, completed my ensemble.

Isaac's and Neha's costumes had cowls. That was because, unlike me, they did not have a force field they could use to protect their heads and neck. They pulled their cowls over their heads. Their facial features altered before my eyes. Isaac's costume was black with light blue bands on his wrists and ankles. His cowl covered his face from the nose up. A fierce-looking, blood-red dragon was emblazoned on his chest. Neha's costume was gray and white. Black smoke shifted around on the surface of it, like storm clouds being blown by wind. Her cowl covered her entire face except her mouth, eyes, and nostrils. Her black hair extended out of the back of her cowl in a long ponytail. Like me, both Isaac and Neha had their red Academy capes on.

We took a moment to admire each other.

"We look pretty badass," I said.

"The Guild should skip the formalities and just give us our licenses now," Neha agreed.

"Well, we're off to see the wizard," Isaac said.

Isaac started to glow, as he always did when he was transforming into a mythological form. His body shrank down and changed shape. In mere moments, Isaac's human form was gone. He was now a big bird, roughly twice the size of a pigeon. His plumage glowed red, orange, and yellow, like the embers of a dying fire. His smoldering coal eyes looked at me and Neha. Isaac cawed loudly.

Then, with a flap of his glowing wings, Isaac took flight. I marveled as I watched him rise swiftly in the air. When I had first met Isaac, he could only turn into a handful of creatures, and each transformation had been a slow process that took a lot out of him. Now Isaac could change forms as easily and quickly as changing his socks. If I ever needed to fight Isaac, I would have my hands full. Sparring with him while training under the Old Man had been bad enough.

A single red and orange feather glowing like a spark drifted down to the ground in Isaac's wake. I picked it up. The feather was warm, but not uncomfortably so.

"Do you know what kind of bird Isaac turned into?" I asked Neha.

"No."

I was shocked that I knew something Neha didn't. It was almost always the other way around.

"A Firebird. It's a figure from Slavic folklore. And," I said, holding up the glowing feather, "finding a Firebird's feather was said to be a premonition that a difficult road was ahead."

Neha snorted.

"Isaac probably let that feather fall on purpose, then," she said. "Even with him as goofy as he is, he has a flair for the dramatic."

Hoping the feather was not really a sign, I put it into my pocket. I launched myself into the air, carrying Neha alongside me as well as a large duffel bag containing changes of clothes for all of us and our Trials' admission letters. In her vapor form Neha could fly, but not nearly as quickly as Isaac or I could.

We caught up to Isaac and began the flight to the Trials.

6

———

We were not in the air for long as the Trials took place in the Heroes' Guild National Headquarters in Washington, D.C.

After a short while, the building came into view. I felt a lump form in my throat as we approached it. I had been to the building before with Isaac and Neha. But back then, we had merely been tourists, gawking with dozens of other people at all the artifacts the building contained from various famous Heroes' adventures. Now we were going to enter the building as Hero candidates. I felt like a devout Catholic approaching the Vatican, or a Muslim making his first pilgrimage to Mecca.

The Potomac River was a ribbon of silver as it glinted in the morning sun behind the Guild building. The sparkling white marble building was fashioned along the lines of an ancient Greek temple. Looking at it made me think this was what an ancient Greek might have seen when the Parthenon was new.

On top of the Guild building was a huge bronze statue. It was a depiction of Omega Man, who was widely considered to be the greatest Hero of all time, as well as one of the most powerful. It was from him that Metahumans with my power level, Omegas, got our name. Omega Man had died in 1966 when he sacrificed himself to destroy the spaceship containing the V'Loth queen. The V'Loths were a hive-mind alien race that had invaded Earth and nearly conquered all of humanity.

"Do you think the legend is true?" I asked Neha as we flew closer to the Guild building. "About Omega Man, I mean. That he'll be reincarnated if Earth faces an existential crisis again?"

"Despite the fact I was raised Hindu and therefore I'm supposed to believe in reincarnation the way a Christian is supposed to believe in the virgin birth, in a word, no. Heroes don't rise from the dead. They're not gods." Neha suddenly smiled. "Then again, I'm flying through the air inside an invisible force field alongside a flaming bird, so what the hell do I know about what's possible and impossible?"

The statue of Omega Man got larger each second as we approached. I couldn't take my eyes off it, a bit awed by what it represented. Although I had never thought of being a Hero until Iceburn had killed my father, I grew up idolizing them.

"Just think—soon we might be Heroes too," I said.

"No. Soon we *will* be Heroes too," Neha corrected me firmly.

"Maybe." The Old Man expressing doubts about me had shaken my confidence a little. More than a little, actually.

Neha looked at me closely.

"What's been up with you lately, anyway? You've been a gloomy Gus ever since you woke up after that bank robbery."

"I'm fine."

"No," she said definitively, "no, you're not fine. Something's bothering you, and has been for a while now. Even if you won't talk about it, whatever it is, you need to shake it off. You need to focus on the Trials. We all do."

Our conversation and flight were cut off by a flying man who streaked seemingly out of nowhere. He slammed to a halt directly in front of us. He wore a green bodysuit and a flowing white cape, the sort only licensed Heroes were permitted to wear. Though Heroes weren't required to wear their white capes, it was protocol to do so on ceremonial occasions, just as it was protocol for Academy graduates to wear our red capes.

The Hero demanded our letters of admission to the Trials. I showed them to him. Then, he scanned us, bathing us with a blue-green beam of light that shone from his eyes. The beam tickled a little, like being stroked all over by feathers.

The Hero then said we could continue to approach the Guild building, and told us where we could land. He then peered off into the distance, squinting as if he was reading fine print. I couldn't see anything but clear blue skies where he looked. The Hero shot off in the direction he had peered, disappearing from view just as quickly as he had appeared.

"When our Guild letters said security would be tight, they weren't kidding," I said to Neha.

"It makes sense, though. All us Hero candidates in one place must make an awfully tempting target for Rogues and others who are not thrilled with the idea of Heroes."

We landed at the foot of the marble steps in the front of the Guild building as the green-clad Hero had instructed us. Isaac turned back into his normal form.

Normally there were tourists all around the building, both lined up at the front to get inside and walking the perimeter of the building, taking pictures. Now though, thanks to the Trials, there were no tourists, at least not close to the building. A huge chain-link fence with razor wire atop it had been placed all around the Guild building to keep tourists out. There was only one gate in the fence. It was through that gate that non-flying Heroes and Hero candidates entered after their credentials were checked by guards posted at the checkpoint. Those guards wore black and tan uniforms. They also wore gold helmets that were so shiny I probably could have shaved in their reflection. They held black assault rifles at the ready. The rifles looked more like something out of a science fiction movie than something in the real world. The guards peered around as if they itched for an excuse to fire their rifles and turn you to ash, electrocute you, break your body up on the molecular level, or whatever else those lethal-looking guns were capable of doing.

On the other side of the chain-link fence I saw curiosity seekers staring at the arriving Heroes and Hero candidates. Some merely pointed and stared; others took pictures. Their voices rose in excitement when they spotted a Hero they recognized.

Beyond the spectators were protesters. They booed and hissed whenever a new costumed Metahuman arrived. Many of them held signs. They were too far away for me to read them, but I supposed none of them said, "Welcome, Metahuman friends." Like Neha had said, not everyone approved of Heroes. Some people thought we were more of a menace than a boon to society.

Isaac shook his head as he joined me in looking at the protesters.

"The next time aliens invade Earth," he said, "who do those dimwits think is going to protect them if not Heroes? Sigourney Weaver? I've got half a mind to stand aside and let the aliens anally probe those yahoos to their little green hearts' content."

"It's not little green hearts the aliens will do the probing with," Neha said.

We turned and walked up the high marble steps. At the top was a portico. We were stopped there by guards dressed and armed as the ones who were at the fence. They had us look into handheld devices that looked like high-tech versions of the old View-Masters. The devices scanned our retinas. While the devices were up at our faces, the guards' hands tightened around their rifles as if they would shoot first and ask questions later at the first sign of trouble. It felt like there was a bull's-eye painted on my chest and back. I had to resist the urge to raise my force field.

Fortunately, I was who I thought I was, and the retinal scanner confirmed my identity, as well as that of Isaac and Neha.

The guards directed us toward the silver-colored double doors that were the main entrance to the Guild building. The closed-door entrance was massive, easily three times taller than I and almost as wide.

"One at a time, step here please," said yet another guard, this one posted by the door. He indicated a silver and gold face mask that was etched into the marble right in front of the door. I took the initiative by stepping first onto the mask. I expected the doors to open to admit me to the building. They did not. Instead, the stones underneath me vibrated a little, as if there was a mini-earthquake happening. I suddenly felt warm all over, like I stood on top of a space heater.

"Now step forward," the guard said.

I hesitated as the doors ahead of me were still very much closed.

"C'mon, you're holding up the line," the guard added.

My mind probed the doors with my powers. They felt as solid as they looked. I felt like a fool, trying to walk into closed doors. But, what if the first test of the Trials was whether or not I could follow directions? On the other hand, if the first test of the Trials instead was "Is the applicant such a dummy he doesn't know better than to walk into closed doors?" I was about to fail.

Holding a hand slightly ahead of myself to keep from banging my head, I stepped forward. My hand passed through the door as if it didn't exist. Surprised, I froze for a moment.

Then, I continued forward. I passed through the door like I was a ghost.

I didn't expect what I saw on the other side of the door. When Neha, Isaac, and I had been in the Guild building before as tourists, the first thing we had seen when we had walked through the front door had been the Hall of Heroes, a long hallway with statues of Heroes on either side.

This was not the Hall of Heroes. There were statues of Heroes all right, but these were not the life-size statues I had seen in the Guild building before. The ivory-colored marble statues here were huge, easily thirty feet tall. They were carved so realistically, I wouldn't have been surprised if they sprang into action if a supervillain showed his face. Omega Man was depicted in the center of the cavernous place I was in. A statue of Avatar was off to the right. Three other statues of Heroes dotted the area.

A bunch of costumed Hero candidates and a handful of fully licensed Heroes milled about in the huge room. The sound of their conversations filled the air. Behind me was simply more of the huge room I was in, not the closed silver doors I expected to see. Floating high in the air around the room were big glowing balls that provided light. In addition to the light sources, flitting around in the air were several teardrop-shaped objects. They were about the size of basketballs. They had the same kind of liquid metal quality that quicksilver did. The way they hovered in the air and then suddenly swooped up or down or side to side reminded me of watching dragonflies hunt for prey when I was back on Dad's farm.

Looking up, I saw the sheen of a translucent dome glinting in the distance, like we stood in the middle of a giant snow globe. Though there had been bright daylight outside the Guild building moments before, outside this dome, it was nighttime. I saw the dark outlines of trees and strange shadowy shapes I could not identify off in the distance beyond the dome.

The moon was full and shone brightly in the heavens above. I stared up at it. No, on second thought, this was *a* moon, but not *our* moon. With this moon, the face of it was all wrong for it to be our Luna. The Seas of Tranquility and Serenity, for example, were nowhere to be found.

In a few moments, Neha and then Isaac appeared next to me as if they had been conjured out of thin air. They gaped around just like I did. As we watched, a huge creature that looked like a bat crossed with a tiger flew high overhead, momentarily blotting out the moon.

"Where the heck are we?" I asked a nearby guard once I found my voice again.

"Washington, D.C.," he said. His eyes looked amused.

"There aren't flying monsters in D.C.," Isaac protested. "Unless you count congressmen and lobbyists."

"In this version of D.C. there are," the guard said. "You're in a different dimension than the one you started out in. You were on Earth Prime. Welcome to Earth Sigma."

Earth Sigma?

What the what?!

"Toto, I've a feeling we're not in Kansas anymore," Isaac said.

"Who the hell is Toto?" the guard asked. I guess he didn't have a Hero sponsor who made him watch a bunch of classic movies the way we did.

"Carolina!" someone cried excitedly. Carolina had been the nickname given to me by Athena, the chief instructor at the Academy. "Smoke! Myth!"

I turned to see a burly guy in a red and black costume barreling toward us. His face was split in a grin and his hand waved excitedly at us.

"Hammer!" the three of us said almost simultaneously. I

grinned back at Hammer as he reached us. Hammer had gone to the Academy and graduated with us. It was good to see a familiar face.

Hands were shaken and backs were patted all around. I reminded Hammer that I went by Kinetic now. He apologized for forgetting.

Hammer was a white guy around my height. He wore a loose-fitting hoodie with the hood up, his Academy cape, and a mask that looked a bit like a necktie wrapped around his head with eyeholes poked out. The color of all of them were the same matching red. When I had first met Hammer at the Academy, he had been what he himself had described as fat. Because of that, a lot of the trainees at the Academy had thought there was no way Hammer would make it through the rigorous physical training there. He had proved the naysayers wrong, though it was rumored Hammer graduated dead last in our Academy class.

There were countless punishing workouts, especially in our early days at the Academy, when Hammer could be found in the corner of the gym, vomiting noisily into a garbage pail. I knew because I often was right alongside of him, with my head between my knees and puking so hard it felt like I was throwing up the bones in my feet. I was more like Hammer than I was like Neha or Isaac. Whereas Neha was brilliant and things seemed to come easily to her, and Isaac was naturally athletic and charming, guys like me and Hammer had gotten through the Academy mainly through sheer determination and mule-headed stubbornness.

It reminded me of what President Calvin Coolidge had said: brains, talent, and education would not make you successful. "Persistence and determination alone are omnipotent," he had said.

Wow, now I was quoting Calvin Coolidge. It was an occupational hazard that came with being the Old Man's Apprentice. Thanks to my studies under him, I knew more about what famous men and women had said than *Bartlett's Familiar Quotations* did. I would kick some serious butt if I ever got on *Jeopardy*.

Although Hammer was still overweight, now that I was seeing him again I would describe him as husky instead of fat as he once had been. He looked good. When I had first met him at the Academy, he was a pasty guy who looked like he ate a lot of pizza and played hours of video games in his parents' basement. Now he looked like someone who played a lot of rugby and drank kale shakes.

"I can't believe we actually made it here," Hammer said. His eyes were filled with wonder as he looked around at all the costumed people around us. Hammer was of course merely his code name. I didn't know his real one. Hammer and I had been friends at the Academy, but we hadn't been close the way I was close with Isaac and Neha. Of my fellow Academy graduates, those two were the only ones whose secret identities I knew and who knew mine.

Hammer said, "I grew up reading superhero comic books and idolizing Heroes on TV. Even when I was little, I dreamed of becoming a Hero like the people I read about and watched. It was all I could talk about. Then, I actually developed Metahuman powers."

He pulled a single red rose out of thin air and handed the rose to Neha with a smile and a half-bow. She blushed behind her mask. I felt a sudden irrational surge of jealousy. "Hammer" was short for "hammerspace," the inter-dimensional realm he could pull items out of.

"Now I'm this close to actually being a Hero," Hammer said. "I keep pinching myself. I can hardly believe it. Becoming a Hero is all I've ever wanted to do."

"What have you been up to since graduation?" I asked

Hammer, partly to distract myself from the claws of the green-eyed monster. Despite the fact Neha and I regularly slept together, she was not my girlfriend. Neha had made that crystal clear. She had told me long ago she didn't want any distractions from getting her license, and a romantic relationship outside the bedroom would be a distraction. So, I didn't have any right to be jealous.

Why, then, did I want to snatch the rose out of Neha's hand and smash it over Hammer's head? I found myself hoping the rose had thorns Neha would cut herself on.

Hammer said, "Since I couldn't get an Apprenticeship like you guys did, I enrolled in a Hero trainee continuing education school in New Hampshire. One of the Heroes there certified my application to the Trials. I had to pester her to death before she would do it." He grinned. "I suspect she only certified me so I'd stop bothering her. But as long as I managed to get here, that's the important thing."

People who had Apprenticed with Heroes after the Academy were more likely to be allowed to stand for the Trials than people who couldn't get an Apprenticeship. The fact Hammer managed to get to the Trials despite not having an Apprenticeship impressed the heck out of me.

"Hey, any idea what those flying things are?" I asked Hammer, pointing up at one of the teardrop things that looked like liquid mercury. It had just scooted across the room to hover over the heads of a group of chatting Hero candidates.

"Yeah, that's one of Overlord's nodes," Hammer said.

"You realize you're speaking Greek to me right now, right?"

Hammer grinned sheepishly.

"Sorry, I'd already forgotten you just walked in. One of the Trials' proctors explained to me earlier what Overlord is. Overlord is the artificial intelligence system that runs the Trials. Well, runs it along with the Hero proctors. Those flying nodes you see hovering in the room are the way Overlord senses things. The way it was explained to me, those nodes are Overlord's eyes and ears. Overlord monitors everything that goes on at the Trials. In a lot of instances Overlord decides whether or not you pass a test in the Trials. It's set up that way to avoid human bias and error. Like much of the high-tech stuff the Guild uses, Overlord was designed by Mechano himself. You know, from the Sentinels."

As Hammer spoke, I noticed Isaac was looking off into the crowd of costumed people. He got a weird look on his face, one I had never seen there before. The look was a combination of anger and disgust, as if he had seen someone kick an old lady's cane out from under her.

Isaac harshly excused himself. He made a beeline toward someone off in the distance, rudely pushing people out of the way as he went. Hammer broke off in the middle of what he was saying, puzzled by what Isaac was doing. Neha and I looked at each other in bewilderment and concern. We had never seen Isaac behave this way before.

Sensing that trouble was brewing, I turned to follow Isaac. Neha and Hammer followed in my wake.

By the time I caught up with Isaac, he was almost literally toe-to-toe with another Hero candidate. Their faces weren't lined up, as the guy Isaac was squared up in front of was an inch or so taller than Isaac. Instead of the two standing nose to nose, the other guy could have used Isaac's nose as a snorkel.

The man wore a black and metallic gray costume that covered him from head to toe except for openings for his nose, mouth, eyes, and the top of his head. Even with his face covered, you could tell he was male model attractive. He was white, and had what appeared to be natural blonde hair. It was perfectly coiffed into elaborate waves that reminded me of the surface of the ocean. His lips were thick and slightly pouty. His eyes were crystal blue, and piercing. His body was built the way most women wished every man's was built. In short, the guy looked like Hitler's Aryan fantasies personified.

"Well if it isn't Demented Man," Isaac said to the guy. His voice dripped with venom. "You've come to flunk the Trials for the third time, I see. Or maybe you'll do the world a favor and die trying instead of embarrassing yourself yet again."

"You know that's not my name," the guy responded. His eyes flashed with anger. "It's Elemental Man."

"Elemental . . . Demented," Isaac shook his head. "It doesn't matter the letters you use, it all spells asshole to me. Tell me, Captain Asshole: do you know you can't stand for the Trials again after you flunk them this time, or are you too stupid to have realized that yet?"

Elemental Man's fists balled up. It looked like he was about to take a poke at Isaac. Before now I had been too stunned by Isaac's uncharacteristic behavior to move. Isaac was usually so easygoing and friendly toward everyone. But now I noticed one of Overlord's nodes had come to float high up above Isaac and Elemental Man. If Hammer had been right, it was recording everything the two of them said and did. I couldn't imagine getting into a fight before the Trials even started would endear Isaac to the Guild.

That thought made me squeeze in between Elemental Man and Isaac before I even consciously realized I was doing it. The chests of both of them pushed against my shoulders.

"Fellas, can't we all just get along?" I said. It was the best I could come up with on the spur of the moment to try to defuse the situation. I wondered how some Heroes seemed to have just the right thing to say at just the right time. Maybe they practiced their quips every morning in the mirror. Or, maybe they had ghostwriters.

"Who's this little twerp? Your boyfriend?" Elemental Man

asked Isaac as he looked down at me. "What watermelon patch did you find him in?" I felt myself flushing. I always forgot about my Southern accent. To me, my voice was simply my voice.

Elemental Man's eyes moved away from me to assess Neha and Hammer. "In addition to this trailer park trash, you're hanging out with a fat fuck and a flat-chested brown bitch. You'll never stop being a loser like the rest of your people if these are the guys you associate with."

Before Elemental Man said all that, I had been feeling charitable toward him since Isaac was the one who started this. That charitable feeling immediately went away.

Elemental Man's lips twisted in a smirk. He said to Isaac, "I'm glad you stopped masturbating while dreaming of your dead sister naked and found yourself a boy toy instead. It's still creepy, but it's a step in the right direction."

His face feral, Isaac's fist reared back to hit Elemental Man. He stopped before the punch landed. His body was frozen in place by my powers.

Isaac's eyes were first surprised, then full of realization of what was happening, then mad. They found mine. "Let go of me," he said through barely moving lips.

"No. Not until you calm down. You're making a scene," I said. That was true: in addition to the Overlord node hovering overhead, the people around us had gotten quiet, watching what was going on.

Elemental Man reached out to pat Isaac on the cheek condescendingly. "Listen to your boyfriend. He just kept you from getting the shit beaten out of you. For the third time, I believe. But who's counting?"

I felt Isaac struggling against the hold I had on him as Elemental Man walked away and was lost in the crowd of people. Once he was out of sight, I released my hold on Isaac.

As soon as I let go of him, Isaac turned on me like a rabid dog.

"How about you mind your own goddamned business?" he yelled, right in my face. He looked like he wanted to hit me now.

I was starting to get irritated. "I'll start minding my own business as soon as you stop acting like a jerk," I yelled back. "You started this. Do you want to get thrown out of the Trials before they even start?"

"What's your beef with that guy anyway?" Neha asked him.

Isaac shook his head angrily. "I don't want to talk about it."

"I don't care what you want. Kinetic stopped you from getting into a fight. Both he and I have the right to know what the deal is."

Isaac shook his head again. "It's so typical for you to take his side."

"What do you mean?"

"I mean that just because you're sleeping with him, you don't have to always take his side. Yeah, I know you're screwing each other, so wipe that surprised look off your faces. I'm not an idiot. You two are about as subtle as cats in heat. You don't have to jump to Kinetic's defense every time there's a disagreement. Which do you want to be: his whore, or his mother?"

Neha slapped Isaac's face so hard, his head was flung to the side. The slap rang out like a gunshot.

Our little group was frozen in place for a moment. Isaac, Neha, and Hammer looked stunned by what had just happened. I certainly felt stunned.

Isaac was the first to recover. Muttering darkly, with a red splotch on his cheek where Neha had hit him, he walked away from the rest of us. He was soon lost to view amongst the others in the huge room.

Neha and I looked at each other. She looked shocked by what she had done. There were tears in her eyes. I had gone years without seeing her cry. Now I had seen it twice in one day. Before today, there were times I had wondered if she even knew how.

As for Hammer, astonishment, not tears, was in his wide eyes. They darted between me and Neha.

After a bit, Hammer said, "Do you three always get along so well?"

7

It turned out that whether you were on Earth Prime or on Earth Sigma, a written exam was just as mind-numbing and as nerve-racking in either dimension.

It was the third and final day of the written phase of the Trials. If I passed this portion, I would go on to the scenarios phase. There, the Trials' proctors had assured us Trials' candidates, we'd be risking our necks and other body parts.

As it was right now, the only risk to my neck was getting a crick in it.

I sat in what looked like a college classroom, furiously typing on a computer keyboard while peering down at the screen sunk into the desk in front of me. Since I had been writing almost eight hours a day for the past three days, I also risked carpal tunnel syndrome along with that neck crick. If I became a Hero but wound up having to wear a wrist brace as a result, I wouldn't blame supervillains if they laughed at me.

I sat high in the tiered classroom along with the thirty-six other Hero candidates taking the Trials. Neha sat to my right at the long, curved desk that took up most of the width of the classroom. Hammer was to my left. I saw Isaac below us, near the front of the room. It was as if he had drawn up a mathematical formula that told him which seat was furthest from me, Neha, and Elemental Man. Hitler's Youth—which was what I had started to call Elemental Man mentally—was a couple of rows ahead of me on the far end of the classroom.

A proctor named Brown Recluse in a brown and tan costume with a huge spider on the front of it wore the traditional white cape of a licensed Hero. He leaned against the metal desk at the front of the classroom, looking bored as he watched us Hero candidates type furiously. Two of Overlord's nodes were overhead, hovering like miniature zeppelins.

Isaac hadn't said a word to either me or Neha since Neha slapped him days before. I had tried to talk to him a couple of times, but Isaac had walked right past me as if invisibility was my superpower. After trying to talk to him the second time only to be ignored like a geek at a sorority party, I had given up in disgust. I now ignored him as assiduously as Isaac ignored us. If he was going to be a big baby, I could be a big baby too.

Like invisibility, maturity was not my superpower.

All thirty-seven candidates taking the exam were in costume and mask, though most of us had left our capes off. The room looked like a cosplay convention. Today's exam was on Hero Law and World History, two subjects I had studied at the Academy and as the Old Man's Apprentice. I was over halfway through the exam. I felt pretty good about it so far. I could not say the same about the exam I had taken on day one, which had focused on Metahuman Math and the Science of Superheroes. Talking with Neha afterward had convinced me I had completely muffed one of the questions where you had to calculate the trajectory and destination of an intercontinental ballistic missile armed with a nuclear warhead launched by Russia. My calculations told me the missile would land harmlessly in the ocean. The correct answer apparently was that the missile would strike New York

City. It was a good thing I wasn't in charge of the United States' defense program.

I was hip-deep in regurgitating facts about the V'Loth invasion in the 1960s and analyzing whether Omega Man really needed to sacrifice himself to take out the aliens' queen when I saw something move on my keyboard.

I blinked a couple of times, thinking I had imagined it. After all, my eyes were bleary from three straight days of staring at a computer screen.

Tiny jet-black objects seemed to be surging with increasing speed out of the raised chiclet keys of my keyboard, like ants swarming out of a disturbed nest. I thought I was hallucinating until the tiny objects started crawling under my fingernails.

The sharp stabs of pain I felt under my fingernails were no hallucination.

I lifted my hands to my face. My nails were now black, their color changed thanks to the swarm of black objects under them. My fingertips started to feel hot, like they were getting closer and closer to an open flame. As I watched with increasing fear and confusion, the black objects began to travel up my fingers, right under the skin. My skin rippled as the objects spread. It was like watching something out of a horror movie.

"Uh, guys?" I said, trying to get Neha's and Hammer's attention. I heard someone shush me. Brown Recluse, maybe. The black objects were now past my wrists, marching up my arms like an advancing army. Intense pain followed in the wake of their advance.

"Guys?" I said louder. I stood up, knocking my chair over in my haste. The room had been quiet other than the sounds of people furiously typing. The chair hitting the floor sounded like a shotgun blast going off. Out of the corner of my eye, I saw people stare at me. Neha was now on her feet. So was Myth. He started to climb the stairs toward me. One of the Overlord nodes dropped from overhead to a couple of feet in front of my face. Maybe I was anthropomorphizing, but it seemed to regard me with silent curiosity.

"A little help please," I said, the words coming out in a near scream. The objects under my skin were now in the middle of my forearms, moving higher and higher implacably. Now it felt like my veins had been injected with molten lava. My skin over where the objects were passing rippled like a shedding snake's. The pain was excruciating. I somehow sensed the objects would keep traveling up my body until they got to my brain. I didn't know what they would do when they got there, but had a feeling it wouldn't be to make me better at calculating missile trajectories. I was faintly aware of Neha touching my shoulder and saying something soothing. I didn't need comforting, I needed saving.

The words *Trust in God, but tie your camel* came unbidden into my head. It was an Arab proverb I had learned in the course of my Heroic studies. It was from a story in which the prophet Muhammad noticed someone dismount from his camel and leave it without tying it. When Muhammad asked the man why he didn't secure his camel, the man said he trusted in Allah to secure it. Muhammad had responded with, "Trust in God, but tie your camel."

In other words, God helped those who helped themselves. That was something my Dad had told me so many times he had sounded like a broken record. If Catholics and Muslims agreed on something, it had to be true.

It's funny what goes through your mind when something is crawling up your arms like a swarm of army ants made of napalm. But, though the Arab proverb might have seemed like useless trivia, it was true: I had to save myself. I couldn't rely on others to do it for me. Besides, maybe this was some sort of weird-ass Trials test. I didn't see anybody else's arms looking like something out of a horror movie, though. Then again, I didn't look hard. I was too busy being in horrific pain and trying to not freak out.

The swarm was now at my shoulders, making it look like I wore weird epaulets under my costume. My arms and shoulders were so intensely and painfully hot, it felt like they would melt right off my body.

I had to do something, and I had to do it now.

I shoved the pain out of the forefront of my mind, though it was like trying to move a heavy sofa with one arm tied behind my back. I also shut out from my mind the increasing cries of the people around me. I needed to concentrate totally on what I was doing as I had never done anything like it before.

I triggered my powers, fixating on my body. I knew what my body was supposed to feel like. I walked around in it twenty-four hours a day, after all. I concentrated on what it normally felt like, focusing on that thought like a sailor focusing on a lighthouse in a storm. Then, I tried to latch onto with my powers everything that was in my body that was normally not there, namely the black objects advancing on my head like an invading army.

At first, it was like trying to grab a handful of water. The objects moved like liquid around and out of the grasp of my powers, still getting closer to my brain.

As I intensified my efforts, it then became like grabbing sand. I could hold onto some of the objects and halt their advance. Still, many of them slipped out of my grasp just like grains of sand. They reached my neck, swirling under my skin like whirlpools. I began to hear faint but ominous rustling, like thousands of dry sticks being rubbed together.

With a herculean mental effort, I imagined the grains of sand eluding my grasp were solidifying into concrete, into something hard I could get a complete grip on.

Slowly but inexorably, I felt my powers latch onto the last of the moving objects in my body. I stopped them from moving further up my neck. They came to a halt right under my chin. I felt them resisting me. It was like holding onto the tail feathers of countless birds who were trying to take flight.

My chest heaved with effort. My cheeks were wet with tears of pain. But I couldn't stop to catch my breath. I had to get these things—whatever they were—out of me before the agonizing pain they caused made me lose my grip on them.

I started pushing the objects back down the same paths they had traveled up my body. It was like trying to push the frozen plunger of a hypodermic needle down to force its contents out.

Unfortunately, forcing the objects back down my body caused just as much pain as I had felt when they had traveled up my body. By the time I had forced all the objects back into my fingertips, I was literally screaming with agony. My throat felt raw.

I lifted my arms. The black objects came back out of my fingertips in a thick black spray, like oil gushing out of a garden hose. I did not release my hold on the objects as I feared they would just attack me again. Instead, I forced them into a spherical, air impermeable force field I created overhead.

Once all the objects were inside, I sealed the force field. I released my grip on the objects. Once free of my powers, the objects began bouncing off the walls of my force field like a swarm of trapped bees bouncing off a giant glass jar. In my mind, I felt them thudding up against my force field like balls thrown at a window. Though I could not hear the objects with my ears—I wasn't even letting sound waves penetrate the force field as I didn't dare risk those painful little suckers escaping—I could hear them in my mind. The dry rustling sound I had heard before was now an angry, frustrated buzz, like the sound of thousands of trapped flies.

My chest heaved with exertion. The tips of my fingers were

bloody. I wanted to collapse on the floor in exhaustion and pain and fear, but I was too afraid I'd lose my concentration and set the black objects free again. I wasn't too tired to notice that both Isaac and Neha were next to me now. Isaac had apparently come up from the front of the classroom while I had been busy wrestling with the—well, whatever in the heck they were.

Brown Recluse came to stand underneath my force field. To anyone other than me, my fields were invisible. Brown Recluse looked up calmly, examining the ball of buzzing tiny objects like he was an entomologist studying a new species of butterflies.

"Hmmm," he said thoughtfully. "I don't believe I've ever seen anything like these things before." He glanced at me. "Do you want to tell me what's going on, Kinetic?"

Based on his question, obviously this incident was not a part of the Trials. Panting, I told him what happened.

"I see," Brown Recluse said once I finished talking. "Are you finished with your exam?"

"Huh?" How could he think I cared about my exam at a time like this? My arms, neck, and shoulders felt like they had been stung from the inside by a huge nest of wasps. I needed a doctor, a painkiller, a nap, and maybe an exorcist, not a fool question about whether I had finished my exam.

But instead of saying all that, I wisely just said, "No sir."

"Can you hold these . . . these whatever they are, in your force field until you finish?"

Oh, hell no. Fuck no. Shit no, I thought.

"I can try, sir," I said instead.

Brown Recluse frowned. "There is no try. Either you can do it, or you can't," he said. Dad, Amazing Man, and Athena all used to say something similar. Apparently all three of them had graduated with Brown Recluse from the School of Positive Thinking, located in the great state of Yes I Can.

"Well, speak up, the exam clock is still ticking," Brown Recluse said impatiently when I hesitated.

"I can do it, sir," I said.

"Then everyone get back to your seats and finish your exams. You all have less than three hours left to complete them."

Isaac walked back down to his seat without saying anything to me. I didn't know whether I wanted to hug him for coming to check on me, or stick my tongue out at him. Neha patted me on the shoulder before she sat back down in front of her computer. Her touch set off new explosions of pain right behind my eyes. In her defense, there was no way she could have known that.

Hammer pulled a couple of handkerchiefs out of hammer-space and gave them to me.

"Dude, that was the weirdest, grossest, scariest, and coolest thing I've ever seen," he whispered eagerly with shining eyes. Though Hammer was around my age, the excitement on his face made him seem much younger. I got a glimpse of what he must have looked like as a kid, breathlessly reading the pages of a comic book late at night by flashlight under the covers of his bed.

Hammer sat back down. I used his handkerchiefs to wipe the blood off my hands and to wipe my face which was wet with sweat and tears of pain.

I poked cautiously at my keyboard, halfway expecting to be attacked again. After a few minutes of remaining unmolested, I relaxed a little and started writing faster with painfully throbbing fingers.

I did not relax entirely, though. In addition to feverishly trying to finish my exam answers, part of my mind was occupied with maintaining the force field containing the buzzing tiny black objects. Maybe it was my imagination, but they seemed to glare down balefully at me, like the eye of a giant monster whose most fervent wish was to chomp you to death.

Another part of my mind thought about what in the hell had just happened, and why. I couldn't help but think about Iceburn trying to kill me and that blonde girl who had planted that explosive in my pocket. Unless I was the biggest magnet for deadly coincidences that ever donned a cape, someone was clearly still out to get me.

A third part of my mind spoke to me mockingly in Brown Recluse's voice.

Good job Kinetic! he could have said to me instead of seeming unimpressed. *That was astonishing, how you improvised using your powers in a new way to save yourself. I couldn't have done a better job myself. Don't worry about finishing your exam or the rest of the Trials —clearly you deserve a white Hero's cape right this second. In fact, why don't you take over as exam proctor? The other candidates have an awful lot to learn from you.*

You don't get a cookie for doing what you're supposed to do, countered someone else's voice. I couldn't tell if it was Athena, Amazing Man, or my Dad. They each had said something similar at one time or another.

There was no doubt about it:

They all must have studied the same clichés in the same school.

8

"They were nanites," said Pitbull, the chief proctor for the Trials. His eyes were so dark, they were almost black. He wore a form-fitting, dark brown costume. He was a short man with big arms and a thick chest. His hands looked like they had been sculpted by someone who liked veins and admired strength. Pitbull radiated competence the way Athena and the Old Man did. I wondered if they issued that air of competence along with the white Hero's cape. If so, I wanted to be first in line for some.

"Nanites?" I repeated.

"Yes. Do you know what those are?

"I think so. Aren't nanites microscopic, self-replicating machines?" I didn't know that because of my Heroic training. Rather, I knew that because of my avid *Star Trek* watching. There had been several episodes where nanites were discussed. It seemed less than Heroic to admit the source of my knowledge, so I didn't. "But those things weren't microscopic. They were big enough for me to feel and see."

"Like your body is made up of microscopic cells, those

devices' component parts are microscopic," Brown Recluse said. "Or at least that's what the technicians who examined them tell me. I wouldn't know a nanite from a nanny. Those little buggers were programmed to spread throughout Overlord's system until they found their target. You, apparently. Once they found their target, they were programmed to go on the attack, self-replicating all the while until their mass was big enough to see and to do damage."

"What would have happened had I let them reach my head?" I asked, though in my heart I already knew the answer.

"If you hadn't acted as you did, I'm told you would not be alive to have this conversation," Pitbull said. To drive the point home, Brown Recluse held his hands up and pantomimed his head exploding.

Yikes! My heart never seemed to be wrong when I wanted it to be.

The three of us were in a tiny room in the Guild complex on Earth Sigma. It was my bedroom during the Trials. It was the day after I had been attacked. Other than a small, uncomfortable bed and my clothes, the only thing in the room was an Overlord access pad that was mounted on the wall. The pad was removable in case a Hero candidate wanted to read in bed or perhaps, in my case, curl up with a swarm of deadly nanites.

Pitbull must have seen me nervously eye the Overlord access pad.

"Rest assured we have scrubbed Overlord of any trace of the nanites," he said. "Once we knew they were there, it was not hard finding the rest of them. We also checked to make sure there were no other hidden threats to you or the other Hero candidates while we were at it. There weren't. Overlord is perfectly safe for you to use now." That was easy for him to say. I'd bet he never had a swarm of microscopic machine assassins try to make his head explode. If he had, perhaps he'd be less blasé about the whole thing.

Pitbull said, "Fortunately you were able to neutralize the threat before irreparable damage was done. The doctor who examined you tells me that, other than some residual pain, you suffered no lasting injury." If by that he meant my arms and neck still felt like they were under a blowtorch, then yes, I suffered some "residual pain." The doctor said the feeling would fade as my body healed itself from the nanites' invasion. He had offered me some painkillers in the meantime, but I refused them. I remembered how being on those painkillers in the Old Man's infirmary had made me so loopy. I didn't want my mind clouded during the Trials. Besides, as much as my body still hurt, it didn't hold a candle to the torture I had experienced when the nanites had been inside me.

"We know what happened, and how it happened," Pitbull said. "What remains is the who and the why. Other than the presence of the nanites, we've found no evidence of Overlord having been tampered with. Can you shed some light on those questions, Kinetic?"

I began to tell him about Iceburn and the blonde girl who left an explosive in my pocket. Pitbull cut me off, waving at me dismissively.

"Yes, yes, I know all about that. I read your application." Hero candidates had been required to state on our applications if we had any known enemies. I had enemies, all right, but unfortunately I still didn't know who they were or why I had them. The Old Man thought it was because I was one of the handful of living Omegas, but he had no proof of that. I could only assume he was right. I could think of no other reason why someone would go to such lengths to hurt me. Before I developed my powers, I was a big fat nobody. In my heart, I still felt mostly like a nobody. But now, I was a telekinetic nobody.

"Do you have any reason to believe that whoever hired this Iceburn fellow or the blonde woman you described is somehow related to this nanite incident?"

"No sir. But I have to assume they are. Three instances where someone's tried to kill me?" I shook my head. "That's way too much of a coincidence for them to be unrelated. My Hero sponsor used to say a coincidence was just a pattern you didn't understand yet."

"Your sponsor is a wise man," Pitbull said. "Alright, let's operate for now under the assumption that the nanite attack is merely a continuation of someone's effort to kill you. We have no reason to believe he will stop now. The Trials are difficult enough without you having to worry about someone trying to assassinate you on top of everything else you must deal with. If you want, you can leave the Trials now. You can return some other year when the situation with this mysterious assassin is resolved."

If there was one thing I had learned from developing powers and Dad's death, it was that you couldn't deal with problems by running from them. Besides, whoever was messing with me was really pissing me off. Maybe they were coming after me to stop me from becoming a Hero. If so, then there was nothing I wanted to do more than to spite them and get my license. And when I did, I'd find them and kick their asses from here to Pluto.

Besides, the Old Man suspected I wasn't tough enough to be a Hero. If I left now, I'd prove him right.

All that went through my mind in a flash.

"No," I said firmly. "The only way I'm leaving here is on a stretcher." *Or in a coffin,* my mind added unhelpfully. Apparently my mind hadn't gone to the same School of Positive Thinking Dad and the Old Man had gone to.

Pitbull smiled at me. He had big teeth and prominent

canines. It was like being smiled at by the dog he took his name from.

"'No' is the right answer," he said. "If you had said anything else, I might have thrown you out."

9

"Congratulations on passing the first phase of the Trials," Pitbull said. He stood behind a lectern in the auditorium all thirty-one of us remaining Hero candidates were assembled in. Six people had flunked the written phase. Fortunately, Neha, Hammer, and I were not one of them. Despite the fact Isaac was still not speaking to me and Neha, I was glad to see him in the auditorium. He obviously had passed as well.

The other six proctors, including Brown Recluse, were on the dais with Pitbull, sitting in chairs. All of us Hero candidates sat in front of the dais.

Pitbull said, "If you're feeling cocky because you've gotten this far, don't. The written phase of the Trials is the easiest. Any reasonably intelligent graduate of the Academy who crams hard can stuff enough information in his head to pass it. Historically speaking, the written phase has a very high passage rate. I can't say the same about the scenarios phase, the phase you will be undertaking shortly. The scenarios phase is where we separate the pretenders from the real deal, the people who merely look good in tights from the people who have what it takes to be a

Hero. In the unlikely event you successfully complete the scenarios phase, you will have earned your Hero's license.

"Now for a few words of explanation. Everyone must pass five separate tests, all on a pass-fail basis. If you pass, you will proceed to the next test. If you fail any test, you're out of the Trials. If you quit any test, you're out of the Trials. Quitters are forever barred from reapplying for the Trials and forever barred from becoming a Hero. The Hero community has no room for quitters.

"The vast majority of the tests will be judged by Overlord. Some tests you will take individually and will be unique to you; others you will take alongside one or more other Hero candidates. The locale and nature of the tests will vary. Some will test you mostly mentally, others mostly physically. Some will take place in a holographic locale; others in other dimensions or on other planets." There was a small murmur among the Hero candidates at that last part. Pitbull smiled wryly. "You're all sitting in a room in another dimension. The fact you might go to other planets or be tested in a holographic locale shouldn't surprise you."

It didn't surprise me. The Old Man had a holographic training facility in the mansion. I had fought many a holographic opponent there while training. I still had the scars to show for it. The fact we might go to other planets was no surprise either considering the conversation I had with that cute nurse who had vaccinated me.

Pitbull continued, saying, "You might be wondering why we don't conduct the Trials back on Earth Prime. The short answer is we can't risk innocent civilians getting hurt." He smiled grimly. "The only ones who will risk getting hurt is you. Risk and danger are what a Hero signs up for. You'll learn that here at the Trials if you don't know it already.

"Those of you who pass the five tests will then face one final challenge. In it, you will be pitted in a one-on-one fight against another Hero candidate. A duel, if you will. Whoever wins that duel will get his or her license. Whoever loses will fail out of the Trials.

"You already know this from prior warnings, but it bears repeating: Each test in this phase of the Trials has the potential to be deadly. Even if you find yourself in a holographic simulation, the simulation's safety protocols will have been suspended. In the Trials, a holographic bullet will kill you just as readily as a real one. We didn't have you sign those waivers of liability in your applications for the fun of it. We did it because there is the real chance of you being killed or seriously injured in this phase of the Trials. And, frankly, that is as it should be. It is better for you to get killed here because you're not ready to be a Hero than for your unreadiness getting innocent civilians killed out in the real world. This is the Heroes' Guild's last opportunity to separate the wheat from the chaff before setting you loose on the world.

"With all that said, now is your chance to get up and walk away if you're not ready to face this challenge."

Pitbull let that sink in for a moment. If he expected anyone to get up and leave, he was mistaken. No one moved. We had all worked too hard to get here to turn tail now. I knew I had.

Pitbull resumed speaking when no one got up. "The specific test you will undergo and who your partner or partners will be, if any, will be determined randomly by Overlord. Furthermore, as I said earlier, Overlord will be the sole judge in most of the tests. This is so who passes and who fails isn't subject to human error and prejudice."

I glanced up at the Overlord node hovering over the dais. Though it looked like a metallic tear like all the other nodes, after my run-in with the nanites, it was hard to not see the nodes as being a little sinister.

Fantastic, I thought. *The same thing that was used as a conduit to try to kill me is also going to decide whether I get to be a Hero. Maybe I should just jump into a volcano now to save Overlord the trouble.*

Pitbull continued to speak, apparently not caring about my mental reservations. Few did. "Overlord will inform you when a test is scheduled to begin and what your objective will be. Overlord may give you hours of notice; or, it may merely give you a moment's notice. As a result, you must always be ready. Just as a licensed Hero must always be ready."

Pitbull paused dramatically.

"Your first test begins now," he said.

The room went pitch dark. People's voices raised in surprise and alarm.

My chair disappeared from under me.

I fell into a dark, empty void.

10

A voice boomed from all around. The sudden voice in the darkness nearly scared me out of my pants.

"This is Overlord," the voice said. It didn't sound like a computer-generated voice at all. If I hadn't known better, I would have thought it was a British aristocrat speaking. "Your objective in this test is to survive."

Those ominous words still rang in my ears when suddenly the lights came back on. No, that's not right. The lights didn't come back on. A light came on. The sun. Or, what looked to be the Earth's sun. I had gone from falling in an inky black void to falling in the bright sunlight. The wind whipped around me. I was high in the air, along with the rest of the Hero candidates, falling toward a grassy clearing in the middle of a wooded area.

Now that I could see what was going on, I activated my powers to slow my descent. Several of the other Hero candidates could fly, and I saw them swooping around to grab ahold of others near them who couldn't. I did the same, grabbing a bunch of people with my powers who obviously couldn't fly. I spotted Hammer nearby. I was about to grab him, but then he activated a jetpack that had materialized out of thin air onto his back. With a sudden whoosh, twin flames licked out of the back of the jetpack. Hammer's descent slowed. So, I ignored him and grabbed some other non-flyers instead.

I didn't see Neha or Isaac anywhere in the jumble of flying and floating bodies, but I knew their powers would get them down to the ground safely.

Before too long, everyone was down in the large circular clearing. Aside from a few tall trees sprinkled here and there, the grassy area we were in was completely clear. We fliers had gotten all the non-fliers down without so much as a twisted ankle.

The clearing was surrounded by a thick circle of tall trees that were off in the distance. Mostly pines from the look and smell of them. It made me think we were on Earth, or at least a holographic simulation of Earth. An Overlord node floated serenely high overhead.

Everyone seemed to speak at once.

"Where the hell are we?"

"Is everybody sure they're all right?"

"What's going on?"

"Where did the proctors go?"

"Is this a hologram, or were we transported somewhere?"

"The Guild's got transporter tech that can move you halfway across the galaxy, lickety-split. I've seen it."

"If that's all there is to this test, it was a snap."

As if on cue, something exploded out of the tree line. No, not something. A bunch of somethings. More somethings than I could count. As they got closer for me to see more clearly, they reminded me a little of *Star Wars* Stormtroopers in appearance, though these guys wore gold and black rather than white and black like Stormtroopers. Their armor glinted in the sun. They carried staffs that were almost as tall as they were. There were nasty-looking blades on the end of them. They looked a bit like oversized surgeon's scalpels.

The armored men advanced on us from all sides, as if they were a tightening noose. They weren't running, but they weren't exactly strolling toward us either.

"Uh, are we supposed to fight these guys?" someone asked, sounding confused.

As if in answer to the question, the advancing men silently lowered their staves until they pointed at us. The blades of the staves suddenly glowed pinkish-black. It reminded me of when the guys in the Chinatown bank had fired their guns at me all at once.

These guys were looking less and less like a "Welcome to our forest" committee.

Pink energy beams lanced out from the tips of the men's staffs. A few of the beams hit the force field I hastily erected around myself and those around me. The beams packed so much concussive force they almost knocked me off my feet before I braced myself better.

Explosions sounded all around as some of the pink beams hit the ground. It was like being in a war zone. There were cries of alarm and pain. Several people took flight, trying to avoid the energy blasts that pelted us like bullets.

Everything was a mad confusion. I had a sudden thought that this was what the Allies invading the beaches of Normandy during the last world war had been like.

"Form a perimeter and fight back," Isaac cried over the pandemonium. He was far off to my left. I only heard him because he had used his powers to swell to the size of a giant. His amplified voice boomed over the mayhem.

I dropped my force field around the people near me so they could retaliate against the advancing men. Some of my comrades charged the men shooting at us; others returned fire with Metahuman projectiles and energy of their own. Hammer was by my side, firing at the men with a strange type of gun I didn't recognize.

I knocked a large swath of the advancing men down with my powers like they were pins in a bowling alley. The hordes of men behind them simply trampled over their fallen comrades like they weren't even there.

That was my first clue something was amiss. Men weren't ants; they didn't simply step through and on their fallen comrades.

Inspired by how I had gotten the nanites out of my body before, I stretched my hand out toward the men to help focus my powers. I reached out with my mind. I went past the surface of the men's armor into the men themselves.

I did not find flesh and blood and bone in my metal probe. I only found metal and wire and plastic.

These guys weren't guys at all.

I snatched a glowing staff out of the hands of one of the marching figures with my powers. I turned it and slashed downward.

I had hoped to incapacitate the thing. I did more than that. Perhaps because of the energy that surrounded the staff's blade like a halo, I easily cut the thing's torso in half diagonally, from the side of the thing's neck down to its waist on the other side of its body. It was like cutting butter with a hot knife.

The thing's body fell apart like a sliced cucumber. Lubricant gushed out. Sparks flew.

"These are robots," I cried out. "You don't have to worry about not killing them! They're just robots!"

I thought at first no one had heard me over the mass pandemonium. I was wrong.

A bullhorn suddenly appeared in Hammer's hand.

"Our opponents are robots," he thundered through the bullhorn, almost deafening me. "I repeat: Our opponents are robots. Use all necessary force."

I didn't think everyone heard, but enough people did that they started fighting back more ferociously. Soon, enough robot parts littered the ground that what was going on became obvious to everyone. Then everyone started fighting against the robot soldiers in a way they never would have with real people.

Soon there were so many robot bodies and body parts piled up I couldn't see to continue to fight effectively. I rose into the air to get a better vantage point and to see if any of my comrades needed help.

Hovering in the air, I saw the robots still poured out of the trees like water out of a breached dam. I took multiple pink energy blasts, but my personal shield protected me. By now, I had several of the robots' staves under my mental command. I used the staves to mow the robots down like stalks of wheat with a scythe. Others I ripped apart with brute force, though it was much more mentally fatiguing to destroy the robots that way.

Isaac, still in a giant's form, was stomping robots left and right. I saw Hitler's Youth somehow conjure up a massive tornado that swept up the robots into the sky dozens at a time. A bright green mist, which I assumed to be Neha in one of her gas forms, spread throughout the advancing robots, causing their bodies to melt and malfunction in its wake.

I spotted a woman in a green and tan costume running toward one of the robots. She nimbly dodged energy blasts from the thing's staff. She got close enough to smack the robot on the chest with the palm of her hand. I expected to see the robot explode or fall apart or at least stop working. It did none of those things. It immediately turned in its tracks and fired on its mechanical brethren. Every robot the woman touched did the same thing. Soon we had a small robot army fighting with us instead of against us.

Though it seemed like forever, eventually the rush of robot soldiers slowed, then halted.

With all of us working together, we incapacitated or destroyed every single remaining robot. It took a while, but by the time we finished, the pristine clearing we had fallen into looked like a war-torn junkyard from a science fiction movie.

After having spent God knew how long in the air, I landed again. I was exhausted, and a little lightheaded. Never before had I used my powers for so long and in so many different ways at once. Even so, I was pretty stoked. Giddy, even. I had never fought alongside so many Metas before. The experience was exhilarating. We had all kicked some serious robot butt.

I looked around. I wanted to share this exciting moment with someone I knew. Soon I spotted Hammer, sitting calmly with his back against one of the few trees in the clearing. His eyes were wide open, appearing to look at a huge pile of robot parts in front of him. He had a faint smile on his face.

I went up to him.

"Tired so soon?" I said, grinning down at him. "And I thought the guys I went to the Academy with could go all day without resting. At least that's what the Academy girls wrote on their latrine's stalls."

Hammer didn't respond. He had the same slight smile on his face.

"Hammer?"

No response.

Now a little concerned, I reached down to gently shake Hammer by the shoulder.

His head slid off his neck. It hit the ground with a small thump.

His open eyes stared up at me. His frozen mouth smiled at me.

There was hardly any blood at all.

11

Pitbull explained to us the next day at a memorial service what had happened.

None of us Hero candidates had ever left the Guild auditorium during our fight with the robots. In fact, the auditorium wasn't actually an auditorium. It was a holosuite capable of projecting holograms so realistic that everything had seemed real. The chairs in the auditorium, the auditorium itself, the Hero proctors on the dais, the clearing, the trees, the sun, the smell of pine—all had been constructs that had seemed so real that they may as well have been.

The robots we had fought had been real enough, though.

Hammer's death and that of another Hero candidate were all too real as well.

Overlord had recorded everything that had happened during the melee. Pitbull told us how Hammer and the other fallen candidate, a woman I had never met named Prism, had died during the memorial service held in their honor.

Prism had been struck down in the first volley of blasts from the robots' energy weapons. She had shoved another candidate out of the path of the blast that killed her.

As for Hammer, he had just straightened up from destroying a robot that was choking another candidate when a different robot swung its weapon from behind Hammer, cutting through Hammer's neck like a sword through a sheet of paper. Hammer's body had crumpled against the tree I had found him leaning on. He was almost certainly dead before he hit the ground.

Overlord had determined that everyone had fought admirably during the robots' attack. So, Pitbull told us everyone had been cleared to pass to the second test of this phase of the Trials.

In light of Hammer's and Prism's deaths, our victory felt more like a defeat to me. The looks on the faces of many of the other candidates told me they felt the same way.

One of the proctors had used his powers to put Prism's and Hammer's bodies into stasis. Their bodies were then placed in mahogany caskets, which were in turn placed on waist-high platforms in the middle of the area we had all first entered the Guild complex at. We all had to pass through that area several times a day. Hammer and Prism would lie in state there for the duration of the Trials. Thereafter their bodies would be returned to their families.

After Prism's and Hammer's memorial service, the proctors had us form a line to walk in between their caskets to pay our final respects. Then we were to return to our quarters. All tests had been suspended until the next day in honor of Prism and Hammer.

White capes signifying Heroes were draped over each casket. Pitbull had told us during the memorial service that any candidate who died while saving another during the Trials was posthumously awarded a license and a Hero's cape.

So, Hammer had achieved his lifelong dream of becoming a Hero. Though I wasn't happy about what it had taken for him to earn his white cape, I was proud of him. When the Trials were over, I hoped to find out Hammer's real identity so I could look his family up. I wanted to pay my respects and see if there was anything I could do for them.

Hitler's Youth was a few people in line ahead of me as we trooped past Prism's and Hammer's caskets.

"They're going to need extra pallbearers to tote this big boy around," Hitler's Youth said to one of his cronies in line behind him, gesturing with his chin at Hammer's casket. They snickered at that until a scowl from one of the proctors silenced them.

It took every ounce of self-restraint I had to not launch myself at the two jackasses. A stab of pain made me realize my fists were clenched so tightly that my fingernails dug into my skin.

I wished Hammer were still alive. I needed him to pull a baseball bat out of hammerspace.

Then I'd use it to put a new part in Hitler's Youth's perfectly coiffed blonde hair.

———

A LITTLE WHILE LATER I LAY IN BED IN MY ROOM. I HAD CHANGED out of my costume and cape, which I had worn to the memorial service. I now had on shorts and a tee shirt. I still had on my mask. As had been the case at Hero Academy, we had been told to keep our masks on at all times during the Trials to keep from revealing our true identities to our fellow Hero candidates.

I stared at the ceiling and thought about Hammer and Prism. I wished I had known Prism.

There was a chime from my Overlord access panel which indicated someone wanted to come in.

"Come in," I yelled out of habit. I was used to yelling to be heard on the other side of the thick door in my room in the Old Man's mansion. Here in the Guild building, I could have whispered it and the effect would have been the same. Through the access panel, Overlord would relay my voice to the person outside my door.

My door dilated open like a camera's shutter. I expected to see Neha. Instead Isaac came in. I had seen him earlier at the memorial, seated far across the room from me and Neha. Like me, he had changed into regular clothes.

"Hey," he said. It was the first word he had spoken to me since the incident with Hitler's Youth.

"Hey," I said, sitting up.

There was an awkward silence for a few moments.

Finally I said, "So does this mean you're speaking to me again?"

Isaac looked sheepish.

"That's actually what I came here to talk to you about. I want to apologize for how I've been acting. Hammer dying drove home what a big baby I was being. If something happened to you or Neha during the Trials and we weren't on good terms—" He trailed off, shaking his head. "Well, I don't think I could live with myself. I wanted to apologize when you got attacked during the history exam, but I couldn't bring myself to do it. Too stubborn, I guess."

Isaac looked me in the eye. His face shone with sincerity.

"Anyway, I was one hundred percent in the wrong. I was an idiot for yelling at you and then not speaking to you. I was being childish. I'm sorry, and I hope you'll forgive me."

It felt like a weight was lifting off my chest. Isaac and Neha were the best friends I ever had. One of them not speaking to me had bothered me more than I cared to admit, even to myself.

"I really appreciate you saying that. I forgive you." I stood up. I hesitated, embarrassed. "Should we hug now? It kinda feels like we should hug now."

Isaac grinned. "As long as you don't cop a feel."

"I can't make any promises."

We hugged awkwardly. After a few seconds, I pushed off of him.

"Okay, that's enough," I said. I wasn't big on male-on-male displays of affection. It was probably the way I was raised. I could count on one hand the number of times I'd hugged my father before he died. "I'm forgiving you, not marrying you."

"Ha! You should be so lucky."

We both plopped down on the bed. It was the only place to sit in the tiny space other than the floor.

"All right, now that we're speaking again, what's the deal between you and Hitler's Youth?"

"Who?" Isaac looked puzzled.

"I mean Elemental Man. Hitler's Youth is what I call him."

Isaac barked out a harsh laugh. "He really does look like Hitler's wet dreams come to life, doesn't he? Hitler's Youth. That's the perfect name for him. I can't believe I didn't think of it myself."

"So what's the story?" I pressed. "He said something about your dead sister. I didn't even know you had a sister."

Isaac looked incredibly uncomfortable, an expression I was not used to seeing on his face. The only other times I could remember him looking this way were when Neha and I asked him why he decided to try to become a Hero. Despite us broaching the subject from time to time, Isaac had never told us. He had always immediately changed the subject, usually by making a joke.

"Look, I realize we just kissed and made up, but I really don't want to talk about Elemental Man—I mean Hitler's Youth. Instead, tell me what's the deal with those black things that attacked you."

I knew he was avoiding the subject, but I let him. I was just happy we were speaking again. So, I told him about my conversation with Pitbull and Brown Recluse regarding the nanites and Overlord.

"Overlord attacked you?" he said incredulously, twisting around to look at Overlord's access panel on the wall. He eyed it with suspicion, as if a monster would spring out of it at any second.

"Not Overlord exactly. More like something someone planted in Overlord."

"Any idea who did it?"

"No. You?"

"No idea."

"Then what good are you?"

"For one thing, I give really good bro hugs." He grinned, then immediately sobered. "Theo, be careful and keep your eyes peeled. This is the second time since you put Iceburn away that someone's tried to kill you. I don't know what I'd do if something happened to you. You're like the brother I never had." He shook his head. "It's a damned shame what happened to Hammer. I really liked that guy."

"Me too." I paused. "What we're doing, becoming a Hero? It's even more dangerous than I thought it would be."

"You can say that again. That's why we have to look out for each other." Isaac stood. "Speaking of braving danger, I need to go apologize to Neha too." He made a face. "What do you suppose the chances are that she'll go easy on me?"

"Dude, you called her a whore. The chances aren't good."

"That's what I was afraid of."

That reminded me. "Why in the world didn't you say something before about me and Neha?"

He shrugged. "I figured it was none of my business. And, that if you guys wanted to tell me, you'd tell me." He hesitated. "So are you dating her?"

"No. I'd like to, but she said we needed to focus on our studies. She said we shouldn't even think of being in a relationship—with each other or anyone else—until we got our licenses behind us. She said to do otherwise would distract us too much." I let out a long breath. "And though I didn't like it at the time, I have to say I think she was right. We have to keep our eyes on the prize." I thought of Prism and Hammer lying in their coffins. "It's too dangerous not to."

There was a weird look on Isaac's face while I spoke of Neha. It puzzled me until an explanation for the look hit me like a thunderbolt.

"Isaac, do you have feelings for Neha?"

The half-guilty, half-defensive look now on his face answered my question before he did.

"No. Yes. Maybe. God, I don't know," he said, suddenly and uncharacteristically flustered. "I toyed with the idea of asking her out until I realized you were sleeping with her. Once I knew that, I tried to put her out of my mind as anything other than a friend." Isaac let out a long breath. "I've got to admit I've had a hard time doing it. If I were being completely honest, I'm a teensy bit jealous of you two."

"Don't be. We're just having sex." My good Catholic father would be shocked at how cavalierly I was talking about having sex with someone. He'd be doubly shocked that I was having sex with someone I wasn't married to. Honestly, the altar boy that still lived inside me was a little shocked by it too. I told him to close his eyes when I did the deed. I suspected he peeked. I knew I would.

Isaac let out a bitter laugh.

"'Just sex' is more than I'm getting from her," he said.

"Have you said anything to Neha about all this? If there's one thing we've learned lately, it's that life is short."

Isaac looked at me incredulously. "I think those nanites infected your brain. They've made you go insane. What would you have me say to her? 'Hey bestie! I know you're sleeping with my other bestie, but I just wanted to let you know that I may or may not have feelings for you. I'm not sure—haven't decided yet. Okay, good chat. Looking forward to you kicking my ass in the gym tomorrow.'"

"When you put it that way, it does sound silly."

"You think?"

Isaac tapped the access panel to open the door. He paused before stepping out.

"When exactly did our lives become an episode of *The Young and The Restless*?" he asked.

I thought of Prism's and Hammer's bodies lying in state. Two people dead, and the second phase of the Trials had barely started.

"Probably around the same time our lives became an episode of *Game of Thrones*."

Isaac grimaced.

"I pray the Red Wedding episode isn't in our future," he said.

He left to go face Neha.

12

"Kinetic, report to Portal Five immediately for your next test," came an insistent voice for the umpteenth time.

I rolled over in bed. Why in the world was I dreaming about pushy British headmasters dancing in a nightclub?

"Kinetic, report to Portal Five immediately for your next test," the voice repeated.

It finally penetrated my tired brain that Overlord's was the British voice I heard. Reluctantly, I pried my eyes open. I sat up. Overlord's access panel was flashing like a strobe light, making my otherwise dark room look like a disco.

"What time is it?" I asked.

"Please specify your preferred dimension and time zone," came Overlord's voice in reply.

Ugh! Thanks to being groggy, I had forgotten I was in another dimension.

"Earth Prime, United States' Eastern Standard Time."

"Two thirty-five a.m." came the immediate response.

Double ugh! I had only been asleep a few hours. It was the

morning after the memorial service for Prism and Hammer. It seemed like Isaac had left my room mere minutes ago.

I got up and hastily pulled off my nightclothes and tugged on my costume. I was about to put on my cape as well when Overlord stopped repeating its Portal Five message long enough to tell me to leave it behind. If I ever became a voyeuristic creep who wanted to spy on the female Hero candidates, I'd need to figure out a way to hack into Overlord.

"Where is Portal Five?" I asked the Overlord access panel.

Its strobe flashing stopped. A map of the Guild complex appeared on the screen. A solid white light threaded from my room through the complex to a room labelled "Portal Five." I was about to also ask what in the heck Portal Five was when Overlord started flashing its strobe light again, blinding me. Its voice sounded more and more insistent.

Triple ugh! I'd have to find out what Portal Five was when I got there.

I left my room and followed the path through the Guild complex Overlord had shown me. The path took me through the main hall where the cape-draped coffins still lay. I felt another sharp stab of grief for Hammer. Not that I needed it, but the coffins were a reminder the Trials weren't a harmless game of patty-cake.

I eventually came to a long corridor with cylindrical metallic walls. I stopped in front of the door that, per Overlord's map, housed Portal Five.

The door dilated open. I walked in. Straight ahead of me was a large, thick, silver ring that was much taller than I. It hovered a few inches off the floor like it was a part of a magician's act. Three steps were in front of it. Inside the ring was what looked like the surface of a lake that was made from liquid emeralds instead of water. The rich green surface shimmered and rippled like something that was alive.

"Step through the Portal," came Overlord's voice from an access panel like the one in my room.

Despite Pitbull's assurance that the nanites had been eliminated from Overlord's system, I was leery of doing something it told me I didn't understand. Once bitten, twice shy.

"Why?" I asked. "What is that thing?"

"Step through the Portal," Overlord repeated.

"Not until you tell me what the heck it's for and what it will do to me."

"Refusing to comply will result in you forfeiting this test and your expulsion from the Trials." Overlord said it matter-of-factly, as if it were merely telling me the time again.

Well that was plain enough. Still, given my history with Overlord, I was reluctant to leap before I looked. Maybe I was being paranoid, but even paranoids had enemies. A scalded cat didn't sit on a hot stove twice.

Since I was fresh out of more clichés to stall with, I mounted the three steps in front of the giant ring containing the rippling field of green. I probed the ever-moving green field with my powers. They were met with a moment's resistance, like I poked my mental finger through a thin sheet of paper. After that initial resistance, I felt absolutely nothing. No nanites, no ticking time bombs, no killer robots, no flesh-eating monster . . . nothing.

Encouraged, I extended my hand to tentatively touch the moving field in front of me. There didn't seem to be anything to touch; my hand met no resistance at all. The field was warm, though it wasn't at all unpleasant. It was like sticking my hand into a sauna.

"Step through the Portal." Maybe it was my imagination, but Overlord sounded slightly impatient this time.

I took a deep breath.

I stepped through the Portal and into another world.

SUDDENLY, I WAS NO LONGER IN THE GUILD COMPLEX. INSTEAD, I stood on a flat, rocky plain. There were no trees, no grass, no vegetation at all for as far as the eye could see.

The first thing I noticed was that I wasn't alone. Another Hero candidate was with me. I recognized her. She was the same woman I had seen fighting the robots with me and the rest of the candidates, the one who could get the robots to fight on our side with a simple touch. We each glanced at each other before looking around.

The sun shining brightly overhead was not the sun I was used to seeing. This sun was much bigger in the sky than the sun I was used to. Usually the sun was the size of a dime in the sky; this sun was the size of a half-dollar. It shone more red than orange, giving everything around us a reddish tint.

The sky was cloudless and bleak, mostly reds lightening to pinks the further you looked from the sun. The air was hot and dry. Though it was breathable, there was a chemical tang in the air that reminded me of bleach.

Both close by and off in the distance stood tall rocky structures, like the ones in Monument Valley in the southwestern United States. About forty feet or so in front of me there was a huge fissure in the ground. It was as if some immense giant had thrust his hands into the ground and then pulled his hands apart, ripping the ground in two like two halves of a grapefruit. The chasm was wide. Not as wide as the Grand Canyon certainly, but still pretty darn big. The huge cleft in the ground extended to my left and to my right for as far as I could see.

Roughly in the middle of the chasm, hanging like some sort of magical curtain, was a gold-colored energy field. It was translucent, and I saw clearly through it to the other side of the chasm. It extended the length of the chasm, its shape contouring to the chasm, but always staying roughly in the middle of it.

Directly across from where I stood on the other side of the chasm was a huge box. It was about the size of one of those green electricity transformer boxes. It probably was white, but under the light of this sun, the box looked pink. The box had a large gold ring emblazoned on its side. The ring was the same color gold as the energy field that hung in the middle of the chasm.

A little bit behind me and the other Hero candidate was a squat, one-story building that reminded me of the storage sheds I had seen on plenty of people's property back in South Carolina. This one had walls that were a beat-up, dull-looking metal.

High overhead, an Overlord node floated against the back-drop of the red-tinged sky.

"Welcome to the planet Hephaestus," Overlord boomed down from above. Despite its words, its tone was too flat and too matter-of-fact to be welcoming. "Your task is to cross the chasm in front of you and destroy the machinery housed in the box on the other side of it before it is too late."

This test'll be easy, I thought. *I'll fly right on over there and smash that box to smithereens with a big rock. Or I'll just squeeze it to a pulp with my powers. Easy peasy, lemon squeezy.*

As if it could read my mind, Overlord said, "Around your neck you will find devices that suppress your Metahuman abilities."

My fingers flew to my throat. Sure enough, I felt a metal band around my neck. I had been so busy soaking in being on a new planet for the first time that I hadn't even noticed the feel of it against my neck.

"On this side of the chasm," Overlord said, "your powers will not work. On the other side of the chasm, past the gold-colored energy field that divides the chasm, your powers will work as they normally do. The box with the gold ring on its side houses the machinery that both generates the golden energy field and that suppresses your Metahuman abilities. Once that machinery has been destroyed, the Portal that transported you here will reappear and you can use it to return to Earth Sigma."

As soon as Overlord stopped speaking, a light shone out of the bottom of its node. Green numbers formed in the air, like digits on a scoreboard, only without the scoreboard. They read "00:60:00." As my companion and I watched, the numbers became "00:59:59." The numbers continued to change as seconds passed. Clearly, this was a one hour countdown. But a countdown to what?

"Is that how long we have to complete the test?" I shouted up at Overlord.

There was no response.

"What did you mean earlier when you said we had to cross the chasm 'before it's too late'?" my companion asked Overlord. I was glad she did. "Before it's too late" was an awfully ominous thing for Overlord to have said.

Again, there was no response.

We shouted several more questions up to Overlord, but to no avail. Apparently it had said all it was going to say. Talking to it was doing as much good as talking to a wall.

We gave up and turned to regard each other. I stuck my hand out, and my companion shook it.

"I'm Kinetic."

"Hacker," she said. Just as when I had seen her before fighting the robots, she had on a green and tan costume. It was form-fitting, displaying Hacker's slim, almost boyish figure. There was a gold band around her neck that hadn't been there the last time I had seen her. Though I couldn't see the choker I felt around my neck, I assumed mine was the twin of hers.

Instead of a mask, Hacker wore black goggles. They looked a bit like the ones welders wore. The rest of her face was bare. Her skin was pale, as if Hacker didn't spend much time in the sun. Her hair was short, albino white with pink highlights, and in a pixie cut. If I had to guess, I would have said she was older than I, but not by very much.

Hacker was cute. Then again, having never had a real girlfriend, I thought most girls were cute. Hunger makes almost any food look good. I didn't like to think of it as desperation; rather, I considered myself open-minded.

I tried to shove thoughts about Hacker's cuteness out of my head. This wasn't the time or place.

"What do you do?" I asked. I felt like we were at a speed-dating event for Metahumans.

"If I can get close enough to touch them, I can control computers. Anything sophisticated enough to think—electronically speaking of course—I can command. You?" I would have thought her power wasn't a terribly useful one for a potential Hero to have, but I had seen how easily Hacker had made the robots that had attacked us fight on our side simply by touching them.

"I'm a telekinetic. With my telekinesis, I can fly and project force fields."

"A shame you can't fly across the chasm and end this test now."

"You took the words right out of my mouth. Actually, hold that thought." It had suddenly occurred to me we shouldn't simply take at face value Overlord's word that our powers wouldn't work. Maybe this was a test of our gullibility.

I held my hands up. The waves of energy that surrounded my hands ever since my Metahuman powers first manifested a few years ago were now gone, as invisible to me as they normally were to others. Nonetheless, I concentrated, trying to trigger my powers. I focused on lifting myself off the ground.

I didn't feel the surge of energy I normally felt when I used my powers. I stayed on the ground like my feet had been nailed there.

"You look constipated," Hacker said somberly as I concentrated hard.

I dropped my hands and gave up.

"It was worth a try."

"Indeed," Hacker agreed. She fingered the gold band around her neck and looked up at Overlord's node. Its normally liquid silver surface was tinted red in the sun's light. "I'm assuming my powers have also been neutralized. If they were working and if I could get up high enough to touch Overlord's node, I could reprogram it, and make it turn off the device that's dampening our powers and open the Portal back up."

I was scandalized at the thought.

"That's cheating," I protested.

Hacker turned her attention back to me. Her serious eyes matched the green of her costume. Her head tilted slightly to the side in puzzlement. The movement was almost mechanical. Hacker seemed slightly artificial, as if she was becoming too much like the computers she could control.

"How is that cheating? No one has said we cannot reprogram Overlord if we need to."

"I don't know," I said, the idea still not sitting well with me. "It may not violate the letter of the rules, but it feels like it violates the spirit of them. We're supposed to pass these tests on our own merits, not by monkeying around with the thing that's judging us."

Hacker looked at me like I was a simpleton, as if I shouldn't be allowed to shave or take a bath unsupervised.

"I'm a hacker. It's right there in my code name. Hacking by its nature is rule-breaking. I love to not follow the rules the way everyone else does. It's kinda my thing." She shook her head with a sigh. "We'll just have to agree to disagree. Besides, it's a moot point. Overlord is out of reach and, if your example is any indication, my powers aren't working anyway."

"Regardless, we need to figure out a way to get past this chasm." I started walking toward it. Hacker immediately joined me. We had to skirt around a huge red rock at least three times my size that thrusted out of the surface of the ground like some sort of weird stalagmite. Something about the huge rock caught my eye. I slowed, then stopped when I was next to it. Hacker stopped alongside me.

The rock was riddled with tiny holes that were about the diameter of my pinkie finger. I put my eye up to one of them. The hole extended all the way through the rock in a straight line that looked like it could have been drawn with a ruler. I could see to the other side of the rock through the hole. I checked a few of the other holes. They were all the same way.

"What in the world are you doing?" Hacker asked. She sounded both impatient and mystified.

"What do you make of these holes?" I looked down, and spotted a fist-sized rock a few feet away. I picked it up. It was as solid as, well, a rock, except that it had a few holes that ran through it just like the much larger rock did. I handed it to Hacker. She gave it a cursory look.

"It's just a dumb rock," she said disdainfully, dropping it back onto the ground. She started walking toward the chasm again, leaving me behind. I got the feeling that anything that wasn't electronic or mechanical didn't interest Hacker much.

I let Hacker proceed without me as my curiosity had been piqued. I checked another rock, and another, and another. They all had holes. Now that I was looking for them, all the rocks around us had holes that were so perfectly and uniformly cylindrical, they could have been drilled into them with a power tool. No power tools I had used back on the farm could have drilled through rocks as hard as these appeared to be, though. I was hardly a geologist, but I had never seen rocks like this back on Earth. If these rocks just naturally formed this way, and I had no reason to think they hadn't, I wondered what kind of otherworldly geological process created them.

Then again, perhaps Hacker was right—maybe they were just dumb rocks. I put the rocks out of my mind and hastened to catch up to her.

By the time I did, she was lying on her chest at the edge of the chasm. Her head and shoulders extended over the lip of it. She twisted to look at me at the sound of my approach.

"Come take a look," she said.

I got down on my hands and knees and carefully crawled forward to join her. After all I had been through since I had gotten my powers, if I got myself killed by falling off a cliff, my ghost would never forgive me.

I looked down into what seemed like eternity. The bottom of the canyon—assuming there even was a bottom on this weird-ass planet—was shrouded in darkness far below, even with the faint glow of the golden energy field in the middle of it. There was the faint but distinct smell of smoke, as if something was on fire far below.

"Look at the walls," Hacker prompted me.

The canyon dropped down at almost a ninety-degree angle below us. There were no hand or footholds that I could see. I rubbed the face of it a little with my hands. It wasn't as smooth as glass, but it was hardly a climbing wall, either.

"It's literally impossible for me to climb down this thing, cross to the other side, and then climb back up without breaking my neck and everything else," Hacker said. "Could you do it?"

I stood up and backed away from the edge of the chasm. Looking down it was making me dizzy. Hacker followed me.

I said, "Maybe Spider-Man could climb down this thing. I can't."

Frown lines sprouted on Hacker's brow.

"Who's Spiderman? Friend of yours? Another Hero candidate?"

"Spider-Man. You know, Spider-Man," I said, miming shooting webbing out of my wrists at her.

Hacker looked at me like I was having a seizure.

"The comic book character," I added, getting exasperated.

"Oh. Well, that explains why I've never heard of him. I don't read comic books. Never have. I have better ways to spend my time."

I was flabbergasted.

"You don't need to have read comic books to know who Spider-Man is. He's an icon. He's a part of world pop culture. There have been movies and TV shows about him. There was even a Broadway musical. How have you not heard of him?" I was having a hard time not raising my voice. Who didn't know about Spider-Man? What kind of weirdo had Overlord paired me up with? If it were inclined to answer questions, I would have asked it.

"What's a 456 Kevlar Macroprocessor?" Hacker asked.

"Huh?" I said, startled by the sudden change in subject. "I don't know."

"Well, just as you don't know about that, I don't know about the Spiderman," Hacker said primly. "Everybody has different bases of knowledge."

She had a point. That didn't change the fact I wanted to shake her and tell her it was not "the Spiderman," but simply Spider-Man.

I changed the subject. The clock counting down over our

heads reminded me we were wasting time. I wondered what would happen when the clock hit zero. Would that mean we had failed?

"We can't fly over the chasm, and we certainly can't climb down it," I said. "We need to figure something else out and do it quick. I can't imagine Overlord's countdown is to remind it to take its cookies out of the oven."

"Let's check out that building. Maybe there's something inside that can help us."

That was as good of an idea as any I had. We hastened over to the building.

Close up, the building looked weathered and beaten-up, as if its metal exterior had undergone multiple sandblastings. There was a single large window on one side of the building. The glass —if glass was what it was—was thick and cloudy, like the bullet-proof windows they had in jail. I knew from personal experience the kind of windows they had in jail thanks to me getting arrested after I fought Iceburn. I wondered if I was the only Hero candidate who was a jailbird.

I paused outside and looked at the weathering on the building's metal more closely. Parts of the metal were pretty thick; other parts were almost but not quite worn through. The parts that were almost worn through were cratered a bit, as if one good punch would poke through them. There were circular indentations all over the building's exterior, like it had been shot countless times with a battery of BB guns shooting oversized BBs. The diameter of the circles looked to be about the same diameter of the holes in the rocks we had seen earlier.

"'Curiouser and curiouser!' cried Alice," I murmured as I examined the wear and tear on the building's exterior.

"What?"

"Nothing." If Hacker hadn't heard of Spider-Man, surely she

hadn't read *Alice's Adventures in Wonderland*. I wondered if Hacker read anything but computer manuals.

"You're wasting time," Hacker said impatiently. She flung open the narrow door set in the middle of one of the long sides of the building and went inside. Unseen, I rolled my eyes at her. She seemed to have the intellectual curiosity of an eggbeater.

I followed Hacker inside, noticing as I did that the entire exterior of the door, including the doorknob, was made of the same beaten-up metal as the rest of the exterior of the building.

It was hot and stuffy inside the building, but it was still cooler than it had been outside as we were now in the shade. Hacker and I both were sweating bullets by now. It would have felt great to strip my costume off and take a nice, cool bath. Preferably with a nice, hot girl. Not Hacker though. Anybody who didn't know who Spider-Man was wasn't my kind of gal.

The interior of the building was all one big room. A skylight made of the same translucent material as the window was embedded in the building's metal roof. Though the skylight was clouded over, it still let in enough of the sun's red light to let us see adequately.

Over on my left against the wall were rows of thick shelves. On the top shelves were stacked a bunch of canned food. Vegetables, beans, fruit, tuna, sardines, that sort of thing. I was hungry, not having eaten breakfast. But food could wait. We had bigger fish to fry. Overlord's countdown continued to nag at me.

On the bottom shelves were plastic bottles. There were two kinds. There were huge multi-gallon clear drums, like the ones used to fill water coolers in office buildings. They were full of a clear liquid. I hoped it was water as I was already thirsty from being out in the hot sun. There were also smaller bottles, like the seventeen-ounce water bottles people carried around. They were unlabeled, and also full of a clear liquid.

I picked up one of the smaller bottles and shook it gently.

The liquid inside moved like water did. I looked carefully at the cap. The bottle appeared sealed, which I considered a good sign. I twisted the cap off, and took a sniff. I smelled nothing. I dipped the tip of my pinkie into the liquid. My pinkie didn't get eaten away by acid, nor did anything else horrific happen. I licked my wet finger. It tasted like water.

Well, if it looks like a duck, swims like a duck, and quacks like a duck, then it's probably not a non-duck that will kill you painfully if you drink it. But, I had learned that it was impossible to be too careful. After all that had happened to me and my friends lately, I should have changed my name to Captain Caution.

I took a tentative swig from the bottle. The liquid was a little musty, as if it had sat in one place for a long time. Otherwise it tasted fine and just like water. I wanted to drink the whole bottle to keep from getting dehydrated, but I forced myself to stop when I had finished only a third of it. If I suffered no ill effects, I'd finish the rest of it later.

Captain Caution was my name, being careful to not get poisoned was my game.

"You want some water?" I called out to Hacker, who poked around in a pile of stuff on the other side of the building. "At least I think it's water."

Hacker nodded, so I lobbed an unopened bottle over to her. She caught it handily, opened it, and took a drink.

I cautioned her, "Don't drink too much of it just yet. Maybe not getting poisoned is part of the test."

Hacker lowered her bottle.

"Thanks for the advice, Captain Obvious," she said with a sniff. "Mansplain much?"

"That's Captain Caution," I muttered under my breath. Now that Hacker was drinking it, I kind of hoped the water *was* poisoned.

Hacker and I were getting along just swimmingly. I would have to invite her to my wedding. If I didn't like my in-laws, I'd be sure to seat Hacker with them.

I realized I was putting the cart before the horse. Step one was find a girlfriend. Step two was to make sure she wasn't Hacker.

I took one last look at the water and canned food. There was enough food and water for two people to live off of for weeks if we were careful with it. Was that how long this test would take to complete?

We continued to explore the building. It was built on a wooden framework. I imagined if I pulled the metal walls away, the building would look like a wooden skeleton. The metal walls were secured onto the framework with thick metal screws. I wondered where the wood had come from since we hadn't seen a scrap of vegetation outside. Had the Guild brought the wood in from Earth Sigma or somewhere else? That assumed the Guild had even built this thing. Maybe there was intelligent life somewhere on Hephaestus we hadn't encountered yet. We had only seen this small part of the planet, after all.

The building was like a miniature junkyard. In addition to the bottles of water and the cans of food, there were various odds and ends: old machine parts; reams of different fabrics; tools; a huge industrial floor scale like one you might see in a factory; a big bucket of nails, screws, and fasteners; more pieces of wood of various sizes than a colony of termites could ever eat; paper of various colors and sizes; pens and pencils; and a bunch of gear I didn't recognize. Hacker told me some of it was surveying equipment. There was even an old motorcycle and a replacement chain for it.

We brainstormed after we finished giving everything in the building a quick overview.

"We could build a glider out of the stuff in here," I said optimistically. "Glide right over to the other side of the chasm."

Hacker tapped her cheek with her finger thoughtfully. I had seen her do it before. It seemed like an unconscious tic.

"You ever build a glider before?" she asked.

"No. You?"

"No. I suspect it might be harder than what you're imagining. We've got plenty of wood to build a framework out of, but is it the right kind of wood? Is it light enough? And the fabric we have? Is it non-porous enough so air wouldn't shoot right through it, making our glider sink like a stone?"

I got a sudden mental image of the old film clips I had seen of inventors trying to fly gliders before the Wright brothers had come along. Them trying to fly their inventions had not ended well, and had resulted in catastrophic crashes. And how long had the Wright brothers tinkered in their workshop before they made their successful flight at Kitty Hawk? I vaguely recalled it had been years. Did I really think we could whip together what it had taken them years to accomplish?

"We'll table the glider for now," I said. "You have a better idea?"

"I don't have a better idea, but I have an idea." Hacker let out a breath. "If that motorcycle works, I can try to jump it across the chasm."

I stared at her.

Then, I burst out laughing.

When I realized she wasn't laughing too, I sobered with an effort.

"Wait, you're actually serious?" I asked, still chortling a little. "Who are you, Evel Knievel? There's no way you can jump a motorcycle over a space that wide."

"I don't have to jump it all the way across. I just have to jump it halfway across, past the curtain that's inhibiting our powers. I practically grew up on a motorcycle. I've done a little stunt riding, too. If we work the angles and the rest of the math right, I could do it." Shockingly, she apparently knew who Evel Knievel was despite not knowing about Spider-Man.

"And then what?" I demanded. "You somehow turn the motorcycle into a computer as you're plummeting to your death? Right before you hit the bottom of the chasm you send an email to the Air Force asking them pretty please to order a missile strike on the box on the other side of the chasm?"

Hacker flushed, turning the same color pink as her hair highlights. "You're right, I hadn't thought it through. It was a stupid idea. Forget it."

I thought about her idea some more. Then, I let out a long breath. I couldn't believe I was about to say what I was about to say.

"I could do it," I said. "No, strike that. We can discuss the highly theoretical but very unlikely possibility that I can be talked into doing it if we're convinced I won't turn myself into a smear on the side of the chasm in the process." I still couldn't believe I was entertaining this nutty idea. "If I could jump past the golden field, I could then use my powers to fly the rest of the way to the other side of the chasm. Then I could destroy the power nullification box and then fly you over to the other side too."

"That would work," Hacker said excitedly.

"There's just one problem. Actually, there are a million problems with this harebrained idea, but there's a fundamental problem."

Hacker frowned. "What's that?"

"I've never ridden a motorcycle. I have absolutely no idea how."

Hacker brightened.

"Is that all? I'll teach you. It's easy. It's like riding a bicycle."

She paused, tapping her cheek again. "Only mechanized. And faster. And harder to control. And much more dangerous. And worse for the environment." Her brow furrowed again. "It's nothing like riding a bicycle, actually. I take it all back."

"You're not exactly inspiring me with confidence."

"We're getting ahead of ourselves anyway. Maybe the motorcycle doesn't even work. Maybe the distance from our side of the chasm to where the energy field sits is too far to cross. We need to collect some data and then reassess. The first thing we should do is figure out how far it is from here to the other side of the chasm. Whether we use the motorcycle or build a glider or do something else, we'll need to know that information."

"Makes sense," I admitted. Talking about the width of the chasm was better for my blood pressure than talking about me trying to jump a motorcycle across it. "How do you propose we calculate the distance?"

"I told you I saw some surveying tools." Hacker went across the building to rummage in a large box on the floor. She held up a small boxy object triumphantly. It looked like binoculars, only skewed, as if it had been built by someone who had heard of binoculars but had never seen them before. Hammer rummaged around some more and pulled out a waist-high tripod whose colors matched that of the boxy object.

"What's that stuff? I asked.

"Well this is a tripod," she said without a trace of sarcasm, gesturing at it. I wanted to throw my water bottle at her. She then held up the boxy object. It had three lenses on the front of it: a big one in the middle, and two much smaller ones on either side of the big one. "And this is a laser rangefinder. It shoots a laser out. The laser will bounce off of something and then back at the rangefinder. Since the device knows the speed the laser travels—namely at the speed of light—the device uses that number along with the time it took the laser to bounce back to calculate how far away the object the laser bounced off is. We'll use it to determine the distance across the chasm."

"Pretty cool."

"Now aren't you glad the part of my brain that knows how to use this equipment wasn't instead filled up with information about the Spiderman?"

"It's just Spider-Man, not *The* Spiderman," I said immediately, but Hacker had quickly covered her ears. She cautiously uncovered them once my lips stopped moving.

"Weren't you even listening? You're liable to shove out of my head with the Spiderman nonsense something that's actually useful. The human brain is a computer. It only has so much space on its hard drive. I don't want you overwriting something important."

She said all that with a perfectly straight face. I was pretty sure she was serious. Hacker was odd. I wondered if she was somewhere on the autism spectrum.

I grabbed the tripod and followed Hacker out of the building. She had the rangefinder. I took my bottle of water with me. I hadn't suffered any ill effects yet from drinking it, so I planned to drink more soon.

We trooped back over to the chasm. Overlord still floated overhead. The countdown shining below its node read less than five minutes remaining. Remaining until what, though? Surely the Guild didn't expect we could figure a way over the canyon in this short of a time.

I took a long look at the canyon with the idea of me jumping a motorcycle across it in mind. It looked even bigger than I remembered.

And I was going to try to jump over half of it? On a motorcycle? As a motorcycle novice? With no superpowers and no parachute?

"Oh, *hell* no!" Too late I realized I had said it aloud.

"What?" Hacker asked, puzzled.

"Just thinking out loud," I said, embarrassed.

At Hacker's direction, I put the tripod down at the edge of the chasm. I was happy when I backed away from the edge again. Standing so close to the precipice made my insides clench. Hacker mounted the rangefinder on top of the tripod and made some adjustments to it. Then she peered through it, pointing it down at the wall on the other side of the chasm. Soon, she turned to me. Her face was lit up with excitement.

"It's only two hundred and twenty point three feet wide," she said breathlessly. "You only have to jump half that length. Knievel jumped over fourteen buses back in the seventies, clearing a hundred and thirty-three feet. And he had to stick the landing. You can do one hundred and ten feet easily, especially because you don't have to worry about the landing. You just have to get past the energy field."

"Oh sure. It'll be easy." I felt a little sick to my stomach. I realized I had hoped in my heart the canyon was way too wide for us to continue discussing this crazy plan. "A walk in the park. I'll just go from never having been on a cycle before to flying through the air on it for over a hundred feet. Simple. You sure I can't travel three hundred feet instead? A mere one hundred sounds like too much of a piece of cake."

Hacker ignored my sarcasm as if she hadn't heard it. Her eyes shone with enthusiasm.

"First we'll have to make sure the bike is working. If it is, I'll give you a crash course in riding. I already checked and saw it has an almost full tank of gas, so that's not a concern." I really wished she had used words other than *crash course*. "We'll need to build a ramp, of course, so you can get the proper elevation to travel the hundred and ten feet. We've got plenty of wood and tools for that. We'll have to do some calculations to figure out the speed you'll need to hit and the right angle for the ramp. But that's just simple math a monkey could do."

Maybe I was becoming as crazy as she was, but the more she broke down the steps we needed to take, the more the plan started to sound feasible. Maybe we could do it. Besides, as long as that glowing timer counting down wasn't the time we had to complete the test, we had all the time in the world to practice and figure out how to pull this off. After all, there was plenty of food and water in the building.

I found myself grinning. Hacker's enthusiasm was infectious. That, or the heat had addled my brain.

"It's a good thing there aren't sharks down there," I said, pointing at the canyon.

"Huh?"

My grin got wider. "I'd hate to jump the shark."

"What?" Hacker looked at me like I had sprouted a second head that was talking about Spider-Man again and the amazing friends he had. "There's no indication there's water down there. Even if there was water, there's also no evidence this planet developed life at all, much less life like sharks."

After the Spider-Man debacle, I wasn't about to explain a *Happy Days* episode to her. "Forget it. I was just making a dumb joke."

"A very dumb one," she agreed solemnly. Hacker must have been really fun at parties.

Hacker nudged me and pointed up. The timer was winding down and was almost at zero. We watched it with apprehension. I knew we both hoped we hadn't flunked this test because we hadn't figured out a way to cross the canyon fast enough.

The timer hit "00:00:00." The digits, once green, now turned red.

Other than that, exactly nothing happened.

No, that's not quite right.

At first, I thought it was my imagination.

Then I realized it wasn't.

The sky was darkening. Not all at once, but like a camera shutter closing in slow motion. Darkness was spreading slowly from all around the edges of the horizon. It was as if someone had spilled a bottle of ink around the edges of a huge funnel in the sky and the ink slowly trickled inward toward the center.

As the sky got darker, I heard a weird noise. It grew louder and louder. It was like someone had made a recording of thousands of chirping cicadas and was slowly turning up the volume. The sound gave me goosebumps and made the hair on the back of my neck stand on end.

As that cicada-like noise increased in volume, there were slight whizzing sounds in the air. At first it was just one or two. Then the number of the whizzing sounds increased as the darkness closed in more above us. The new sound was like bullets zooming past us. Unfortunately, thanks to my time as the Old Man's Apprentice, the sound of whizzing bullets was one I was all too familiar with. I suppressed the urge to duck. I had no idea what I would be ducking from.

Hacker and I looked at each other, not knowing what the heck was going on or what to do about it.

Suddenly, the water bottle in my hand jerked. I felt the pants of my costume getting wet.

I looked down to see a stream of water coming out of a hole on the side of my partially full bottle. Confused by how that had happened, I lifted the bottle to eye level to look at it.

There was now something in the water bottle. It was worm-like, and about the size of my pinkie. It was shiny black with gruesome orange stripes. One end of it glistened red, pink, and white, like a fresh open sore. The other end of it tapered into what appeared to be a tail.

The thing swam in a frenzy in the water, around and around

the perimeter of the bottle. I got the impression the water confused the thing, as if it wasn't used to it. The creature made a slight sound as it swam, like the cicada sound now coming from all around us, but in miniature.

The rest of the water drained out of the bottle. The creature glistened at the bottom, coiled up like a tiny snake. Then it suddenly straightened out like a snapping whip. The red, pink, and white part now pointed straight at my probing eye.

I don't know exactly what made me jerk my head out of the way. But, some survival instinct made me do just that. I jerked the bottle to one side, and moved my head to the other. The creature burst out of the bottle like a bat out of hell, right over my shoulder. It sounded like a bullet whizzing past my ear.

My heart thudded at the near miss. I looked at the empty bottle. There were now two holes in it: one high on it, the other near the bottom. The holes were perfectly round and about the size of my pinkie.

Just like the holes all around us in the rocks.

Overlord's countdown, its statement that we needed to find a way across the chasm before it was "too late," the worm that had exploded into and then out of my bottle, the unseen things whizzing by us, the ever-increasing cicada-like sound, the darkening of the sky, the holes in my bottle matching the holes in the rocks all around us . . . the pieces fell into place in my mind like the tumblers of an opening lock.

The approaching darkness in the sky wasn't darkness at all.

It was a swarm of worms that could make Swiss cheese out of hard rocks.

13

If these swarming worm things could bore through hard rocks, what in the world would they do to human flesh?

Then another thought hit me: The building didn't have holes in it. Just countless pinkie-sized indentations.

I dropped the water bottle like it was a hot coal.

"We need to get into the building. Now!" I cried.

I'd say this for her—Hacker didn't hesitate and she didn't ask a bunch of questions. She seemed to catch on immediately to the danger we were in. She took off like a gazelle toward the building, with me hot on her heels.

The approaching cicada sound grew deafening. Alien worms whizzed all around us. There were so many I could see some of them now. They rocketed past in all directions like miniature black missiles. I felt a stabbing pain in the back of my right thigh.

For the first time I was grateful for all the running I had done at the Academy and during my Apprenticeship. Despite the pain in my thigh, I sprinted past Hacker.

I got to the building before she did, no doubt smoking all my previous sprint records. I flung the door open. I paused impatiently, waiting for Hacker to catch up. A worm hit the door's metal right over my head with a loud ping, making me flinch.

Moments later, Hacker barreled past me through the open door. I spun inside and slammed the door behind me.

Once inside, I heard worms hitting and bouncing off the building's metal walls with increasing frequency. The sound reminded me of sitting in a parked car during a hailstorm.

Hacker was bent over, with her hands on her knees, panting. I knew how she felt. My legs ached from the sudden sprint. My chest heaved from exertion.

Hacker said something. I couldn't hear her over the thunderous pelting the building was now getting from the alien worms. The sound competed with the equally loud cicada-like sound.

Hacker moved closer. She yelled in my ear so she could be heard.

"Remember when I said you were dumb for examining the rocks?"

"Actually, you said the rocks were dumb," I yelled back.

She pondered that, tapping her cheek again. I had a hard time keeping my eyes off her heaving chest. Her small breasts were so close they almost touched me. They rose and fell like a bellows. What a bizarre time for my creepiness to kick in.

"You're right," Hacker yelled. "I forgot. What I had said aloud was that the rocks were dumb. What I said in my head was that *you* were dumb. Anyway, I was wrong. Sorry about that."

I didn't know how to respond, so didn't say anything. Hacker didn't say anything else, either. She didn't move away from me. You couldn't tell from looking at her face, but I got the sense she was scared. Or maybe I was just projecting.

I certainly was scared.

Instead of dwelling on my fear, I twisted to look at my right thigh. It was bloody right above the back of my knee. Apparently one of the worms had hit me during our run here. It had sliced through my high-tech protective costume like it was made of tissue paper. Fortunately, the wound was not deep. The worm must have merely grazed me. Dumb luck.

Hopefully the worm didn't carry diseases. Getting infected by alien cooties was the last thing I needed. We were in enough trouble as it was.

The interior of the building was now dark and gloomy thanks to the worm swarm. They had blotted out most of the sunlight coming in through the window and skylight. The skylight and the window were black with tiny flashes of red and orange, the worms were now hitting the building that furiously. This must have been what going through a Biblical plague was like.

Hacker and I stood silently in the near darkness. I feared that any second now the window or skylight would crack open and a horde of writhing worms would come swarming in and put a permanent end to my fears.

Thankfully, that did not happen. In fact, after a while, the opposite happened: the onslaught outside slowed. The thickness of the worms on the surface of the skylight and window visibly thinned.

Then, like a switch had been flipped, the pandemonium suddenly stopped. The incessant pelting ended. The sudden silence seemed stark and unnatural. The interior of the building brightened again as sunlight shone through the window and the skylight.

The onslaught probably only lasted a couple of minutes, though it seemed much longer. Apprehension your insides were about to be ventilated by a mass of alien worms tended to slow down one's perception of time.

"Do you think it's safe to go back out now?" I asked Hacker. I spoke louder than I probably needed to, but my ears still rang from the cacophony of sounds we had just undergone.

She shrugged. "Do I look like the worm whisperer?"

Helpful.

I went to the door and cautiously cracked it open. A mass of alien worms didn't rip through my throat and give me a tracheotomy. I opened the door wider. Everything outside was as still and quiet as it had been when we had first arrived here. The sky was clear and the sun shone brightly overhead once more.

I stepped outside. Off in the distance by the canyon, Overlord still floated overhead, unaffected by the recent swarm of worms. As I watched, the countdown glowing under it reset, going from all zeroes to 48:00:00. It changed to 47:59:59 and then 47:59:58 and so on, the seconds ticking down again.

It didn't take a rocket scientist to figure out what was going on.

"According to Overlord's countdown, in two days the worms will return," I called out to Hacker who was still in the building. "Hopefully we can get over the canyon by then. On the plus side, if we can't, we can always take shelter in the building again."

"Maybe not," her voice called back to me. "Come take a look at this."

I went back into the building. Hacker stood next to the far wall. When I got close to her, I saw it immediately.

Three circular holes, grouped together like bullet holes on a target at a gun range, were punched through the metal walls. This was in one of the spots where the walls had been nearly worn through before the worm swarm had occurred.

Hacker and I looked at each other silently. Without even speaking to coordinate it, we spread out and carefully examined the rest of the building's walls.

We found several more worm holes, each one punched through a part of the wall that had been worn thin previously.

The building was no longer secure from the worms. We had gotten lucky this time in that the few worms that had penetrated the building hadn't hit us. We might not be so lucky next time, especially since the building's walls were already holey in spots and looked even more worn than before.

It was as clear as the noses on our faces: We had to get over the canyon and end this test in less than two days. If we couldn't do it in that time, we would turn that old expression on its head:

Instead of the early bird catching the worm, we late birds would catch the worms.

Literally.

14

When it became obvious we were up against a hard deadline—with emphasis on the *dead* part—Hacker and I swung into action.

First, Hacker made sure the motorcycle ran. It started right up after Hacker tinkered with it a little. She even took it for a spin to check out how it operated. When she returned, she said it ran like a top even though it was a "poorly made, Chinese-built 250cc single cylinder." The Chinese part I understood. Everything else was Greek to me.

Using the scale in the building, we weighed both the motorcycle and me. Then, using the paper and pencils in the building, we did some calculations to see if it was even possible to jump the canyon with the motorcycle with both my and its weight factored in. For the first time ever, I was glad Metahuman Math had been a requirement at the Academy. We did the calculations separately to make sure we came up with the same answers.

We did not. My calculations varied widely from Hacker's. When we checked each other's work, it turned out I had made a boneheaded mistake that had thrown my end results off wildly from what they should have been. Hacker looked smugly superior when she pointed out my error. I wished, not for the first time, I had been paired with Isaac or Neha instead of her.

Once we were on the same page mathematically, what we needed was clear. We needed to build a ramp at a certain angle. If I then rode off of it going at least fifty-five miles an hour on the motorcycle I would easily sail past the gold energy field that suppressed my powers.

I had hoped the math would show Hacker could have driven the motorcycle with me behind her, but our combined weight would be too heavy for it to work. Thanks to the implacability of math and physics, jumping off the ramp with the motorcycle would have to be all on me.

Fantastic. No pressure at all.

We got to work building the ramp. Fortunately, the building had all the tools and wood we needed, including an incli-nometer so we could get the angle right. Unfortunately, Hacker didn't know a Phillips-head screwdriver from the screwdriver drink, so I took charge of designing and building the ramp. I resisted the urge to rub her nose in the fact I knew useful stuff she didn't. Hacker helped once I taught her how to use a hacksaw without cutting her fingers off.

Hacker looked at me in near awe as the ramp started to take shape, as if I were performing a wondrous magic trick.

"Where did you learned to build stuff?" she asked as I hammered a board into place. "They don't teach this at the Academy."

"My Dad taught me. I grew up on a farm. We didn't have a lot of money, especially after my mother died. A farmer, especially a poor one, must be a Jack of all trades. My Dad could butcher a hog, build a house, do electrical work, repair a tractor, and a bunch of other stuff. He was versatile."

"What's his name?"

"James."

"He sounds like a great man."

"He was." My eyes unexpectedly blurred with tears. So Hacker wouldn't see, I turned my head and pretended to examine a piece of wood. Even though Dad had been killed a couple of years ago, I still missed him. Grief still stabbed me like a knife sometimes when I thought of him.

To avoid getting dehydrated or sun stroke as we built the ramp under the hot alien sun, we took frequent breaks to drink water. We also took a break to eat some canned food as we both were famished. We had to pry the cans open with screwdrivers as there was no can opener in the building.

A motorcycle but no can opener? If we ever got back to Earth Sigma, I needed to have a chat with the Guild's supply clerk.

Eventually, eating and drinking took their toll.

"I wonder where the bathroom is," Hacker said.

I pulled out the nails I had between my lips. "You're kidding, right?"

"No. Why do you ask?"

I spread my arms out to encompass the unpopulated alien landscape around us.

"The whole world is your bathroom."

Hacker looked disbelieving.

"You expect me to do my business outside?" She sniffed disdainfully. "I'm not a savage."

"Well you're going to be an awfully backed-up non-savage if you don't."

Hacker frowned and continued to work on sawing boards into set lengths as I had instructed her.

As she worked, she got more and more fidgety. Finally, with a curse, she threw her saw down on the ground. She stomped over to the building and went inside.

A few seconds later, she walked back out. Though I was a good distance away from her, she appeared to carry white sheets of paper and a bottle of water. She glanced at me. She then walked further away until she was but a dot in the distance. She stayed there for a little while.

Eventually, she walked back to where I continued to work. Her hands were empty. She got back to sawing.

I was dying to say something. I held it in as long as I could. A heroic effort counts for something, right?

"Everything come out okay?" I finally said, vainly trying to suppress a grin. "I hope you didn't get a paper cut."

"I hate you," Hacker said, without looking up. Despite her words, a slight smile played around her lips.

It took about eighteen hours of almost non-stop work to get the ramp built and adequately secured in the ground so it wouldn't be pushed over the cliff into the canyon as soon as the motorcycle hit it. Though I knew my way around a toolbox, I was hardly a professional carpenter. It undoubtedly would have taken less time if I had been, or if Hacker was more help than she was.

As I put the finishing touches on the ramp, I told Hacker to go to sleep for a couple of hours. When I finished, I woke her up and in turn went to sleep myself for a few hours. It would be hard enough to learn to ride a motorcycle without being so tired I'd risk falling asleep on it.

By the time Hacker woke me, a little under twenty-four hours was left on Overlord's countdown. While I had slept, Hacker had used her hands and a rake to clear a mostly rock-free path leading to our new ramp. She also marked off with rocks how far away I would need to start riding from the ramp in order to accelerate to the necessary speed of at least fifty-five miles per hour.

I got on the motorcycle behind Hacker. We made a few practice runs up and down the path she had cleared to give me a feel for being on the bike. I also got a good feel of Hacker since I had my arms around her as she drove. It would have been a lot more titillating had we not been fighting for our lives.

After several practice runs, Hacker gave me a crash course in riding a motorcycle, quickly but thoroughly explaining the operating parts and how to use them: the clutch, the front and rear brakes, the gear shifter, and the throttle. It would have been a lot more confusing if I didn't already know how to drive a manual transmission car. My car before I had set off to try to be a Hero had been a manual Chevy Cavalier with a sun-faded, powder-blue paint job and rusted-out floorboards. If I could pull off learning to ride a motorcycle and I survived this test, maybe I would one day buy a bike. It was sure to attract more positive female attention than my beat-up Cavalier had. It would be nearly impossible not to.

Under Hacker's critical eye, I put the bike into neutral and then started it with a push of a button. The engine roared to life. Good. Step one: Start engine. Step two: Don't die.

Straddling the bike with my feet on the ground, using only the clutch, I walked the bike slowly forward, getting a sense of the bike's balance.

Now feeling more confident, I eased into first gear, taking my feet off the ground and putting them on the bike's foot pegs as the bike moved forward. I gave it a little gas, and the bike surged forward like a spurred racehorse.

I was doing it! I was riding a motorcycle. Pride swelled within me. I could check "riding a motorcycle like a badass" off my bucket list.

I should have known better than to anger the motorcycle gods by being prideful. As the Good Book says, "Pride goes before destruction, and haughtiness before a fall." In this case, the fall was literal. I must have gone all of forty feet before I lost my balance. The bike and I hit the ground with a crash. Fortunately, I pulled my right leg free before the motorcycle fell on it. Even so, the fall wasn't like falling into a pile of feathers.

Hacker rushed over to see if I was okay. No, strike that. I *thought* she was rushing over to see if I was okay. She stepped right over me and bent down to make sure the bike was alright.

With a friend like this, who needed enemies?

Despite the fall shaking me up a little, both the bike and I were none the worse for wear. After taking a few minutes to collect myself, I got back on it and tried again. While I practiced, Hacker got the rake again and cleared a longer path so I could practice going longer distances at higher speeds.

I wound up falling a few more times. But, in a few hours, I was whizzing up and down the path we had laid out like I was one of the Hells Angels. Well, that's not exactly true since I couldn't really turn. I was too scared to try. I would skid to a stop, put my feet down, and walk the bike in a circle so I could make another run down the path. I didn't need to be able to turn, anyway. I just needed to go down our path and hit the ramp at the necessary speed.

By the time we had about an hour and a half left on Overlord's countdown, I felt confident. By now, I was zooming up and down the path we had made in excess of sixty miles an hour. This was going to work.

I was about ready to stop practicing and actually ride over the ramp and leap the chasm when it happened.

There was a sudden clatter as I zoomed down our path, and the motorcycle slowed. Freaked out, I braked and brought the bike to a stop. I got off. Hacker came over and together we checked out the bike.

As it turned out, the "it" that happened was the motorcycle's chain had broken, probably due to age and neglect. We found the broken chain back along our path, flung there when it was ejected by the motorcycle.

I glanced up at the countdown clock. There was less than one hour and twenty minutes until the worms made their appearance again.

I looked at Hacker. She tapped her cheek with her finger furiously. She looked like she held back tears of fear and frustration.

I knew I was.

Hacker and I hustled to push the motorcycle back to the building. We had seen a replacement chain in there. Plus, there were more tools inside than we could shake a stick at. Surely we'd be able to fix the motorcycle. How hard could it be to put a replacement chain on? Maybe it was like putting a new chain on a bicycle. I had done that lots of times when I was a kid.

As it turned out, it was not much like putting a chain on a bicycle. Unfortunately, Hacker didn't know how to do it, being tool and mechanically-challenged despite her years of motorcycle riding. Fiddling around with computers, not mechanized devices, was her bailiwick. We had to figure out how to install the chain on the fly.

By the time we got the chain on, we were both streaked with grease and oil. But, it was on.

The problem was, what would probably have taken us less than ten minutes had we known what we were doing took us well over an hour.

We were cutting this incredibly close.

"Stay here," I said to Hacker as I wheeled the motorcycle out of the building. I saw there wasn't much time left on Overlord's countdown. "If I can't pull this off, even with holes in it, this building is the safest place to be."

Hacker flung herself against my back and hugged me awkwardly. Her breasts pressed against me. The unexpected and uncharacteristic display of affection nearly made me drop the bike.

"Good luck," she murmured before letting go of me. Once the bike was clear of the door, Hacker closed it behind me. Maybe it was my imagination, but there seemed to be a lot of finality in the sound of that door clicking shut.

Overlord's countdown was now a red row of zeroes. The sky was darkening again. The cicada-like sound got louder and louder as I hurried toward the path we had cleared leading to the ramp. I pushed the bike as fast as I could. If I could have hopped on the motorcycle and ridden it to the path instead, I would have. The problem was the ground was too rocky here. I was sure I'd wipe out if I tried to ride the motorcycle on anything other than the cleared path.

I wanted to push the bike all the way to the end of our cleared path. I knew from my practice sessions I would be able to accelerate the bike well past the needed fifty-five miles per hour if I started the bike off from there.

The problem was, I didn't think there was time for that. The sky was too dark and the sound of the approaching swarm was too loud. Already I heard whizzing in the air.

Once I hit our path, despite the fact I was nowhere near the end of it, I hastily mounted the motorcycle. My heart was in my throat. Blood pounded in my head like a drum. My hands were sweaty on the motorcycle's handlebars.

For a split panicked second, I drew a complete blank on how to start the damned motorcycle.

Then, I suddenly remembered. The bike's engine roared to life, throbbing between my legs like something alive. I started to roll forward, praying to God I wouldn't stall the engine in my haste to get the bike moving and up to the necessary speed.

I accelerated faster and faster toward the ramp at the end of the path. I was focused so hard on the ramp that my vision tunneled. I felt more than saw a worm shoot right past my nose.

There was no time for do-overs. I had to get this right the first time.

I hit the ramp dead-on with a thump that rattled my bones. As I zoomed up it, I glanced at the speedometer.

I flew off the ramp. I sailed into the air with a roar of the bike's engine. The wind whipped past me.

The speedometer had read forty-eight miles per hour. I needed at least fifty-five.

I wasn't going fast enough.

I wasn't going to make it.

15

Math doesn't lie. Equations don't miraculously change because you want them to.

But the variables you plug into those equations can.

I hadn't hit the necessary fifty-five miles per hour. I couldn't change that variable. The ramp's angle was fixed. I couldn't change that variable either.

The only variables I could change were me and the bike.

In a vacuum, the fact the bike weighed more than I wouldn't be relevant. If there was no wind resistance, we would fall out of the air at the same rate. Galileo proved that back in the sixteenth century when, according to urban legend, he dropped two spheres of different weights off the top of the Leaning Tower of Pisa. The balls had fallen at exactly the same rate.

But here's the thing: The bike and I weren't airborne in a vacuum. Wind resistance had to be factored in here. A motorcycle flying through the air was not aerodynamic. But *I* could be, at least far more than the bike was. Me studying the most efficient way to fly at the Academy had taught me that.

That all flashed through my mind once I saw I wasn't going fast enough when I hit the ramp.

As soon as the bike cleared the ramp, I let go of the bike. I put my arms down at my sides and closed my legs, straightening my body out like a skydiver cutting through the air. I knew trying to minimize the wind resistance and traveling further than our calculations had shown the bike and I would travel together was my and Hacker's only chance.

The bike and I separated. It dropped behind and below me as I cut through the air more efficiently than it did. The golden energy field was straight ahead, getting closer and closer with each instant.

I punched through it like a shot bullet.

Though I didn't feel any resistance as I moved through the gold field, I did feel something familiar as soon as my body passed through it.

My hands were burning.

My powers were back.

Yes!

Able to fly again, I needed to change my trajectory. My current descending one was hurtling me toward the wall on the other side of the canyon where I would go *splat*.

I angled up, out of the canyon. I turned in midair to get my bearings.

The power nullification box was below me. The sky was now almost completely dark. There was whizzing in the air around me. I raised my force field, but I had no idea if it would stop the worms or not. The only thing I had seen stop the worms so far was the metal walls of the building Hacker was still in.

The whizzing sound as the worms passed by increased. A couple of worms zoomed right in front of my face, barely missing my nose and chin. They had passed through my personal shield like it didn't exist.

Wonderful. That resolved the question of whether my shield was effective against the worms. The answer was a big fat *NO*.

Overlord had told us at the beginning of this test that if we destroyed the power nullification box, the Portal to take us back to Earth Sigma would reappear. Just as there had been on the side of the canyon I had just left, there were massive stone structures poking out of the ground on this side. I ripped one of them out of the ground with my powers like it was a weed. I rapidly moved it to high above the power nullification box like it was slung inside an invisible crane. I then turned off my power's hold on the huge rock structure, and let gravity do the rest.

As soon as I let go of it, I realized it had weighed many tons. It was the heaviest thing I had ever handled. By far. And yet, I had ripped it from the ground and picked it up almost without effort.

Maybe the Old Man had been right in our conversation from an eternity ago: maybe stress had acted to kick my powers up another notch.

SMASH! The massive stone structure crashed into the metal box on the ground. It crushed the box the way a stomping foot crushes an ant.

The gold energy field immediately disappeared as if someone had neglected to pay the light bill. Simultaneous with the gold field disappearing, the Portal that had sent me here flicked back into existence. It floated off the ground maybe fifty feet from the mangled debris of the power nullification box.

The cicada-like noise the worms made and their whizzing increased in intensity as the main body of the swarm got closer. The sound of them was now almost deafening. I felt like the leading man in a horror flick.

Safety was now right at hand, though. The emerald field inside of the Portal rippled, seemingly gesturing invitingly. I could fly through the Portal and back to the Guild complex on

Earth Sigma. The worm swarm was so close, it was likely I'd only manage to kill both of us if I went back for Hacker. Surely no one would blame me if I saved myself and left Hacker behind.

The smart thing to do would be to save myself.

Sometimes I'm not very smart.

I rocketed toward the building Hacker was in like a stone shot from a slingshot. Worms rained down around me. I felt a sharp pain in my right arm, and yet another in my backside as I approached the building. I cried out in pain. I opened the building's door with my powers. I shot toward the small opening in the building like a billiard ball racing toward the side pocket.

As soon as I zoomed through the door, I slammed it shut behind me with my powers. The sound of the worms pelting the outside of the building was thunderous.

I barreled toward the wall opposite the door. I was going too fast. I couldn't stop in time.

I slammed into the wall like a cannonball.

I bounced off it, leaving a Theo-sized dent behind. I sailed backward, hitting the floor hard. I skidded along the floor like a slapped hockey puck before finally coming to a stop. Fortunately my shield was still up, otherwise I probably would have broken bones. As it was, my insides were shaken around like I had just been in a car accident.

I looked up to see Hacker standing over me.

"You came back for me." She sounded surprised. She had to yell to be heard over the ear-splitting sound of the worms pounding the building.

"Of course," I said. If I weren't in pain and scared silly, maybe I could have come up with a clever quip. As it was, "of course" was the best I could do.

I tried to stand. It was harder than it should have been. Hacker bent over to help.

"You'd have done the same for me," I said once I was back on my feet.

"No I wouldn't have," she said matter-of-factly. "It's not logical. The only thing you've accomplished by coming back is to put yourself in a position to be killed too."

"You ever think about changing your name to Negative Nelly?"

As if on cue, two cans of food jumped off the shelves with loud *pops*, like they had been shot. We ducked at the noise. The cans hit the floor. They moved around there as if they were full of Mexican jumping beans. Worms were clearly getting in through the holes they had made in the building during their last swarm.

The worms in the dancing cans amply demonstrated Hacker had a point about how we were now both in danger. My plan had been to fly in here. I didn't have a plan as to how to get me and Hacker out.

"If you fail to plan, you plan to fail," Dad had often said. What a terrible time for him to be proven right.

The building's skylight and window were completely covered with colliding worms now. Thanks to the sun being obscured, the interior was now almost totally dark. The worms pounded the building's outsides. If I tried to fly Hacker out of here now, the worms would turn us into Swiss cheese before we flew twenty feet.

A few more worms punched through the building's walls and whizzed by. They ricocheted off the opposing walls. At any moment they might punch holes through me or Hacker.

I needed a plan. Immediately.

Vegetable juice oozed from one of the cans on the floor. The fact the cans still moved around on the floor like something possessed indicated the worms remained in them. Why hadn't the worms already flown out of the cans?

The question reminded me of how the worm that had gotten into my water bottle earlier seemed confused by the water.

I got an idea. I felt a sudden surge of hope.

"Come on!" I cried. I grabbed Hacker by the hand and pulled her to the door. Once there, despite my butt's and arm's painful protests, I bent over and easily picked her up and held her. Before my Heroic training, it would have been easier for a woman to pick me up rather than vice versa. The countless squats and deadlifts I had done during training were serving me well.

"What are you doing? Put me down!" Hacker made it sound like I was groping her.

"Shut up," I snapped, distracted. "I need to concentrate."

Think of a ten-pound dumbbell. Picking one up by hand and moving it around was simple. The same was not true of ten pounds of water. If you dipped your hand in a bucket full of ten pounds of water, picking all the water up by hand would be impossible. The water would flow through your hands like, well, water. That's because the molecules of a liquid like water flow and slide past one another. By contrast, the molecules making up a solid object like a dumbbell are compressed together tightly, making the entire object easy to pick up.

Just as picking up a ten-pound dumbbell by hand was easy and picking up ten pounds of water by hand was impossible, me moving a solid with my powers was easy, yet moving a liquid was almost impossible because it was tough to grab onto a liquid. The molecules in liquids just moved around too much.

Almost impossible, but not impossible. At least theoretically. Late one night when I had been in the Academy, I could literally feel with my powers the molecules and atoms of everything in the building I had been in. That had been the first, but not the only, time that had happened. *One day,* I had thought during those times when my powers had seemed to kick into overdrive and let me feel things on a molecular level, *maybe I'll not only be able to feel things on a molecular level, but manipulate them too.*

That day needed to be today. It had to be. If it wasn't, it would be buh-bye Hacker and Kinetic. We'd get our Heroes' capes alright, but they'd be draped over our caskets instead of draped around our necks.

Feeling encouraged that my powers seemed to be stronger than usual since I had managed to move that massive rock, I stretched out my mind to the water bottles on the shelves. I dove deep into the water with my mind, down to the molecular level. I grabbed ahold of the chains of hydrogen and oxygen. It was like grabbing onto strands of spaghetti swirling in a boiling pot. I tugged hard on the water molecules.

The water bottles exploded. Both the big drums containing gallons and the small ones containing mere ounces exploded open like a bomb had been planted into each of them. I levitated off the ground a bit with Hacker in my arms. I had picked her up earlier rather than levitating her separately because this way there was one less thing my powers would be distracted by. I made the water rush toward us. It formed a thick liquid sphere around us. The view of everything got distorted. It was like looking through glasses of the wrong prescription.

I felt myself sweating with the mental exertion of maintaining the sphere of water around us. Would the worms penetrate the surrounding water, or would they be confused by it as we had observed previously?

Holding my breath in apprehension, I diverted enough of my attention away from holding the water in place to use my powers to open the door.

What seemed like a Biblical plague swarmed inside. The inside of the building immediately filled with flying worms like a swarm of black and orange locusts.

And yet, Hacker and I remained untouched. I felt some of

the worms enter the water around us. They swam around in it, but did not penetrate to where we were.

Whew! I let out the breath I'd been holding.

Despite the fact we hadn't been immediately shot to pieces by the worms, this was no place to linger. The worms might eventually get through the water to us. Plus, my hold on the water was tenuous. I literally shook with the effort it took to maintain my hold on the liquid. I felt like a quaking bodybuilder holding too much weight over his head.

Still carrying Hacker and still surrounded by the water, I flew us out of the building. Thanks to both the water and all the worms, I couldn't see where the Portal was. I knew in what general direction it was, though. I diverted a tiny bit of my attention away from the water to extend mental feelers out for the Portal's metal. I groped around for it like a man groping for his car keys in a dark room.

I found it. I flew toward the Portal as quickly as I could without letting the water around us fall. Even with the sound-muffling liquid around us, being in the thick of the worm storm was deafening.

Moments later, Hacker and I shot through the Portal like a smashed tennis ball.

Then, we slammed into something hard face-first. I hit it with such force, it felt like my brain sloshed around in my skull. My hold on both Hacker and the water was jarred loose. Surprised, I inhaled water. I felt myself falling.

A moment later, I hit the ground. Hard. The air whooshed out of my lungs.

Wheezing and coughing up water, I wiped wetness from my eyes. I looked around, expecting to be slapped with a faceful of worms.

There were none to be seen. We were back in the room containing Portal Five in the Guild complex on Earth Sigma.

Other than Hacker and I—who were both a coughing, wet mess —the room was as empty as it had been when I had first entered it. Based on the huge wet splotch on the wall above us, Hacker and I had slammed into it before falling to the floor.

Unsteadily rising to her hands and knees, Hacker made a bunch of choking sounds. She then threw up all over the floor. Some of it got on me. I was too busy coughing up water to mind much.

It would be mighty ironic, not to mention embarrassing, if I had survived all that on Hephaestus only to choke to death on Earth Sigma.

"Congratulations, Hacker. Congratulations, Kinetic. You both passed test two," intoned Overlord's voice from the wall panel. "If you suffered any injuries, please report to the infirmary for treatment. You would be well advised to hurry. Test three could begin at any time."

I still coughed. When I could finally speak again, I asked Overlord, "Where did all the worms with us go?"

"No extraterrestrial life-forms may pass through the Portals," Overlord said. Apparently it was more inclined to answer questions here than it had been on Hephaestus.

Hacker was done throwing up. She now stood, bent over, panting, with her hands on her knees. I tried to get up as I was lying in puke and water, but my body wasn't working correctly. So I stayed where I was, exhausted, gasping for breath. Standing was overrated anyway. If standing was so awesome, why didn't infants do it?

"You saved my life," Hacker said, looking down at me.

"We saved each other," I rasped. "I never could've jumped the chasm without you."

"That is true. My performance was exemplary." Her lack of social graces seemed more charming here than it had on

Hephaestus. Not fighting for one's life apparently made one more forgiving of others' quirks.

Hacker started tapping her cheek again. She said, "Even so, you came back to rescue me when the most sensible course of action would have been to leave me behind to die. I am in your debt. If there's anything I can ever do to help you, just let me know."

"Thanks. I'll keep that in mind." I tried unsuccessfully to stand up again. My head pounded and my body ached. My arm and butt throbbed painfully from where the worms had shot me. I didn't seem to be coordinated enough anymore to get to my feet. Using my powers in new ways apparently had taken the starch out of me. "Well, for starters you can help walk me to the infirmary. I seem to have hurt my—" I broke off, not sure how to finish the sentence. My head? My butt? My arm? My bones? I hurt all over.

"My everything," I concluded.

Hacker put her arm around me. She helped me stand, and then started walking me to the Guild infirmary. I knew I wasn't feeling so great because I didn't notice how her breast pressed into my side as she aided me.

Well, okay, I did notice it a little. I was hurt, not dead.

On the way to the infirmary, we saw another cape-draped casket had been added to Hammer's and Prism's.

16

"All right everybody, huddle around and listen up," Hitler's Youth said at the beginning of my third test of the Trials' scenarios phase.

We seven Hero candidates all hurried to cluster around him. If Hitler's Youth wasn't the king of the douchebags, he certainly was douchebag aristocracy. Despite that, Neha and I hastened to gather around him like the five other candidates did. We didn't want to be left out.

Even though I didn't like him, I understood why people tended to listen to Hitler's Youth. With his tall, strong body, rugged jaw, and flashing blue eyes, he was like a Hollywood casting director's idea of how a Hero should look. That, plus the fact he was assertive and had natural charisma—as much as I hated to admit that last part—made it hard to not do as he asked.

Hitler's Youth said, "Like it said, Overlord has given us forty minutes to find and deactivate the bomb hidden in this mall. If we don't, we fail the test. Plus, hundreds will be killed or injured."

Even I couldn't fault Hitler's Youth for adding the people

being injured or killed part as an afterthought. This wasn't a real mall we were in, of course. The Guild would never endanger a bunch of civilians by planting a real bomb in an actual mall. We were in one of the Guild's holosuites in the Trials' complex. Other than us candidates, everything around us was merely a cunningly wrought, high-tech combination of photons, tractor beams, and force fields. Beyond knowing that, I was too technologically challenged to understand exactly how the holosuite worked. It seemed like magic, though I knew it wasn't.

You never would have known we were merely in a holosuite based on the sights and sounds around us. We had just walked from outside the mall where it was sunny, hot, and muggy, to inside the mall where it was cool and temperature-controlled. According to the mall directory we had just consulted by the entrance, the mall had three stories and lots of high-end stores. Thanks to a star labeled "You are here" on the directory, we knew we were on the first floor. It looked, felt, and sounded like we were really in a big city's shopping mall. The mall was busy, with plenty of people laden with shopping bags bustling by. There was a steady hum of conversations and music playing softly over the mall's loudspeakers. There was even a faint whiff of odors from the mall's food court.

Floating overhead near the mall's high domed ceiling was an Overlord node. A green-glowing countdown indicating thirty-nine minutes and counting was below it. It gave me flashbacks of my time on Hephaestus days before. I still had bandages on both my left buttock and my right arm where worms had shot through them. Otherwise, I felt much better than I had when I first returned to Earth Sigma. Though the Guild doctor who had treated me didn't have Metahuman healing powers the way Doctor Hippocrates did, he knew his stuff and had done a good job stitching me up.

"This place is massive, so we'll need to split up," Hitler's

Youth said. All of us were dressed in normal clothes issued to us by the Guild for purposes of this test. As per Overlord's instructions, we were supposed to find the bomb without letting the mall-goers know they were in danger. That's why we wore mufti and why we weren't supposed to use our powers too obviously in locating the bomb. Fortunately, though, once we found the bomb, we could use our powers to our heart's content in deactivating it.

Hitler's Youth said, "Dervish and Glamour Gal will search the third floor; Flare and Chance, you've got the second; Samson and I will take the ground floor. Once you locate the bomb, alert the rest of the group. We'll converge on it and figure out how to defuse it." Overlord had provided us with communicators mounted in our ears. I felt like a Secret Service agent with it in.

The group began to scatter to carry out their assignments.

"Hey, what about me and Smoke?" I protested to Hitler's Youth.

He stopped in mid-stride. He smirked down at me.

"Just stay out of the way. The rest of us will handle this," he said. With a jerk of his head, he motioned for Samson to follow him toward the escalators. Samson—who was as big as you'd expect from his name—hesitated, looking at me and Neha with a confused frown. Then he turned to trail after Hitler's Youth.

Neha and I looked at each other. If we stood here twiddling our thumbs while everyone else did the work, we'd flunk the test for sure. Hitler's Youth had to know that. With us being friends of Isaac's, apparently Hitler's Youth had decided the friends of his enemy were his enemies.

Neha said, "If that lunkhead really thinks we're going to stand here with our heads up our asses, he's very much mistaken." With one exception, Neha had taken the words right out of my mouth.

"Lunkhead? Interesting word choice." I grinned. "What are you, a character out of *Archie Comics*?"

"I'm trying to cut back on my motherfucking cursing."

When irritated, Neha tended to curse like a raunchy stand-up comedian. She also talked dirty when we were in bed together. There had been many times when her command of profane language had simultaneously turned me on, made me blush, and expanded my vocabulary. Her pillow talk was the fucking trifecta. Pun intended.

Despite the fact we were in the middle of a test, just looking at Neha right now got me a little turned on. She was dressed in black boots, tight skinny jeans, a purple fitted turtleneck, and an unzipped leather jacket. If it hadn't been for metallic Big Brother hovering overhead in the form of Overlord, I would have kissed her.

The only thing that marred Neha's appearance was a black and blue shiner on her right eye. It stood out in vivid contrast to her light olive skin. It was a memento from her previous test. When I had asked her about it earlier, she had smiled happily and said, "If you think this looks bad, you should see the other guy." I had the feeling Neha was enjoying the Trials more than I was.

With an effort, I pulled my thoughts away from how good Neha looked in her jeans.

"Any thoughts on how best to go about finding the bomb?" I asked. "It could be anywhere and look like anything. The other guys searching by hand is better than nothing, but trying to find something in a place this huge is worse than looking for a needle in a haystack. It's like looking for a needle in a needlestack."

"Yeah. We need a way to look at everything here at once. Fortunately, the mall's already got just such a system in place."

She pointed at a light fixture on the wall. I didn't see what she pointed toward at first.

And then I did. Hidden within the nest of lights was a black globe that obviously housed a camera.

"Of course! You're a genius," I said. "There must be hidden cameras all over the place. If we can access the cameras' feeds, maybe we can figure out where the bomb is."

"Technically, I'm not a genius. I'm a near genius. Dad had me tested when I was a kid. He was very disappointed I didn't have a genius-level intellect like him. Not that his brains are doing the world much good." Neha's father was Doctor Alchemy, a noted supervillain. Helping to thwart his plans for world domination was the main reason Neha wanted to become a Hero.

"Okay, okay, you're not a genius. Just a near genius. And overly literal on top of that. Alright Miss Almost-A-Genius, where does that big brain of yours tell you we should look for the hidden cameras' video feed?"

"I don't need my intellect to tell me. Experience tells me. Big malls like this usually have a central office where security officers review the camera footage for problems. I know because I got caught shoplifting a couple of times by them." She must have seen the look on my face because she added, "Don't look so shocked. I wasn't always a Hero's Apprentice, you know. Back when I ran away from home after Mom was murdered by one of Dad's enemies, I had to do what I had to do to survive. A girl's gotta feed and clothe herself somehow."

"You're a fellow jailbird? No wonder we get along."

Neha shook her head. "I said I got caught. I didn't get arrested or go to jail. It's amazing what you can get away with if you're a cute girl and you can cry on command." Apparently unlike petty larceny, false modesty has never been one of Neha's vices.

"Come on," Neha said. We walked for a bit through the

146

shoppers until we came across a patrolling security guard. He had a red jowly face and a short haircut. His belt rode low on his waist. His big belly swelled over it. If he were a woman, I would've assumed he was pregnant. Clearly mall security guards —even of the holographic variety—did not need to be in the kind of shape Hero candidates were in.

"Hi!" Neha said brightly to the man. Overlord had told us to treat the holographic people as we would actual humans as the holographic constructs were programmed to behave like people. "My friend and I are reporters for the local newspaper. We're supposed to meet the head of security. Mister . . . mister . . . oh my goodness, I forget his name. Theo, didn't you write it down?"

I caught on in time. I pretended to check my pockets for a non-existent note.

"Mr. Jenkins," the guard supplied helpfully. Neha snapped her fingers triumphantly.

"That's right, Mr. Jenkins. Anyway, he wanted us to meet him where you all review the hidden camera video footage. Can you tell us where that is?"

The guard looked dubious. "Are you sure he wanted to meet you there? I thought only security guards were allowed in there."

"Mr. Jenkins made an exception this one time. We're writing a story about how you hard-working guards keep everyone safe. It'll make the front page for sure. It's long past time for you guys to get your due. The working title is *Heroes of the Mall*." Neha's eyes shone with enthusiasm. She had thrown her shoulders back so her chest stuck out. She looked at the guard like she wanted to pin the Medal of Honor on him right after fellating him.

The guard stood up a little straighter. "Well in that case, I'm sure it's all right." He pointed down the mall's concourse. "See Macy's down there? Well, on the third floor, to the right of the store's entrance is an unlabeled door. If you go through it and down the corridor, you'll find Room 305 on the left. That's the video surveillance room."

"Thank you so much," Neha said. She glanced down at his name tag. "I'll make sure to mention your name in our article, Mr. Byrd."

"Aw, you don't have to do that." He hesitated. "But the first name is Douglas in case you should decide to mention me anyway."

"Douglas Byrd. Got it. We definitely won't forget."

Mr. Byrd walked away to resume his patrol. There seemed to be an extra bit of swagger in his step now.

Neha and I started toward the escalators.

"What?" she demanded once we were gliding upstairs. I had eyed her suspiciously ever since we'd walked away from the guard.

"You looked at the guard just now the same way you looked at me when you told me our sex was the best you've had. I can't help but wonder if you were lying to me too."

"Of course I wasn't lying." Her hazel eyes twinkled. "The day I told you that, that was the best sex I had that whole day."

"You're not funny."

Following the guard's instructions, once on the third floor, we made our way to the unmarked door near the Macy's entrance. Once we were inside the white corridor that lay behind it, the sounds of music and shoppers were left behind as if we had left the mall altogether.

Unlike the rest of the mall which was slick and affluent, this corridor had a rough, unfinished look. We went down to Room 305. I checked the door. It was locked. Using one of my power's new tricks, I probed inside to see if it was occupied. My powers passed through two holographic constructs shaped like men. Running my powers over them was weird. It reminded me of the slightly clammy feeling I got when I stuck my hand into a heavy fog.

I raised a hand before me, about to force the door open with my powers. Before I could do so, Neha stayed me with a hand on my arm.

"This is supposed to be a stealth operation, not a prison riot," she said.

"Is that remark a not-so-subtle dig at my jail time?"

Neha smiled mysteriously. "Maybe."

Her body became translucent and cloudy. In gaseous form, she started to seep into the gap between the floor and the door. In a few moments, she was completely gone.

I heard a muted thump from the other side of the door. Seconds later, Neha opened the door. She was back in her solid form. Two security guards were behind her. One lay on the floor; the other slumped over in his chair. Both were unconscious. In front of them was a big bank of monitors showing various parts of the mall.

"Knockout gas," Neha said in explanation of the guards' unconsciousness.

I dragged the guard on the floor out of the way with my powers. He was even bigger than Mr. Byrd had been, but fortunately my powers were far stronger than my muscles. The chair of the seated guy was on rollers, so him I just rolled out of the way.

When I focused my attention on the bank of monitors, Neha was already examining them.

"To be honest, I don't know exactly what to look for," I admitted with my brow furrowed after looking at the monitors for a bit. There was simply too much to watch. I didn't know how in the world actual security guards were able to do their jobs effectively. "Somehow I don't think the Guild was helpful enough to label something B-O-M-B," I said, spelling out the letters.

"Look for anything suspicious," Neha said. "Remember what the Old Man taught us about scanning for a threat in a crowd of people—we're looking for anything or anyone that doesn't seem to belong. Someone who seems nervous, who's dressed inappropriately for the weather or in big bulky clothing, someone who doesn't take his hands out of his pockets, that kind of thing."

We watched the monitors like two electronic hawks. After a while, we had stared at the monitors for so long I felt like I would go cross-eyed. I stood the entire time because it was a literal pain in the butt to sit. The stitches in my butt itched. I wanted to scratch, but refused to do it in front of Neha. We were close, but not that close.

We hadn't heard anything from the rest of the candidates in the test. When we occasionally spotted them on the monitors, they looked increasingly agitated. I knew how they felt. I was agitated too. I felt like doing something more proactive than merely staring at a screen. Scratching my butt, while it would make me feel better, didn't seem to fit under the category of "proactive." Then again, standing here looking at these monitors seemed like a more effective use of our time than running around like chickens with their heads cut off the way the rest of the candidates were.

Knowing that in my head and feeling that in my heart were two different issues though. Part of me wanted to go back out into the mall and start tearing things apart with my powers in search of the bomb. Overlord had admonished us that an obvious use of our powers prior to locating the bomb was a no-no, though.

Time was inexorably ticking away. If we didn't find the bomb soon, we would surely all fail this test and be forced to leave the

Trials. I knew better than to think Overlord would accept "But we did our best!" as an excuse.

Someone caught my eye on a monitor on the far left. I had noticed him enter the mall earlier. He was a lean white guy who was by himself, wearing a baseball cap, and pushing a baby stroller. He slowly made his way toward the center of the mall on the first floor.

Many decades ago a guy pushing a stroller by himself would have been weird, but men took a more active role in childcare these days. Even so, something about the guy and his stroller nagged at the edge of my consciousness. I couldn't figure out what it was.

We had been here so long, Neha and I had figured out how to zoom in on things a while ago. I hit a key to select the monitor the man with the stroller was on, and then used a joystick to zoom in on him. I studied the blown-up footage. Nothing about the man himself seemed terribly unusual. Then I focused in on the stroller. It was one of those strollers designed for the baby to lie flat in it. The sun shield—or whatever in the heck that part of the stroller is called that shields the baby's head—was up. Between it and the thick-looking blankets covering the kid, I couldn't see the baby. All I could see was a lump under the blankets. The lump didn't move. The baby was no doubt asleep.

"The collapsible part of a baby stroller that covers a baby's head—what's it called?" I asked Neha.

"The canopy," she supplied absent-mindedly. She was busy looking at a different monitor.

I smiled to myself. I had just known Neha would know. She seemed to know just about everything.

Then what had been gnawing at the edge of my mind hit me like a brick upside the head.

There were thick blankets covering the kid in the stroller! The man had just come from outside where it was hot and muggy. There was no way you'd cover your kid like that on a day like it was outside. Plus, the lump under the blankets hadn't budged an inch since I had been watching.

I straightened up from the control panel. Excitement rose in me like a tide.

"It's in the stroller!" I exclaimed. "The bomb is in the stroller." I hastily sketched out my suspicions to Neha. She took a long look at the monitor I had been examining.

"Makes sense," she said. "Let's go check it out."

"Shouldn't we tell the others?"

"Let's hold off on that. If we're wrong, we don't want to pull the others away from the search."

We hustled out of the room and back into the mall proper. We moved quickly through the shoppers, not running, but not exactly walking either. When we got to the center of the mall that had a huge open area stretching from the mall's third floor ceiling to the bottom floor, we could see Overlord's countdown.

We had less than four minutes to go.

Neha and I looked at each other.

"If we're right, there's no time left for subtlety," she said. After a quick running start, she jumped over the safety railing and plummeted out of sight toward the bottom floor.

I loved the fact she was a badass.

Then, a realization hit me like a lightning strike:

I loved her, period.

The unexpected realization made me freeze at the railing. I watched Neha turn translucent as she assumed a gaseous form and floated gently down to the first floor. I was in love with Neha. I now realized I had been for a while now. Since Neha had made it clear she wasn't interested in any kind of relationship other than a sexual one until we got our licenses, I supposed I had hidden my true feelings from even myself.

I snapped out of my reverie. Had I suddenly wandered into a

Lifetime movie? Now was not the time for emotional awakenings or professions of undying love.

I leapt over the railing and dropped like a stone. Since I didn't have to break as soon as Neha did, I hit the ground on the first floor mere seconds after she did. Some of the nearby shoppers gaped at our sudden appearance from above like giraffes had materialized in front of them.

We ran toward where we had seen the man with the stroller on the cameras. He soon came into view. His back was to us. As soon as we made visual contact with him, I stretched out my awareness with my powers to probe the baby carriage.

What I felt with my powers was not baby-shaped. It was as round as a softball, but bigger.

I tapped my ear communicator as we ran toward the man. "We found the bomb," I said breathlessly as we weaved through shoppers toward the man. "It's in a baby stroller on the first floor near New York and Company."

We slowed to a walk behind the man. Neha tapped him on the shoulder. He turned his head. He was a tall guy with a scraggly beard.

"Y-Y-Yes?" he stammered, looking nervously at us. If I hadn't known he was guilty of trying to bomb the mall, I would think he was guilty of something just from how he acted.

Without so much as a *How do you do?*, Neha clipped the guy with an uppercut to his chin. The man's eyes rolled back. He slumped to the ground like a sack of potatoes. There was a murmur from the shoppers around us. "Somebody call the cops," someone said. I ignored them as my mind was fully occupied with the contents of the stroller.

Careful to not move the lump that lay beneath the covers, I gingerly lifted the covers off the little bundle of boom the stroller contained. I was surprised to see the round device under the covers looked identical to the explosive that had nearly taken my head off after the foiled Chinatown bank robbery, only this device was much larger.

Someone dropped from above and landed next to me. It was Hitler's Youth. His eyes quickly took in the situation, sweeping over the unconscious man on the ground and the device in the baby carriage.

"Good job guys," he said grudgingly, like the words had caught in his throat. "I'll use my wind powers to fly this thing high up into the sky where it can't hurt anyone." He stepped forward, reaching for the device. Neha immediately moved in front of him to bar his path.

"Don't be stupid," she said. "It might explode if you try to move it. Kinetic, what do you think?" I had told her all about the recent augmentation of my powers. She needn't have prompted me as I was already gently roving over the object with my mind.

"There's a pressure switch under the device," I concluded. I knew more about explosives than a terrorist thanks to the Old Man's training. "If we try to move it, it'll blow."

A hard pit of dread formed in my stomach. The pressure switch wasn't the worst part of what I found when I probed the device. I hadn't found merely photons and force fields as I had expected.

"But that's not all," I said. "This thing's not a hologram. It's real. If it explodes, it'll not only kill us, but probably take out half the Guild complex with it."

17

"What do you mean, the bomb is real?" Hitler's Youth said incredulously. By now, all the candidates except Dervish and Glamour Gal had arrived and gathered around us. "Everything except us is supposed to be a holographic projection. You must be wrong."

"I'm not wrong," I insisted.

Chance's brown eyes turned milky white for moment before returning to normal.

"Kinetic's right," she said. "There's a one hundred percent chance we will all die if we do nothing and the bomb explodes. There's a ninety-six percent chance a third of the people in the rest of the Guild complex will die if we do nothing." Her powers allowed her to assess the probabilities of any situation.

"So what do we do?" Samson asked. It was disconcerting to see a big man look so scared.

"Kinetic, can you secure the bomb in the stroller so it doesn't budge and then fly the entire stroller out of the mall?" Hitler's Youth asked.

"To what end?" Neha said. "The bomb would still be in the holosuite and still in the Guild complex." She raised her voice.

"Overlord, there is a real bomb in the test that poses a threat to everyone in the Guild complex. We need you to suspend the test and end the holographic simulation so we can get the bomb out of here."

Overlord remained silent. Nothing happened other than Overlord's countdown continuing to tick down. I suspected it was programmed to never interfere in an ongoing test.

We had less than two minutes to go.

Dervish and Glamour Girl came running up. Hitler's Youth rapidly explained the situation to them. We all looked at each other, uncertain as to what to do.

Nobody rushed forward to save the day, though somebody had to do something before we all were turned into hamburger.

Since nobody else had an idea, I guess that somebody had to be me.

Ugh!

"I'll contain the explosion in one of my force fields," I said.

Neha looked at me like I had proposed to walk on water today and rise from the dead tomorrow.

"You can't do it," she said flatly. "The bomb is too big. I've seen what you can do with your powers, and you can't do that." My feelings would have been hurt at her lack of faith if it weren't for the fact she was probably right.

"I can do it," I said, stating it with far more confidence than I felt. I hoped there was something to the concept of the power of positive thinking. Neha was right: I hadn't done anything like this before. But, I found myself wanting to save Neha, maybe even more than I wanted to save myself. If this was love, it had made me foolhardy. Or just stupid. "Besides, even if I can't fully contain the explosion, maybe I can suppress enough of it so not as many people in the Guild complex are killed or injured."

I moved to stand in front of the stroller. While holding the bomb in place with my powers so I wouldn't accidentally trigger the pressure switch, I gently lowered the stroller's canopy. The bomb looked even bigger now that it was fully exposed.

"Fuck this noise," Samson exclaimed. His eyes were wide and wild with panic. "You guys can stand here and have your heads blown off if you want. I'm outta here." He spun and ran, knocking shoppers to the ground with his big body as he retreated. After a moment's hesitation, Glamour Girl, Dervish, and Flare turned tail and ran too. Their reaction was understandable, if not probably futile. If a bomb this size went off uncontained, it would almost certainly incinerate everyone in the holosuite.

Still, I could hardly blame them for running.

I wanted to run away too.

Only Neha, Hitler's Youth and Chance remained. I didn't know if Chance had weighed the odds and decided I would be able to pull this off, or if the odds told her she was likely to die regardless of what she did.

"I hope you can actually do this," Hitler's Youth said to me. Then, he turned to the throng of shoppers around us.

"There's a bomb!" his voice thundered. "Everybody run!"

I had to give credit where credit was due. Instead of panicking and running the way those others had, he hadn't forgotten we were still in the middle of a test that was being judged. In the real world, if a bomb was about to go off in a crowded place, the first thing a Hero would do would be to evacuate the area.

Despite Hitler's Youth's warning, none of the shoppers budged. Few seemed to hear him. In their defense, we were in civilian clothes. In our costumes, people would pay more attention to us and our warnings. I had learned in the Academy that was one of the main reasons we wore costumes and capes.

Hitler's Youth cursed at the crowd's lack of a reaction. He raised his hands high over his head and cupped them together.

A fireball shot out of them, hurtling toward the mall's high ceiling.

BOOM!

The fireball exploded against the ceiling, seemingly harm-lessly, but with a light show that could rival a Fourth of July fire-works display. Though a couple of people screamed, the rest of the shoppers froze in fear and confusion.

"Bomb! Run!" Hitler's Youth repeated. His loud voice rever-berated through the mall like a foghorn. Another fireball shot from his outstretched hands. *BOOM!* It thundered against the ceiling.

Being told to run a second time was apparently the charm. Everyone around us began to scatter, like cockroaches when the lights unexpectedly turn on. Panicked screams and the sounds of scrambling feet echoed against the walls. Both Hitler's Youth and Chance went to help the people getting trampled in the others' mad dash.

I tore my attention away from the madhouse swirling around me. My eyes flicked up to Overlord's countdown.

Less than thirty seconds to go.

It was now or never.

I felt Neha's lips press against my cheek. Was it a goodbye or a good luck kiss? Both, maybe.

I stretched my hands over the bomb like a witch consulting her crystal ball. I concentrated mightily, forming a spherical force field around the bomb within the contours of my clawed hands. In my mind's eye, I pictured my force field as an immov-able object nothing in the world could budge. I tried to tune out everything else around me.

Seconds ticked away. Soon, thanks to the force of my concentration, everything else became gray and distant. I even stopped feeling my heavy breathing and the pounding of my heart, as if they now belonged to someone else. There was nothing else in the world but my power, my force field, and the bomb.

The bomb flashed like the lights of an oncoming locomotive. It exploded.

Fire and fury and destruction raged between my hands. The terrific pressure felt like it was blowing my hands and mind apart. I hung on to maintaining my force field like my life depended on it because, well, it did. The mother of all migraines exploded in my skull, spreading to every nook and cranny of my tortured mind like a virus run amok. Simultaneously, it felt like a giant dominatrix in stiletto heels stepped on the base of my skull, harder and harder, until her full weight bore down on me.

The explosion in miniature taking place between my hands grew bigger. I could feel my hold on my force field slipping, like it was grains of sand trickling faster and faster between my fingers.

It wasn't going to work. I wasn't going to be able to contain the explosion. The bomb's energy was about to escape. My mind and hands were about to fly apart. We were all going to die. Neha, the only girl I had ever loved, was about to die.

A thought pierced my agonized brain like a bolt from the blue. Maybe I was going about this all wrong. The law of conservation of energy dictated that energy can neither be created nor destroyed; rather, it merely is transformed from one form to another. Instead of trying to contain the explosion's energy, maybe what I needed to do was transform it into something else. I did it all the time when I used my powers, but usually on a much smaller scale. When the bank robbers had shot at me, for example, I had not stopped the kinetic energy of their racing bullets by making it disappear. Rather, I had absorbed the energy into my own body.

Like a drowning man desperately clawing for a life preserver, I immediately switched tactics. I went from trying to stop the force of the explosion to instead trying to absorb it. I went from trying to be a big rock that stopped the force of a wave smashing against it to trying to be a sponge that absorbed the wave.

The terrific light show exploding between my hands dimmed slightly. The hair on my body stood on end as I slowly siphoned away the explosion's energy and absorbed it into my own body. I soon felt like I had chugged a gallon of coffee and then stuck my fingers into an electric outlet.

The energy fighting for freedom within my force field slowly faded, and then disappeared. I staggered backward, gasping for breath.

"Son of a bitch!" Hitler's Youth said. His voice was full of disbelief. "The little twerp actually pulled it off."

"Remarkable," Chance exclaimed.

"Oh my God, Theo!" Neha said, uncharacteristically slipping and calling me by my real name in front of others. Her voice was equal parts shocked and awed. "You did it."

Well, not quite. I slammed my mouth and eyes closed, afraid the energy I had absorbed was going to shoot out of me to disastrous effect. Now instead of the bomb exploding and killing everyone, I felt like *I* was going to explode and kill everyone. Every fiber of my being buzzed with barely suppressed energy. It was as if electrified buzzing bees ricocheted off the walls of every cell in my body. My body felt like it was about to fly apart like a jet pushed well past its design specifications. I just had to release the massive amount of energy I had absorbed before it blew me apart.

Out wasn't an option, because that was where the others were.

Up seemed like the only reasonable alternative.

I turned my face up like I was praying to God. I threw open my mouth and eyes. I channeled the energy inside of me, forcing it out through my gaping eyes and mouth.

The energy I had absorbed shot out of me like an erupting volcano. It felt like I was projectile vomiting every ounce of energy pent up in my body's cells.

The blasts of energy from my eyes and mouth hit the mall's ceiling like a laser cutting through butter. Part of the ceiling disappeared with a massive concussion. Rubble fell. The energy destroyed part of the holographic illusion, exposing the shimmering walls of the holosuite. The energy blasts cut right through the holosuite, through the floor above us in the Guild complex, and then through the floor above that. They hit the dome that covered the entire Guild complex high above. The dome rang deafeningly, like a struck bell. Everything around us shook, like we were going through an earthquake.

I gushed energy like an exploding geyser.

Then, suddenly and unexpectedly, all the explosive energy was out of me.

I fell to my knees, unable to stand. I was as weak as a newborn kitten. My chest heaved. I exhaled smoke like a chimney. My throat and nose were raw. My eyes burned like acid had been thrown into them.

As if from far away, like I was at the bottom of a well and someone was calling down to me, I heard someone speaking. It was Neha.

"Well!" she said. Wonder filled her voice. "*That's* new."

A SHORT WHILE LATER, PITBULL LOOKED UP AT THE GAPING HOLE I had cut through the holosuite all the way up to the dome covering the Guild complex. Neha, Chance, and Elemental Man were still here with me. I was making a real effort to think of Elemental Man as that instead of as "Hitler's Youth." Though I still didn't like him or how he treated me and Neha, I respected the fact he hadn't run away from the bomb the way some of the other Hero candidates had.

We four Hero candidates had each given to the proctors statements about what had happened. Through the holes I had blasted through the Guild complex, I saw one of the Hero proctors flying high above us. From this distance, he looked like a buzzing gnat flitting right below the dome housing the Guild complex. He was repairing the dome. I had cracked it when I blasted the dome with the bomb's redirected energy. Earth Sigma's native life apparently wasn't friendly, and the Guild didn't want to give the creatures on the other side of the dome a chance to breach it through a damaged portion.

Pitbull shook his head as he examined the damage I had caused.

He said, "Just when I think I have seen everything, someone turns up and shows me something new. First the nanites, now this." He then looked at me. "You certainly have a flair for being in the thick of things, Kinetic."

"Not by choice," I said. I was as unsteady on my legs as a newborn colt. My eyes and nose burned, like I was having the mother of all allergy attacks. My voice was raspy, like I was recovering from a bout of laryngitis. Spewing out energy like you were Mount Vesuvius was apparently hard on one's orifices. Who knew? "If one of the infirmary's doctors specializes in flair removal surgery, let me know."

Pitbull snorted and then looked back up at the damage I had caused.

Overlord had already told us four Hero candidates we had passed this test, and why: Neha and I for locating the bomb, me for containing and redirecting the bomb's explosive energy, and Chance and Elemental Man for not abandoning their mission and doing what they could to ensure the safety of the civilians in the mall. Dervish, Glamour Gal, Samson, and Flare had failed and had been sent packing. For all I knew, they were back on Earth Prime by now, sleeping in their own beds. I envied them. Not the flunking out part, but the sleeping part. I was so exhausted I felt like I would give Rip Van Winkle a run for his money when I finally got some shut-eye.

"There weren't supposed to be any real explosives used in this test," Pitbull said. "Only a holographic one. If the test had proceeded as designed and you all weren't able to defuse the holographic bomb in time, you might have been injured a bit. You certainly wouldn't have been killed. And the rest of the complex certainly shouldn't have been in any danger. Our preliminary overview of Overlord's recorded footage gives no indication of how someone snuck a real bomb into this test. We're launching an investigation as to how and why this happened."

"Isn't the 'why' obvious?" Neha said. "Someone's trying to kill Kinetic. First the nanites, now this. Plus, Kinetic says this bomb looked like the big brother of the one someone tried to kill him with before he entered the Trials." She could have added Iceburn's assassination attempts, but probably didn't want to risk exposing too much of my personal life in front of the other Hero candidates.

"Why would anyone go through the bother of trying to kill someone like *him*?" Elemental Man said, eyeing me contemptuously. He said "him" the way someone might say, "Eeew! A cockroach!"

And just like that, the goodwill I had felt toward him vaporized. My nickname for him was reborn. Rest in peace Elemental Man. Long live Hitler's Youth.

"How about showing him some respect and gratitude, asshole?" Neha said hotly. "He just saved your life. He saved all our lives." I would've added "Yeah!" but I was too busy concentrating on remaining upright.

"I would've found a way to defuse the bomb if the twerp hadn't been around," Hitler's Youth said with confidence.

"How exactly? By smothering it with your ego? Or you could have told it this is your last shot at the Trials. Maybe it would've felt sorry for your raggedy ass and deactivated itself."

Hitler's Youth flushed. He loomed intimidatingly over Neha. Despite my exhaustion, I knew if he took one more step toward her I'd toss him through the hole in the holosuite's ceiling and through the cracked dome. Maybe he'd get along better with the bat-tigers that flew around out there.

"If you weren't a girl, I'd slap you into next week," he warned Neha.

"And if you were a man, you might try," she snapped back. She looked about as intimidated by him as a pit viper was by a mouse.

"All right, that's enough," Pitbull said. Though he hadn't even raised his voice, his tone commanded compliance like a cracked whip. "We've got enough trouble with someone trying to harm Hero candidates without you two doing his job for him."

Neha and Hitler's Youth glowered at each other. They looked like they wanted to smack the taste out of the other's mouth. My money was on Neha.

"Once we know how and why this happened, we'll let you know," Pitbull said. "In the meantime, there's nothing more we need from you at this time. You should get some rest. As you know by now, you never know when you'll be called on to take your next test. You in particular Kinetic look like the walking dead."

"The walking dead" accurately captured exactly how exhausted I felt.

But, in light of the repeated attempts to kill me, I really wished Pitbull had used a different phrase.

18

That night, I dreamed about a bomb the size of my head blowing up as I held it. Once I was blown to bits, I would slowly re-form, my bloody bits reassembling like a gruesome jigsaw puzzle until I was unhurt again. I would repeat the process, over and over, in a continuous loop of explosions and re-forming.

I didn't need a doctorate in psychoanalysis to figure out the origin of that dream. Oh, and by the way—whoever said you can't feel pain in a dream lied. I felt excruciating pain every time the bomb blew me to smithereens, and then yet again when I coalesced back together.

Though it seemed like I had only been asleep for a short while, I was nothing short of relieved when Overlord's voice and flashing strobe light awakened me. I slowly sat up in my bed. I hadn't even begun to recover from channeling the bomb's energy. I felt like a corpse rising from his coffin.

"All right, all right, I'm awake," I said irritably to Overlord. It was an effort to speak. "How long have I been asleep, anyway?"

"Three hours," came Overlord's voice.

Three hours? What crazy thing was the Guild about to throw

me into while I was sleep-deprived and feeling like the living dead?

My sleep-fogged mind was in the middle of mulling over if this treatment constituted cruel and unusual punishment under the Constitution's Eighth Amendment when Overlord spoke again.

"Precisely twelve hours from now, you will report to Portal Two," Overlord said in its usual unemotional British voice. "From there, you will be transported to a planet where you will meet your fellow Hero candidate Elemental Man. You will battle him in a one-on-one gladiatorial contest. Whoever prevails will advance to the next round of testing. As this duel will be to the death, both you and he are being provided with advance warning to enable you to prepare and to allow you to bid farewell to whomever you deem necessary. Any farewell messages may be recorded on your room's access panel. They will be forwarded to whomever you wish in the event you do not survive."

With that, Overlord's strobe light stopped flashing. The room fell dark.

I collapsed back into bed, relieved I could get more shut-eye before contending with another test. I was so exhausted from dealing with the bomb that fighting Hitler's Youth right away would be a slaughterfest. If I had to fight him immediately, I'd be tempted to just forfeit now to save everyone the time and trouble.

It took several more seconds for what Overlord had said to fully penetrate my denser-than-usual skull.

Once it did, I shot upright like a jack-in-the-box. I was abruptly wide awake as if I had been dunked into boiling water.

A duel to the *WHAT*?!

"YOU CAN'T KILL HIM, THEO. YOU KNOW THAT," NEHA SAID.

"What choice does he have?" Isaac demanded. "Roll over and let that jackass kick him to death? He has to do it."

"There's a third option," she said. "You have to forfeit the match, Theo. Don't fight him at all. Quit."

"And forever give up the chance to get his Hero's license? After all the time and effort it took to get here? After all he's already been through? You're crazy."

We were in Neha's room. Other than the fact her bed was in a slightly different position, her room was identical to mine in its spartan and sterile blandness. It was several hours after I had gotten Overlord's pronouncement. I hadn't gotten a wink more of sleep. Telling someone he had to fight someone else to the death in a few hours tended to keep you awake. Who would've guessed? That effect was a fact I had been happily ignorant of a few hours ago.

Isaac and Neha sat on her bed as they argued about what I should do. I paced at the foot of the bed like a caged tiger. Maybe like a lamb being led to slaughter would be a better analogy.

What in the world was I going to do?

"If I fight him and lose, I'll die. If I fight him and win, I'll have killed someone. Hitler's Youth is hardly my favorite person, but I don't want to murder the guy. If I refuse to fight him, I'll get thrown out of the Trials and be forever barred from getting my license." I shook my head in frustration. "I don't know what to do."

"You don't have a choice. You have to kill him," Isaac said definitively.

"The only part you're right about is that Theo doesn't have a choice." Neha glared at him. "He has to quit."

She turned to me.

"Theo, we all know how important getting your license is to you. We know you want to use it to find who hired Iceburn. I know how hard you've worked to get here. We've *all* worked incredibly hard to get here. But you can't kill Elemental Man. How many times did Amazing Man and our instructors at the Academy tell us Heroes don't kill? I'm not saying quitting is a good option. But, it's the best of your bad options."

Isaac interjected. "Heroes can kill in self-defense. That's what this is—self-defense. It's kill or be killed."

"Oh come on, you can't really believe this is self-defense," Neha said. "This is like breaking into someone's house, shooting the gun-toting owner, and then justifying the shooting by saying if you hadn't shot the owner, he would've shot you. You should've never gone into the house to begin with. What the Guild wants Theo to do is wrong. He has a moral obligation to never step inside the house."

No one said anything in response.

Neha shook her head in frustration. "I can't believe I'm the one who's pointing out the morality of the situation. I'm the daughter of a supervillain. Usually I'm the one who wants to do something morally questionable. The fact I'm saying this is a clear case of wrong versus right should tell you guys something."

Even Isaac didn't have a counter to that.

"And, I should also point out there's no guarantee you will win," Neha said. "Every Hero candidate here knows how to fight, or else they wouldn't have gotten this far. I don't want to have happen to you what happened to Hammer." She actually teared up a little. "If something happened to you, I wouldn't be able to stand it." Even at a time like this, my heart soared. Maybe there was a chance she cared about me the way I did about her.

"Stop being such a worrywart. When did you become such a milksop? Theo will go in there and kick his ass." Isaac said it with a confidence I did not share.

Neha turned on him like a cat protecting her kittens. "This is Theo's life we're talking about. The worst-case scenario is that he dies. The best-case scenario is that he murders somebody. Even the best-case scenario is terrible." She was almost screaming now. "What the fuck is wrong with you? If it weren't for the fact you have some sort of bad blood with Elemental Man, you would be agreeing with me right now."

"The fact Elemental Man is a piece of shit has nothing to do with this." Isaac must have seen the look of disbelief on both of our faces, because he continued in a defensive tone. "I'm not gonna lie: the world would be a better place without that jerk-off in it. But that's beside the point. Theo's worked too hard for too long to quit now."

"All right, I let this go before because it really was none of my business," I said to him. "Now that my life's on the line, it's very much my business. What's your problem with Elemental Man?"

"I told you before, I don't want to talk about it."

"What you want is not relevant anymore," Neha said. "Like Theo said, his life is on the line. You're going to tell us what your issue is with Elemental Man, and you're going to tell us right now. If you don't, I'll force you to inhale a gas that'll make you tell us." Her left forearm and hand ominously turned a cloudy yellow-white.

Isaac jumped up off the bed as if he had been scalded by it. He looked down nervously at Neha's now translucent arm.

"That's a violation of my privacy. It's unethical. You wouldn't dare," he said.

Neha looked scornful. "Have you met me? I'll do it with a song in my heart and sleep like a baby afterward."

Isaac's eyes darted over to me as if I would intervene to stop her.

"Don't look at me," I said. "I'm with her. If you know anything that will help me decide what to do, I need to hear it."

Isaac's eyes then shifted to the door. He looked like he was considering leaving. I doubted he'd make it two steps before

Neha tackled him. Since my neck was on the line, I had just about decided I'd help her when Isaac puffed his cheeks and let out a long sigh. He sounded like a balloon with a hole in it.

"You're right," he said, looking deflated. "I'm just so used to avoiding talking about this that it's gotten to be a habit."

"Avoiding talking about what?" Neha demanded. She still looked like she was going to fling herself at Isaac if he moved toward the door.

"About Elemental Man. His real name is Frank Hamilton. He's the third male in his family to have that name, so people usually call him Trey. I mostly just call him 'Asshole.' His father is married to my mother. So technically, he's my stepbrother. As far as I'm concerned, though, he's no brother of mine."

Isaac's eyes were full of pain.

"He raped and killed my sister," he said.

19

There was stunned silence in the room at Isaac's bombshell.

"How is that possible?" Neha finally asked. "The Guild runs a background check on Metas before they let them into the Academy. The background check is even more thorough before you're allowed to stand for the Trials. There's no way a rapist and murderer could slip through the cracks."

"Well, it's not as though Trey put a gun to Lilly's head and blew her brains out," Isaac said. "He may as well have, though. As for the rape, there's no official record of it. He was never arrested or charged."

My mind was awhirl at Isaac's revelation. As if I didn't have enough to think about as it was.

"Whoa, whoa, back up," I said. "Start from the beginning and tell us everything."

"It all started when my father died. He was a California state trooper. He was a great man. Tough, but kind; strong, but giving. A lot of people want to be cops so they can carry a gun and push people around. Dad had always wanted to be a cop so he could help and protect people. When I was a kid, I wanted to grow up to be just like him. Still do, as a matter of fact. It's the reason I'm trying to become a Hero.

"When I was fourteen and my sister Lilly was twelve, Dad pulled over a guy for a busted taillight. Little did Dad know the guy had a couple of outstanding warrants for armed robbery. When Dad asked for his license, the guy pulled out a gun instead. He shot Dad twice in the chest. When Dad fell to the ground, the guy got out of his car, stepped over him, and shot him three times more in the head. The dash camera in Dad's car recorded it all. I've watched it so many times, I could draw you a picture of it."

Isaac said all this tonelessly, as if he were talking about an incident that had happened to someone else's family on the other side of the world. Only the tightening of his jaw muscles betrayed how he really felt.

"Good God Isaac, that's terrible. I'm so sorry," I said.

"How does Trey play into all this?" Neha asked impatiently. I wanted to kick her. I loved her, but sometimes she had the sensitivity of a wolverine.

"Theo asked me to start at the beginning, so I'm starting at the beginning," Isaac said. "Anyway, Mom was understandably inconsolable. You find out what someone's really like when they are going through stress and grief. Mom processed hers by climbing into bed with just about any man who would have her. It was as if she couldn't stand to be alone, as if she and Lilly and I weren't enough to make her feel complete. The entrance to her bedroom became a revolving door through which any Tom, Dick, or Harry could stroll. Especially Dick." The last part was said bitterly, without a trace of humor.

"Mom desperately wanted to remarry. Now that I'm older, I realize that since she married Dad when she was just nineteen, she never had a chance to form an adult personality independent of a man. My Dad was older than her. When she married him, she went right from her father's house to Dad's house. Until Dad died, she never had the need to stand on her own two feet. Now that I look back at it all with adult eyes, Dad was as much of a father figure to her as he was a husband. After he was killed, instead of learning to be independent, she immediately opened up auditions for the new guy who would take care of her.

"The problem was, she wasn't a dewy-eyed, tight-bodied, nineteen-year-old anymore when Dad died. She was older, less attractive, and had two kids to boot. The fact she's black didn't help any. Even childless black women often have trouble finding good men. Guys weren't exactly lining up to shoulder the responsibility of an instant family. They did line up for some free booty, though. They'd sleep with my mother, but they weren't interested in settling down with her. Why buy the cow when someone's giving the milk away?

"Then Frank Hamilton, Junior—Trey's father—came along when I was sixteen. I was with Mom when she met him. We were grocery shopping. Frank's a tall, handsome white guy who looks and sounds like he has money. That's because he does: he's an Ivy League-educated owner of a brokerage house that he inherited from his father, Frank Senior. I could practically hear Mom's brain assessing Frank's net worth as she looked at his expensive shoes, clothes, and watch. I could also practically hear Frank wondering how long it would take him to get into Mom's panties as he stared at her boobs. As usual, they were on display in a too small, too tight top. After Dad died, she always dressed that way. To my mortification. She always looked like a street-walker, and the day she met Frank was no exception. I guess she figured she'd always keep bait on the hook because she never knew when a rich fish would bite.

"In case you're wondering how long it took Frank to get into Mom's panties, the answer is less than an hour from the moment they met. Even over the headphones I always blasted when

Mom invited a guy over to the house, I could hear them, howling and grunting like animals at the zoo."

Isaac shook his head at the memory.

"I expected Frank would just be another notch in Mom's bedpost who would get his rocks off a few times and disappear. Just like so many others who had come before him. But to my surprise, they started dating. It turns out Frank is into race play as a fetish. In case you don't know what that is, it's as disgusting as it sounds. Frank and Mom didn't even have the decency to keep their master-slave relationship confined to the bedroom. Frank had a real taste for dark meat. 'Dark meat.' Those are Frank's words, not mine, by the way. He'd call Mom that, often in front of both Lilly and me." Isaac shook his head in a combination of wonder and disgust. "Mom has very dark skin, unlike me. I took after Dad's side of the family that way. 'Smile so I can see you,' Frank would say to her. If someone said that to me, I'd punch him in the mouth. Instead, Mom would just giggle and rub herself against him. Even now, it makes me want to throw up just thinking about it. If you think there aren't worse words to call a black person than the N-word, you're wrong. I know because I'd hear Frank loudly calling Mom them when he'd play his sick fantasies out with her in the bedroom.

"Eventually, as things got more serious between Mom and Frank, I met Trey. He must've been eighteen at the time. The instant I laid eyes on him, I saw the rotten fruit hadn't fallen far from the putrid tree. For both of us, it was hate at first sight. Unlike my mother, I didn't have big boobs and a big butt to mitigate against the unpardonable sin of having been born black."

Isaac paused and swallowed.

"But Lilly did. Like Mom, she was dark-skinned. Also like Mom, she was well-developed, even at fourteen, which was how old she was when Frank and Trey came along. As Frank put it in his oh-so-charming way, Lilly was 'built like a black brick shit-house.' Can you believe a grown man talking about a fourteen-year-old like that in front of her and her brother?" Isaac's voice dripped with disgust mingled with disbelief. "Anyway, it was obvious Trey hated me the moment he laid eyes on me. It was equally obvious he lusted after Lilly. Like weirdo father, like weirdo son.

"Before I knew it, Mom had moved us in with Frank and Trey. Frank had a huge house that was like something out of MTV Cribs. Mom was delighted, of course. She thought she had won the lottery with Frank. From a monetary standpoint, maybe she had. I was less happy. When they weren't ignoring me like I was invisible, both Frank and Trey treated me like I was dog doo they had stepped in. The moment I was an adult, I planned to move out. I didn't know how or where, but anywhere was better than living with Frank and Trey.

"They didn't ignore Lilly, though. You know how a dog looks at your plate when you're eating a steak? That's how those two looked at Lilly—like the moment your back was turned, they would pounce on her. Lilly thought Frank was creepy. She was certainly right about that. As for Trey, she was flattered by the attention from him. As much as I hate him, even I have to admit he's a good-looking guy. He's tall, muscular, blonde, and has good bone structure. He looks like something a white supremacist would cook up in a lab. Lilly loved the fact that an older guy who looked like he belonged in a boy band was paying attention to her.

"I tried to warn her. I tried to tell her Trey was no good. But she wouldn't listen. To her, I was just a dorky brother who didn't know anything.

"One day I came home to what I at first thought was an empty house. When I passed Lilly's room, though, I heard crying behind her closed door. I knocked, but she wouldn't let me in. It was clear from the sound of her voice she was upset.

Worried, I broke down the door. I found her on her bed, half-dressed, with the few clothes she still had on ripped. Her thighs were bloody, as was her bed."

Isaac's face was screwed up in anger, like he wanted to punch something.

"Lilly didn't want to tell me at first, but I eventually got it out of her. Trey had raped her. They were doing that whole grouse mating dance they always did, but this time Trey had pushed her further than usual. Lilly had told him no. Flirting with him was one thing; having sex with him was an entirely different thing. She was only fourteen. She was still a virgin. She hadn't even kissed anyone yet.

"Lilly told me that after Trey forced himself on her, he had gone to play basketball with his friends. Knowing what I know now, I should've called the police so they could see the way Lilly looked when I found her. Instead, all I could think about was getting my hands around Trey's neck and choking the life out of him. So, I left Lilly at the house and went to confront Trey." Isaac barked out a humorless laugh. "I choked the life out of him all right. I choked him so well, I was in the hospital for almost a week afterward. I didn't know until I confronted him at the basketball court that Trey had powers. Instead of me beating the stuffing out of him, he beat the stuffing out of me. Gave me this lovely little memento of our encounter."

Isaac pulled up his shirt to reveal a dark blotch on his otherwise light brown skin that was the size of a large grapefruit. I had seen Isaac without his shirt on many times, so had seen the mark before. When I had asked about the blemish previously, Isaac had told me with a wink that it was an old sex injury.

Unfortunately, he had not been entirely lying.

Isaac shook his head. "Nothing happened to Trey. He denied raping Lilly. He denied sleeping with her at all. He was eighteen and legally an adult; Lilly was under the age of consent. It would have been statutory rape even if Lilly had agreed to it. Trey knew that. There was no way he was going to admit what happened, even if the sex had been consensual." Isaac shook his head at the memory. "There was no way it was, though. I saw Lilly. Her clothes. The blood. The stricken look on her face, like she was a little kid who was told that, not only was there not a Santa Claus, but the Tooth Fairy was a serial killer."

"But what about the forensic evidence?" Neha asked. "Surely your mother had the cops do a rape kit."

Isaac snorted.

"Mom refused to report the incident to the police. She said that by the time she got home, Lilly was just fine and there was nothing amiss in her room. When Lilly came to visit me in the hospital, Lilly told me she had made up what she had told me about Trey. She couldn't even look me in the eye when she told me that. I didn't have to be a master detective to know it was a big fat lie. Though I have no definite proof of this, my strong suspicion is Mom cleaned Lilly and her room up when she got home and that she strong-armed Lilly to say nothing had happened between her and Trey. I didn't need telepathy to figure out what Mom was thinking. In her mind, she had found the golden ticket when she had hooked up with Frank. She wasn't about to do something that would jeopardize her gravy train, even if that something was standing up for her own flesh and blood against a sexual predator."

Isaac's voice was bitter. "Lilly was never the same after that. Can you blame her? She was living with a guy who had defiled her, an older guy who always looked like he wanted to defile her, a mother who wouldn't protect her, and a brother who *couldn't* protect her."

Isaac's eyes glistened.

"I wasn't even all that surprised when I found Lilly dead on the floor of her room a couple of weeks later. An empty bottle of Mom's sleeping pills was on the floor next to her.

"The fact I wasn't surprised didn't mean I wasn't mad, though. I was mad at Trey, of course. He didn't pour those pills down Lilly's throat, but he might as well have. I was also mad at Lilly for giving up on life and leaving me. I was mad at Mom for choosing Frank over her own family. I was mad at Frank for spawning a piece of crap like Trey. And, I was especially mad at myself for not being able to give Trey the thrashing he richly deserved. I wished I was stronger, more powerful, so I could take Trey on again.

"I didn't know it at the time, but if you have latent Metahuman powers, they are usually triggered in times of great stress and emotion. Like yours were, Theo. As I knelt there over Lilly's lifeless body, rage built up in me like a dam about to burst. I started getting dizzy, and it seemed like the room was shrinking. Then I realized it wasn't the room that was shrinking, but it was I who was growing. I had just been watching *Game of Thrones*. Apparently it had made quite an impression on me, because my powers were turning me into a dragon. My first transformation was a humdinger. My anger and sorrow fueled me. It took a lot of training and years of study before I could turn into something so powerful again.

"Imagine my surprise when I opened my mouth to cry out in confusion as my body shifted and morphed. Instead of crying out, I let out a roar that made the entire house shudder. The roar was followed by a stream of fire that blew a hole right through the wall. Once I realized what was happening to me and that I was a Metahuman, it struck me that the universe was giving me a second shot at Trey. I ripped a hole through the roof of Frank's house and took flight. I didn't know where Trey was, but he was easy to find. It turns out that dragons have an acute sense of smell. Tracking him down was as easy as following the stench of a skunk.

"We fought again." Isaac's hands clenched and unclenched, as if he were reliving the battle. "Though I couldn't believe it at the time, Trey beat the crap out of me again despite my dragon form. I later found out he was so adept in the use of his powers because Frank had been paying an unscrupulous Hero to train his worm of a son to prepare him to enter the Academy. Trey has been planning for years to get a high-paying gig with one of the big Hero teams, like the Sentinels or the Pacific Protectors. Frank had happily opened his wallet to help his dirtbag son achieve his ambitions.

"In our fight, Trey knocked me unconscious. When I awoke, I was in human form, and once again in the hospital. I've no doubt Trey would have killed me if a death wouldn't have been a black mark on his record when the time came for him to try to get his Hero's license.

"Frank tried to get me prosecuted for battery and for unlicensed use of Metahuman abilities. Fortunately, the District Attorney had more compassion for a kid who had just lost his sister than she had a need for Frank's campaign contributions. She refused to prosecute me, especially since it was my first Metahuman transformation and I didn't yet have control over my powers.

"Since I had attacked his son not once, but twice, and he couldn't get me thrown into jail, Frank gave Mom an ultimatum: either she had to throw me out of the house, or he would throw both her and me out." Isaac snorted derisively. "I guess my mother wasn't inspired by the example of the District Attorney who had let me off the hook. After listening to all this, you won't be surprised to hear Mom had my bags packed before I even got home from the hospital. I was shipped off to live with my paternal grandparents. I stayed with them until I entered the Academy."

"So you want to become a Hero for what reason, then?" Neha asked. "To get revenge on Trey? You don't need to become a Hero to do that."

Isaac shook his head.

"No. Like I said earlier, I idolized my Dad when I was a kid and wanted to be just like him. I always figured I'd grow up to be a cop. But when I developed my powers, I decided I would try to become a Hero instead. If you think about it, a lot of Heroes are essentially cops with superpowers anyway. And, thanks to our powers, we can help a heck of a lot more people than a cop ever could. Now don't get me wrong. I'm not going to say Trey trying to become a Hero didn't play a role in my decision. I figured if that asshole could do it, I could do it too. Plus, I didn't like the fact he beat me up twice. I never again wanted to be in the position where someone like him could hurt me or someone I loved. Sure, I've daydreamed about taking him on a third time. But that's not why I'm trying to get my license."

"Why haven't you told us all this before now?" I asked. We had previously asked Isaac why he decided to try to become a Hero, but he had always sidestepped the subject.

Isaac shrugged.

"The way I was raised, I guess. Dad was an old-school kind of guy. He used to tell me, 'The only thing a man accomplishes by complaining or talking about the past is to convince others you're not in control.' I don't like to talk about this kind of stuff. It makes me feel weak. I don't like that feeling. I've felt it too often in my two run-ins with Trey."

It was true, I thought. Though Isaac was easily the most talkative of the three of us, he rarely spoke of his emotions or how he felt about something. Isaac was about as chatty as the Sphinx when it came to what was in his heart. In a flash of insight, I realized his humor was as much of a mask as the one on his face was.

The room fell silent as Isaac's revelations sank in. I thought about the fact we all had some seriously messed up backgrounds.

Neha's mother had been murdered by an enemy of her supervillain father Doctor Alchemy. That murder had forced him off his rocker, and put him on the path of attempted world domination. Then Neha had been homeless for a while.

Isaac's policeman father had been killed in the line of duty. Then his mother had fallen into the clutches of a man who probably thought of the Antebellum South as the good old days. That same man had a son who raped Isaac's sister, leading to her death.

My own story wasn't one out of a fairytale, either. Until I developed superpowers, I had been bullied most of my life. My mother had died of brain cancer when I was twelve. Then my father died in a fire set by a supervillain trying to kill me. Someone apparently was still trying to kill me for reasons I did not understand.

No wonder the three of us had become fast friends at the Academy. Collectively, our pasts were a hot mess. I guess the cliché was right: Misery really did love company.

I said, "The three of us are like something out of a Dickens novel."

Neha said, "Yeah, and you know how the chapter about you fighting someone to the death should start out? It was the worst of times, and it was the worst of times."

"It'll be the best of times when Theo wins," Isaac said.

"*If* he wins," Neha said.

"The one good thing about you knowing Trey is you can tell me about his powers," I said to Isaac. "I saw him create a tornado in the fight against the robots. I know from our experience in the mall he can also generate fire." I had a sudden thought. "First Iceburn and his fire powers, now Trey. If God is trying to make a point about how life is sometimes hellish, I wish He'd lay off. I get it already."

Isaac said, "His code name Elemental Man is a reference to the elements the ancient Greeks believed made up everything."

"Air, fire, water, earth, and aether," Neha supplied.

"Exactly. Aether, of course, doesn't exist. At least not how the Greeks envisioned it. As for the other so-called elements, Trey can manipulate them. As much as I hate him, he's a pretty powerful guy."

"Does he have any weaknesses?" I asked hopefully. Maybe I could borrow a cup of Kryptonite from somebody.

Isaac shook his head. "Other than the fact his arrogance makes him overconfident, he doesn't have any weaknesses I know of."

Fantastic, I thought. *The only thing worse than a death match with a trained Meta is a death match with a powerful, trained, confident Meta.*

My dismay must have been evident on my face because Isaac hastened to add, "But I have no doubt you can take him."

"You said before this is Trey's third time taking the Trials," Neha said to Isaac. "What happened the other two times?"

"Beats me. Trey didn't stand for the Trials the first two times until long after I was kicked out of the house. All I know is that he Apprenticed with some Hero in Texas after he graduated the Academy. It's not like we get together over coffee to giggle about girls, chat about old times, and talk about why he flunked the Trials." Isaac's eyes bored into mine. "That's another reason why you have to take him on. A guy like that has no business getting a Hero's license. He ought to be in jail, not flying around with legal authorization to use his powers. If you forfeit the match, what happens with Trey?"

Neha and I both looked blank.

"Exactly," Isaac said. "You don't know, and I don't either. Maybe he gets a pass to the next test if you forfeit. He'd be one step closer to his license. Or, maybe he just gets assigned another opponent. You're an Omega-level Meta, Theo. Of all us Hero candidates, you're the one with the best shot at defeating Trey."

Neha shook her head. "I'm just as sorry as I can be about what happened to you and your family, Isaac. Theo and I knew Trey was a tool, but we had no idea just how much of a tool. Clearly the Guild needs to revamp its psychological testing if a guy like him can stand for the Trials. But it's not Theo's job to keep a bad seed from becoming a Hero."

"And I say it is," Isaac insisted. "One of the jobs of a Hero is to protect the public. Keeping Trey from donning a Hero's cape is a public service. It'll be like putting down a rabid dog before he can bite again."

"You're operating under the assumption Theo will win. No offense, Theo, but I'm not so confident. Not when your life is on the line. Trey beat you up, Isaac. Twice. What makes you think Theo will be any different?"

"Trey beat me up before I was trained," Isaac said stubbornly. "If I had to face him again, things would be different now. Just like they will be for Theo."

"Your understandable hatred of this guy is blinding you to the risk Theo will be running. Theo shouldn't chance getting himself killed. He also can't risk killing someone himself. If he did kill, he would be violating everything we've been taught about being Heroes."

"Normally I'd agree," Isaac said. "But this fight is sanctioned by the Guild. That makes it okay."

Neha shook her head stubbornly. "You'd never say that if it

were someone other than Trey. What the Guild is asking Theo to do is murder, plain and simple. He can't do it."

I sat on the bed next to Neha. Her and Isaac's argument continued to swirl around me as I thought. They were just repeating the same old arguments, anyway. Though I appreciated their input, it was my butt on the line, not theirs. I would have to be the one to make the decision as to what to do.

If I fought Trey and won, I will have murdered someone. Isaac could call it self-defense and whatever in the heck else he wanted until he was blue in the face, but that's what it would be: murder. If I wasn't willing to murder Iceburn, the man who had killed my father, how could I murder Trey? Yes, he was a rapist. As far as I was concerned, a rapist and child molester deserved death, not a Hero's cape. But that didn't mean I should be the one to do the killing. Who made me judge, jury and executioner?

On the other hand, if I fought Trey and lost, I would be dead. If I had a voice in the matter, I'd try to come back and haunt Trey. I didn't think it likely I'd have a voice in the matter.

Kill, or be killed.

Neither was appealing.

That left door number three: Quitting. Neha was right. I didn't have to do this. I could quit the Trials before facing Trey. Yes, that would mean I'd never get my Hero's license, the goal I had been working toward with single-minded devotion the past few years. On the other hand, quitting guaranteed my survival. Maybe it was better to be a live jackal than a dead lion.

Trey was a big, strong, imposing-looking guy. I had the sudden mental image of him pinning me down and twisting my head off my neck like it was a bottle cap.

I shuddered at the thought. Door number three looked better and better.

Trey reminded me so much of the people who had beaten,

bullied, and tried to bully me in the past. The Three Horsemen at the University of South Carolina at Aiken. Hank Thune, who called me white trash and beat me up in the third grade because my family didn't have money like his did. Chet Buck, who had thrown me to the ground and pummeled me when I was in high school, not because I had done anything to him, but because I was small and weak.

I'd say there were countless other bullies, but they weren't countless. I knew exactly how many of them there were. I knew exactly what each of them looked like, and I could recite their names on command. Their names and faces were seared into my brain like a brand of shame and embarrassment. Trey was cut from the same cloth as those other guys. He was but the latest in a long line of dirtbags.

As Isaac and Neha continued to argue, I had a sudden thought—quitting the Trials wasn't tempting simply because it was arguably the moral thing to do.

It was tempting because I feared Trey.

I feared him just as I had feared the Three Horseman, Chet Buck, Hank Thune, and all the guys who had bullied me in the past. Despite my powers, all my studying, all my training, how much I had changed since entering Hero Academy, a scrawny little boy who was terrified of standing up to a bully still lived inside me.

Maybe the Old Man was right. Maybe I simply wasn't tough enough to become a Hero.

After all I've been through? All the work? All the sacrifices? was my next thought.

Oh, hell no!

I stood abruptly.

"That's enough," I said to my squabbling friends. "I've made my decision."

Neha and Isaac turned to focus on me.

"What are you going to do?" Neha asked.

"I'm going to go into the test and kick Trey's ass," I said.

Despite my outward bravado, the scrawny, scared boy who still lived inside me was dubious.

Maybe he was right.

But, like the Old Man, that scared little boy could go fuck himself.

Despite my fear, I'd do what I had to do.

20

"I've got to hand it to you Kinetic—I didn't think you'd have the stones to actually face me. I'm impressed. It's not going to stop me from doing what I need to do to advance to the next test, though."

I could have said something back to Hitler's Youth, but chose not to. Instead I stared Hitler's Youth down, doing my best fearless Hero impersonation. Fake it until you make it.

Besides, if I tried to speak, having my teeth chatter would expose my Heroic facade as a fraud.

Hitler's Youth stood yards away from me in a large, flat clearing. Despite the fact I now knew his real name, it was easier to think of him as Hitler's Youth. Maybe it would make it easier to do what I needed to do. In wars throughout history, men dehumanized their opponents. Thinking of your enemy as not being like you, as being the "other," made it easier to kill him. In World War Two, for example, American soldiers often didn't call the Germans Germans or the Japanese Japanese. Instead they were the Krauts and the Japs.

If a psychological tactic was good enough for World War

Two's G.I. Joe, it was good enough for me. I'd continue to think of Hitler's Youth as just that despite the fact I knew his name.

Nuclear blasts set off by the American Metahuman John Tilly in Hiroshima and Nagasaki had brought World War Two to an end. I would've liked to further emulate G.I. Joe by dropping nuclear warheads on Hitler's Youth's perfectly groomed blonde hair. Alas, I was fresh out of warheads. If Batman were real, he'd probably have a couple of nuclear bombs in his utility belt for an occasion just like this one. Unfortunately, us both being orphans was the only thing Batman and I had in common.

Normally, I would have given up both of my pinkie fingers in exchange for Batman's Batmobile and Bruce Wayne's bevy of busty bikini babes. Now that I was staring at Hitler's Youth, I'd turn my nose up at all that fun stuff in favor of a big BatBomb instead.

It's weird the stuff that goes through your mind when you're staring potential death in the face. You think of Batman and World War Two history and scantily-clad gold diggers. Your life definitely doesn't flash before your eyes. That was a myth. The fact I knew that for certain demonstrated I had lived a pretty crazy life since leaving the farm.

Hitler's Youth and I certainly weren't in South Carolina now. The group of trees over to my right sported leaves that were every color of the rainbow. Whatever made them those colors, it sure as heck wasn't chlorophyll. Wherever the Guild's Portal had delivered me and Hitler's Youth only moments before, it definitely wasn't Earth.

It was Earth's close cousin, though. The sky was blue, though more vividly blue than Earth's sky. Even the sun was yellow. A large stream was to the left of us, and another tree line was off in the distance past that. Unlike the leaves on the trees, the grass underneath my feet was green. However, the grass wasn't greener, metaphorically speaking, than it was in the Guild complex on the other side of the Portal. I wondered if I would see the complex or my friends again.

It was a bright, cloudless, hot day. Despite a slight breeze, sweat trickled down the back of my neck. I didn't know if I was sweating due to the heat, or due to fear. It was probably six of one, half a dozen of the other.

The sun was almost directly overhead, beating down on my uncovered head. The appropriateness of it being high noon was not lost on me. I had watched a lot of old westerns while living with Amazing Man. If he were here now to refer to me as Gary Cooper, I would know what he meant.

Other than my cape, which I had left off because I figured it might get in the way, I wore my full costume. Hitler's Youth had on his full costume sans cape as well. The metallic gray in his costume glinted a little in the sun, accenting the swell of his well-developed muscles. His blonde hair looked almost white in the day's brightness. Not a hair was out of place. Hitler's Youth certainly looked the part of the all-American Hero. As much as I hated to admit it, he looked more like a Hero than I probably ever would even if I started mainlining steroids and carried a Captain America shield. Unlike me, Hitler's Youth probably wasn't sweating like a pig eyeing the slaughterhouse. He probably didn't sweat, ever. He probably glistened. Or, maybe he just sparkled like those vampires that were all the rage.

An Overlord node was to the side and overhead, recording everything taking place. A countdown glowed green underneath it, ticking down the seconds until the test officially began.

What was Overlord's obsession with countdowns? Maybe Overlord had been a stopwatch in a past life.

Add timepieces to the list of strange things my bizarre brain fixated on when my life was on the line.

Overlord's countdown turned red once it hit the ten second mark. Oddly, as the seconds ticked toward zero, I calmed down considerably. I had drilled endlessly for fights against other Metahumans both in the Academy and under the Old Man's tutelage. Yeah my conscious mind might be terrified, but my muscle memory and instincts weren't. Fighting off another Metahuman was now as automatic and unthinking as breathing. I was ready for this. I could do this.

Then again, Hitler's Youth, being both an Academy graduate and a Hero's Apprentice, was well-trained for this too.

I really wished I hadn't thought that last part. My nervousness surged again. Later—if there was a later—I'd have to have a serious chat with my consider-all-sides-of-the-issue brain about whose side it was on.

Overlord's countdown hit zero. I took flight immediately. It didn't seem a good idea to fight on the ground when my opponent could literally control the ground.

I had reacted fast, but my opponent's response was equally fast. With a sound resembling an earthquake's rumbling, an earthen arm rocketed out of the ground after me. Its hand wrapped around my ankles like a giant's fist before I could dodge out of the way.

As quickly as a retracting yo-yo, the arm sank back down into the ground, but not before slamming me into the turf like a professional wrestler. Everything inside me bounced around as if I had run headlong into a brick wall. If my personal shield hadn't been up, I would no doubt have gone *splat!*

The sun, the moon, and the stars exploded behind my eyes. I shook my head, trying to clear it after the impact. The earthen fist was still around my ankles. I reached out with my powers, trying to break the hard dirt fist up into pieces. I was successful, but Hitler's Youth added to the fist as quickly as I tried to break it up.

Before I could shift tactics to free myself, the ground underneath me opened up. It swallowed me whole, like a boa constrictor swallowing a mouse. I plunged into total darkness. There was a grinding sound that sent vibrations through my entire body. Under different circumstances, the overwhelming smell of fresh dirt would have been pleasant. Under these circumstances, it was the smell of a limited air supply—namely the air trapped in my shield—and of imminent death. I immediately lost all sense of which way was up and which way was down. The dirt squeezed tight against my force field. Despite my best efforts, the earth prevented me from expanding my shield and giving me some room to maneuver.

If I didn't do something and do it double-quick, either Hitler's Youth would crush me, or I'd run out of breathable air. Either way, I'd be just as dead.

Being buried alive had not been a part of my plan. But, as Mike Tyson said, everybody has a plan until they get punched in the mouth. Or in my case, buried alive.

Doing my best to swallow the panic rising within me like nausea, I stretched out my powers. I used them to grope all around in a wide area like a blind octopus for the flesh and blood form of Hitler's Youth. For the first time, I was grateful for those nanites that had attacked me during the written exam. If it hadn't been for them, I wouldn't have developed the technique I used to try to locate my opponent.

Found him!

I locked onto his body with my powers. I flung him as hard as I could. He went flying. I wasn't aiming in any particular direction as I was too disoriented to pick one. I was like a pitcher who had been blindfolded, spun rapidly around in a circle, and then forced to unleash his best fastball.

Me turning Hitler's Youth into a human fastball must have broken his concentration on the earth binding me. The dirt that had been pressing against my shield like a giant trash compactor relaxed. The ground was no longer trying to squeeze me to death. However, I still had to get out of here before Hitler's Youth recovered his hold on the ground and before I suffocated.

Fortunately, me finding Hitler's Youth with my powers had told me which way up was. The cessation of the terrific pressure around me allowed me to reshape my force field. Imagining myself as being in the center of an invisible drill bit, I spun out of the ground. I soon shot into the air like a missile launched from a silo.

Sudden bright sunlight blinded me for a few seconds. Still, it was a welcome change from the total darkness I had just been in. Even more welcome was fresh air. I inhaled it hungrily.

As soon as I could see again, I spotted Hitler's Youth. Apparently, I had been fortunate enough to fling him against a tree. He staggered to his feet at the base of it. His hair was no longer perfectly coiffed. Now it looked like it had been caught in a windstorm. It was streaked with blood.

I had gotten lucky in throwing him blindly into that tree. Sometimes it was better to be lucky than good.

Hitler's Youth saw me above him. I must give him credit for how quickly he reacted. He threw two fireballs at me. They rocketed up toward me, growing larger as they approached. I didn't bother dodging them, though I could have easily. Instead, I made my personal force field impermeable to air right before the fireballs hit me. They hit my shield, causing me no injury.

In fact, it was quite the opposite. The fireballs only served to strengthen me. As I had with the bomb in the mall, I absorbed the fireballs' energy. No doubt Hitler's Youth was shaken from hitting that tree, otherwise he would have remembered the incident at the mall and not tried to attack me this way.

The energy absorbed from the fireballs surged through me

like an electric current. The energy built up, demanding release. I concentrated, willing the energy within me to be channeled out again. My eyes burned. Beams of pure energy lanced out of them. Hitler's Youth tried to dodge out of the way. My energy beams hit the base of a tree he sought cover behind.

There was a massive explosion. Hitler's Youth was thrown through the air from the force of it. I locked onto his body with my powers, not wanting to lose track of him in the wooded area he was thrown deeper into.

The tall tree I had hit toppled to the side, the base of it having been pulverized by my energy beams. Branches of other trees popped and crackled as the falling tree ripped through them.

THOOM!

The tree hit the ground. The sound of it added to the echoes of the explosion seconds before.

I dropped down out of the sky into the wooded area toward where my powers told me Hitler's Youth was. Out of the corner of my eye, I saw Overlord's node drop out of the sky as well, continuing to record the action.

I landed on the forest floor. It was noticeably cooler here as the tall trees and their multicolored leaves blotted out most of the sun. Hitler's Youth was on his hands and knees, obviously hurt, but struggling to get to his feet. If he had been anyone else, I would have admired his persistence.

I picked him up with my powers. I threw him against yet another tree. I was none too gentle about it. He cried out in pain at the impact. I pinned him against the large tree trunk like an insect in a bug collection. I forced his hands together over his head, not wanting him to throw more fire at me. I cast out with my mind, and then used the ropy vines I found to bind Hitler's Youth's hands, ankles, and waist to the tree.

In seconds, he was trussed up like a Thanksgiving turkey.

Hitler's Youth glared at me. There was a cut over his left eye. Blood dripped into that eye, making it demonically red. As if by magic, a miniature cyclone sprang up in front of me. Debris including leaves, dirt, dead branches and the like hit my force field and whipped past me as they were sucked into the powerful small twister. Hitler's Youth was lost to view in the sudden pandemonium. The twister danced on top of the forest floor, advancing toward me ominously. I wheezed painfully. The breath was literally ripped from my lungs by the twister, no doubt with an assistance from my opponent's air-manipulation powers.

I had learned my lesson from grappling with the earthen arm that had attacked me earlier—don't go after the manifestation of the power. Go after the power source.

Despite Hitler's Youth not being visible thanks to all the swirling debris, I still felt him with my powers. I grabbed his head with them. It was like picking up a rag doll by the hair. While I struggled like an asthmatic for a breath that would not come, I slammed Hitler's Youth's head against the tree. I used his head like it was a hammer and the tree was the nail. The twister still approached. I still could not breathe. I flung my opponent's head forward, and then back against the tree hard.

Again.

Again.

The fourth time was the charm.

Like a switch had been flipped, the cyclone died away. I could breathe again. My nose and lungs burned as air filled them. Everything that had been sucked into the twister fell back down to the ground. The sound of the debris hitting the ground was like a burst of machine gun fire.

Once the dust settled, I could see again. Hitler's Youth was still bound to the tree. His body was limp. His face was down. A steady stream of crimson trickled down his head to plop onto the ground below. Hitler's Youth's head hung listlessly between his shoulders. His hair was a bloody mess, more red than blonde now.

I ran my powers over his neck, feeling for a pulse. I had been around the block too many times by now to go up to him and check for one manually. He could be playing possum.

There was a sickening, sinking feeling in the pit of my stomach when I felt nothing at first.

Then I found a pulse. Though Hitler's Youth bled like a stuck pig, he was still very much alive.

Good.

I turned to the Overlord node which hovered silently nearby like a silver ghost.

"I came here to see if I could beat him," I said to the node. My throat felt raw. I cleared it and spat. "I had my doubts as to whether I could. But I had to prove to myself and to all the people who ever belittled me that I could beat him. And now I have. It wasn't even as hard as I thought it would be. I guess I'm stronger and tougher than even I had thought."

I shook my head.

"But I'm not going to kill him. Everyone whose opinion I give a damn about—both Hero and non-Hero—has taught me killing is wrong. They're correct." I thought of Athena and the other instructors at the Academy, Amazing Man, and my parents.

I also thought of God. I had been raised Catholic. I had literally been an altar boy. I definitely was no altar boy now. I hadn't followed all the rules I was raised to believe in. Me sleeping with Neha before marriage, for example, was a definite no-no in the eyes of the Church. I didn't know exactly what I believed in anymore. Too much had happened to me and my family for me to swallow what I had been taught about an all-powerful, all-good God without a big bucket of salt to go with it. If God was so good and so great and so loving, then why were my parents dead? Why was Isaac's sister dead? Why did He let her get raped? It just didn't make any sense.

Maybe God didn't exist. Or maybe he was a watchmaker who created the universe, wound it up, and just let everything play out without further interference. Or maybe He was a sadistic SOB who enjoyed playing with us and our emotions.

Or, maybe I was just too stupid and near-sighted to know the mind of God.

Regardless, if there was one thing I had been taught that I still believed was right, it was that "Thou shalt not kill." If God couldn't or wouldn't do what was right, that didn't mean the rest of us didn't have too. To do anything less would lead to chaos. Especially for people with superpowers like me. My abilities gave me greater capacity than most people to do harm. Or, to do good. If I didn't have the right to kill Iceburn, the man who had destroyed what was left of my family, I certainly didn't have the right to kill Trey.

"If I can't be a Hero because I won't kill my opponent in your stupid test, then so be it," I said to Overlord. I was tearing up. "Being a Hero is all I want to do. It wasn't always that way, but it's that way now. It breaks my heart to walk away from the idea of becoming a Hero after working so hard and coming this far. But if you think I'm going to win a Hero's license at the price of losing my soul, you're crazy. You tell the proctors that. Also tell them, for trying to force me to violate everything a Hero is supposed to stand for, that they can go straight to hell. I don't want to be a member of any group where they make you kill to become a member."

I paused. It was not for effect. Rather, I just wanted to be absolutely sure of what I was about to say. I felt like Julius Caesar about to cross the Rubicon.

"In other words, I quit," I said.

Alea iacta est. "The die is cast." There was no turning back now. Since I wasn't going to be a Hero, maybe I could find a job pulling historical quotes out of my butt.

Maybe I would have noticed it had I not been ranting and raving at Overlord. Maybe I would have noticed it if I weren't sleep-deprived. I'd like to think I would have. But the fact was I didn't.

The "it" I didn't notice wrapped around my head like a kidnap victim's hood. It forced itself up my nose and into my mouth and down my nose. It burned like acid.

Water from the stream! I thought as I started choking, likely to death. I really should have made sure Hitler's Youth was unconscious before I started making speeches. I'd have to remember that next time.

Not that there would be a next time.

A watery helmet surrounded my head, dampening sound and blurring my vision. I coughed—or at least tried to—to get the water out of me. I only succeeded in choking harder as the water forced itself further into me like an invading army.

A person can drown in a tiny amount of water if it's covering his mouth and nose. That was exactly what was happening to me.

Caesar had made it into the history books for his military exploits. I was about to make it into the history books for stupidity and for being the first person to drown, standing up, in the middle of a forest, with everything but my head bone-dry.

With my powers, I tried to latch onto the water and force it out of my body and from around my head. I had manipulated water before when I used it to protect me and Hacker from the alien worms on Hephaestus. Now, unfortunately, the water did not heed my powers' commands. Hitler's Youth had years of experience manipulating water with his powers. I did not stand a chance against his adeptness.

My body shrieked for oxygen. I felt the dark elevator doors of unconsciousness closing around my mind. My vision was darkening. I was desperate. I fell to the ground, twisting in the dirt and decaying plant matter, hoping the ground would absorb the water writhing around my head like a constricting snake.

If flailing on the ground had an effect, it wasn't noticeable.

A blurred shadow loomed over me. It was Hitler's Youth. He must have burned through the thick vines I had used to bind him.

He said something. I couldn't hear a thing over the water gurgling around me and in my ears.

As if Hitler's Youth could read my mind, the water in and around my ears cleared away. I could hear again. I couldn't focus enough to bring my powers to bear on him, though.

"Your problem is, you've been hanging out too long with Isaac," Hitler's Youth said. Even with my blurred and ever-darkening vision, his face looked triumphant. "You talk way too damn much."

His hands glowed red with fire.

I wonder which will kill me, was my last thought. *Suffocating or burning?*

Suddenly, the Overlord node came into my field of vision. A golden beam of energy shot out of it and bathed Hitler's Youth.

The fire in his hands died. The glob of water around my head collapsed.

Barely conscious, I rolled onto my stomach. I coughed up water, feeling like I had been forced to stand under Niagara Falls. The coughing soon became vomiting. Fortunately, I had the presence of mind to lift myself up a bit on enfeebled arms to avoid inhaling my own vomit. Death by drowning was bad enough. Death by drowning on one's own vomit was a bridge too far.

After throwing up what felt like everything I had ever eaten in my entire life, my stomach finally stopped heaving. Feeling as weak as a sick puppy, I managed to haul myself to my feet. Hitler's Youth was still bathed in Overlord's energy beam. He was frozen in place like a paused movie. Only his eyes moved. The look in his eyes was part murderous, part confused.

"Why did you stop him?" I demanded of Overlord. Not that I wasn't grateful. The answer to my question came to my sluggish mind even as Overlord answered me.

"Contrary to what you both were told, this was not a duel to the death," came Overlord's proper British voice from the silver-colored node.

"You lied to us," I said. My throat hurt. My mouth tasted the way pond scum looked.

"Indeed I did. Not of my own volition, of course. I was under instructions from the proctors. The Trials are dangerous, and there is an unfortunately high death rate. The proctors would never expect one of you to kill the other, though."

It didn't matter. Even though he hadn't killed me, Hitler's Youth would have had Overlord not intervened. I had clearly lost the duel. I had failed this test and flunked out of the Trials.

"Congratulations, Kinetic," Overlord said. "You have passed this test. Elemental Man, I regret to inform you you have failed."

At first I thought I hadn't heard right. Then I saw Trey's eyes. They looked like they would bulge out of his head. My mouth dropped open. Since my breath smelled like a sewer, I immediately closed it.

"What do you mean, I passed and he failed?" I asked. It wasn't until much later that it occurred to me I shouldn't look a gift horse in the mouth. "He clearly defeated me. He would've killed me if you hadn't stopped him."

"Indeed he would have," Overlord agreed. "That is why I have immobilized him and temporarily nullified his powers. And, that is why he failed. With certain limited exceptions, a Hero does not kill. You all should know that based on your Heroic studies. If someone asks you to kill, even someone with authority over you, you are duty-bound to refuse. Kinetic, not only did you fight Elemental Man, but you spared his life after you had him at your mercy. Since you expected to fail this test by doing so and expected to forgo the opportunity to pursue a Hero's license, your act of mercy was a great personal sacrifice. That is the sort of person who should be a Hero. Not someone who will kill on command."

I glanced at Hitler's Youth. Dismay filled his eyes.

"What's going to happen to him?" I asked Overlord.

"Since Elemental Man demonstrated a willingness to kill, for both his and your safety I will hold him here with my immobilization beam until the proctors come to escort him back to Earth Prime. I have already sent a message to Earth Sigma about the results of the test. As Elemental Man has failed the Trials twice before, with this new failure, he will be forever barred from either receiving his license or using his powers. As for you, you will return to the Heroes' Guild complex via the Portal and await word of your fifth test." As soon as Overlord finished speaking, a Portal appeared out of thin air.

I was in disbelief. I hadn't flunked out. This was incredible.

Before moving toward the Portal, I took one last look at Hitler's Youth. Though I could scarcely believe it, he was crying. Tears streamed down his face as though he had just learned his best friend had died. I knew how he felt. After all, I had just thought our roles were reversed and that I would be the one leaving the Trials.

Hitler's Youth was no innocent. He had raped Lilly. He had treated Isaac like he was dirt. And, he had nearly killed me.

Despite all that, I kinda felt sorry for the guy. Not a lot. But a tiny, miniscule, walk a mile in the other man's moccasins amount.

Dad had often said to me, "Everyone thinks, rightly or wrongly, that they are the heroes of their life story. Remember that when you're tempted to judge someone. From his perspective, almost everything someone does is perfectly justified."

Why was it a Jamesism—one of my Dad's life lessons—popped into my head whenever I wanted to hate someone? Maybe you could take the altar boy out of the altar, but not the altar out of the boy.

"Can you ease up a little on your field holding Elemental Man?" I asked Overlord. I hastened to add, "Not enough to let him use his powers or move. Just enough to talk." Though I felt the tiniest bit sorry for the guy, I didn't feel sorry enough to let him take another crack at me. Yeah, maybe I was still part-altar boy, but I wasn't all-the-way stupid.

Overlord's energy beam flashed white for the briefest of moments.

"Proceed," it intoned.

I wanted to curse Hitler's Youth out. Not just for almost killing me, but also for what he had done to Isaac's family. But instead, with Dad's Jamesism ringing in my head, I took the high road.

"I just wanted to say I feel bad that you've worked so hard and won't be able to become a Hero. Despite what happened here today, there are no hard feelings," I said, partly lying through my teeth.

At first I thought Overlord hadn't freed Hitler's Youth up to speak. He just glared at me balefully through bloody and teary eyes for several long moments.

Finally, he said something.

"Fuck you, you little country piece of shit!" he hissed hatefully at me. He then fell as silent as a clam again.

What little sympathy I had felt for him disappeared.

"Well that was a cathartic chat," I said to Hitler's Youth. "I'm glad we had it. I for one feel a lot better about things."

I turned and walked toward the Portal.

It took every ounce of willpower I had to not flip Hitler's Youth the bird as I stepped through the Portal.

21

"Ah yes Kinetic, come on in," the Hero proctor said. He smiled at me. "You're right on time I see."

It was two days after my fight with Hitler's Youth. Overlord had instructed me to report to this room in the Guild complex for my fifth test.

I had gotten plenty of sleep and rest since I had faced Trey. I no longer felt as ragged as a cheap, overused toy. Even the wounds where the two worms had shot through me were healing nicely.

So physically, I felt pretty good. Mentally was a different story. My wariness meter was now permanently set on High, and it bordered on Freaking The Frak Out. So far, the Trials had made me feel like an abused spouse. Yeah, this Hero was smiling at me now, but what fiendish things would he do to me later?

I cautiously entered the room the Hero invited me into. If a Rogue named Boogeyman leapt from behind the door and tried to stab me in my uninjured buttock, I wouldn't have been the slightest bit surprised given my track record at the Trials so far. I didn't know what to expect with this test, but I was dead certain it wasn't going to be good.

Years ago, when Dad was still alive and I was in high school, I had volunteered at a dog shelter for a few months. There had been a female Rottweiler named Kiara there who had been severely abused by her prior owner. I made a point to visit her each time I went to the shelter, especially because some of the other volunteers were too afraid to deal with a big, scary-looking dog like Kiara. Despite the fact she had come to know me, every time I went to pet her she recoiled from my touch as if I was going to hit her.

That was why, despite the fact this Hero smiled at me, I half-expected him to pull a cast iron skillet from behind his back and whack me over the head with it.

Maybe I needed to change my name from Kinetic to Kiara.

The Hero asked me to sit in the chair in the center of the small room. The padded black and white chair reminded me of a dentist's patient chair. The part that supported the lower body was almost parallel to the floor, whereas the part supporting the upper body was at a forty-five degree angle. In fact, the entire office reminded me of a dentist's office in that it was cold and sterile. If a cute dental hygienist smelling of spearmint and antiseptic came in and started scraping away at my teeth until my gums bled, I wouldn't have been surprised. If she then tried to knock my teeth out with a baseball bat, that wouldn't surprise me either. These were the Trials, after all.

Instead of a cute hygienist to take my mind off of whatever new craziness was about to happen to me, all I got was Lotus. That's what the Hero told me his name was as I settled down in the thickly padded chair. Pain ran from my butt to my brain like an electric current as the chair pressed against the stitches sewn into my rear end. I suppressed a grimace. I didn't want Lotus to ask me if something was wrong. *A worm shot me in the butt, sir,* seemed like a less than Heroic thing to say. I wanted to ask Lotus for one of those doughnut-shaped chair pads people with hemorrhoids used, but that seemed like a less than Heroic thing to say as well.

Lotus was a tall, spare man in a green and black costume. His white mask matched the whiteness of his ceremonial Hero's cape. His eyes had a faraway look to them. It was as if, when he looked at you, he was simultaneously looking somewhere else far away.

That look made me even more nervous than I already was. I shifted a bit in the chair. Between the chair's soft padding and me practically lying down, I would be quite comfortable if I hadn't been as nervous as a virgin in a brothel.

"Where's the Overlord node?" I asked Lotus. There was only an Overlord access panel on the wall. There was an access panel in every part of the Guild complex except the infirmary. Overlord wasn't allowed to monitor the infirmary out of respect for patient privacy. "There was a node present at all my other tests so far." I spoke mainly to have something to say. It was hard to stay quiet when you didn't know what potentially lethal test you would face next. Those facing firing squads must have talked people's ears off. Maybe that's why they were shot, to shut them up.

"Overlord will not be proctoring this exam. I will be," Lotus said.

"Oh," I said. "What am I being tested on?" I hoped it wasn't my articulateness. In addition to "oh" not being the height of oratory, I wasn't certain "articulateness" was a word.

Lotus looked down and through me with his faraway eyes.

"You'll see," he said.

He put his hands on my head like a faith healer laying hands on a congregant. Though I hadn't been sleepy before, I suddenly felt like I hadn't slept in a week.

My eyes slammed shut like a closing book.

I AWOKE IN MY BED. AMAZING MAN PEERED DOWN AT ME.

No, wait. This wasn't my bed. And that wasn't Amazing Man. It was merely an Amazing Man poster mounted on the wall across from me.

I sat up. Bright sunlight shone behind the blinds of the room's two windows. If I didn't get up, I was going to be late. But for what, exactly? I was groggy and confused. This was my bed. And yet, it wasn't. This was my bedroom. And yet, it wasn't.

This was the bedroom in the brick rancher I had grown up in. The walls were painted blue. Blue for boy. I had picked the color out myself. My parents had built the house when I was a little kid. My Mom, who was appropriately named Felicity, had asked me then what colors we should paint the bedrooms. She always had a knack for making me feel like my opinions mattered.

"My room should be blue," I had told her. I was six at the time.

"Why?" she had asked with a twinkle in her green eyes.

"Because I'm a boy. Blue is for boys."

"What color should my and your Daddy's bedroom be?"

I had considered the question with the somber intensity only a child was capable of.

"Green," I had finally concluded. "Because Daddy's a farmer who grows green stuff. Plus, your eyes are green."

"And what about the guest bedroom?"

"Yellow," I had answered immediately.

"Yellow? Why yellow?"

"Because yellow's yucky," I had said firmly. "The color'll make 'em leave. If someone comes to visit, we don't want 'em to stay long. Daddy says fish and visitors stink after three days."

Mom's eyes had sparkled with amusement. "I think your Daddy stole that expression from Benjamin Franklin."

"Who's that? One of our relatives?"

Mom had thrown her head back and laughed for reasons I hadn't understood at the time. Then she had hugged me hard and kissed me on the cheek. I had wiped away the kiss, pretending to not like it or the hug. I was a big boy. I was six and three-quarters years-old, after all. I projected an air of being far too dignified to enjoy my mother hugging me. The truth of the matter was I liked her hugs and kisses. Mom always smelled of the pies and cakes she baked fresh for me and Dad almost every day, with a slight undertone of the floral perfume she favored. Being hugged by her was like coming home after a long trip.

Even later, when her metastasized brain cancer had eaten away her insides and she smelled of decay and death instead of cakes and pies, her hug was still like coming home.

I shook my head, still confused by the fact I had awaken in a house I hadn't been inside of since Dad had sold it. He sold it after Mom died to cut costs and help pay down some of the crushing medical debt he'd been in thanks to Mom's illness. The two of us had then moved into a cheap mobile home Dad had plopped in the middle of one of his fields.

I got out of bed. I couldn't shake the nagging feeling I had somewhere to be. The fog clogging my mind began to clear as I looked around the room. No, wait. None of what I had thought seconds before had happened. Dad had never sold this house. This didn't used to be my room. It *was* my room. It was as familiar to me as the inside of my mouth.

Two cheap bookcases sagging with books, mostly science fiction and fantasy, were against two of the bedroom's walls. Ever since I had been a little kid, I had loved and admired Heroes. As a result, Hero action figures were on top of my dresser and desk.

"Those are dolls, not action figures," Mom had sometimes teasingly said to me as I got older.

"Since you often confuse *Star Trek* and *Star Wars*," I had always responded with mock dignity, "I'm not sure what you think counts."

In addition to the very manly and not at all doll-like action figures, there were models of various *Star Trek* starships on my dresser. To the left was the Enterprise from the original television show. To the right was the Enterprise from *The Next Generation*. In the center was the USS Defiant, the starship from my second favorite of all the *Star Trek* shows, *Deep Space Nine*. My favorite show was *Enterprise*, but I didn't go around advertising that fact. Many *Star Trek* fans saw *Enterprise* as a monstrosity, and weren't shy about mocking and shaming you if you felt otherwise. *Star Trek* was about tolerance and diversity. The irony of fans being intolerant of others' opinions seemed lost on them.

Despite the fact the room was mostly as familiar to me as the back of my hand, as I looked around, in subtle little ways it was bizarrely as alien to me as the surface of Mars.

The dresser, for example, wasn't where it should be. It was in the center of the wall across from me. It should have been all the way on the right, covering a hole in the wall. I had busted a hole in that wall by throwing my bookbag with all my might against it when I had come home from middle school one day.

My parents had scrimped and saved to enroll me in Saint Theresa, a private Catholic school, because they had thought—correctly, as I later realized—that the local public schools had sucked. I, a nerdy farmer's son, had stood out like a sore thumb among the other kids, most of whom were from rich families. A lot of the kids had been too busy looking down their noses at me to speak to me. When they did speak to me, it usually was to make fun of me.

Four older kids had picked on me all week the week I had

punched a hole in my wall. They had said I was a nerd loser and had mercilessly made fun of my clothes, my haircut, how I spoke, and everything else about me. Well, the fact I was a nerd was certainly true. But, being a nerd and being accusingly called a nerd were two different matters. After taking the name-calling for as long as I could stand, I had finally snapped. I was not only sick of being teased by those four kids, but by the kids in my school in general.

I had defended myself against the four by telling off their ringleader. I knew he was failing English and that his parents were divorcing. I had verbally stabbed at his soft underbelly.

"It's better to be a nerd than be someone who can't even spell nerd," I had said. "I'd tell you to ask your mom how to spell it, but I hear her mouth is too full of her boss' dick to educate you."

The results were predictable. I was precocious, and often wrote checks to bullies with my mouth the rest of my scrawny body couldn't cash. I knew more about warp drives than I did about fighting. The four kids had all jumped on me and beaten me like I was a piñata they were trying to punch and kick candy out of. When I had gotten home, I'd thrown my bookbag against the wall in anger and frustration, causing a hole.

But now, the hole in the wall was gone. It was as if that incident with the four kids had never happened.

That was not the only thing that was not quite right about my room. A laptop was on my desk. Until becoming Amazing Man's Apprentice, I never had a laptop or any other computer. I hadn't been able to afford one. Every time I needed to use a computer, I used one at my school or at the public library.

Another thing that wasn't right about my room was that it seemed smaller than it should be. It was as if it was a wet wool sweater someone had foolishly put in the dryer. It was still recognizable as my sweater, just shrunk down in size.

A third thing that wasn't right about the room was, out of the corner of my eye, I saw a gray-white fog that was about the size and shape of a large door. Every time I turned to look at it directly, though, it disappeared. Then it would reappear seconds later, again in the corner of my eye.

Either I hadn't fully awakened, my room was haunted, or I was going crazy. My vote was definitely in favor of the former.

A fourth thing that wasn't right was there was a poster of the Hero Avatar to the right of Amazing Man's. I didn't remember having a poster of Avatar in this room. And yet, here Avatar was, seemingly lifelike, looking right at me in a heroic pose. Then again, Avatar probably looked heroic when he went to the bathroom. He was a big, muscular man dressed in red gloves, red boots, and a gray, one-piece, skintight outfit. A bright red stylized "A" was on the center of his chest, and his red cape billowed out behind him. His matinee idol face was chalk-white, giving Avatar an otherworldly appearance.

It was said that the only thing that matched Avatar's Metahuman power level and good looks was how moral he was. It was a real loss to the planet when someone had figured out a way to kill him. The fact that someone like Avatar and someone like me were both Omega-level Metas must have been God's idea of a really funny joke.

Wait a minute. What the heck was wrong with me? I wasn't a Metahuman, Omega-level or otherwise. The only thing Avatar and I had in common was we were both male. We were similar in the same way a sardine and a shark were similar—both fish, but otherwise, nothing alike.

And Avatar most definitely wasn't dead. I saw him on television just two nights before, when he prevented the crash of a 747 whose engines had failed. Avatar had flown under the out of control airplane and had carried it gently to the ground, saving everyone on board.

I didn't have superpowers. I hadn't gone to Hero Academy, or been Amazing Man's Apprentice, or had friends with names like Smoke and Myth. I had never even met Amazing Man. People like him and Avatar were distant, larger-than-life figures, like the President or the Queen of England. If I ever was lucky enough to meet Amazing Man, I'd probably squeal like a little girl and ask for his autograph.

I was no Hero-in-training. I was just a college student, finishing my second year of mechanical engineering at the University of South Carolina at Aiken. I had recently been admitted into the Massachusetts Institute of Technology and would move to Cambridge after this semester was over to finish my degree there.

Dad had never sold this house. This was the only home I had ever lived in. And my room wasn't smaller than it should be. It was exactly the same size it had been when I went to bed last night. For some reason, when I first woke up, I had viewed it the way I had remembered it when I was a kid. When you're little, everything seems huge. Now that the confusion that had fogged my brain was fading away, I saw the room the way I had always seen it.

And I hadn't been bullied, either. I had always gotten along well with my peers and had a ton of friends. If anyone ever had gotten it into his head to bully me, he would wind up having to fight almost everyone in school. I was popular.

I shook my head at myself as my confusion continued to fade away. I must've had a dilly of a dream last night to wake up with all these crazy thoughts in my head. Me, a superhero? What bizarre dreams would I have later tonight? Would I be an international rock star? The Sultan of Dubai? Married to Taylor Swift?

I paused, intrigued. *Oh please God let me have a dream about being married to Taylor Swift,* I thought.

Then I remembered why the thought I needed to get up had

been nagging me. I was supposed to meet with some friends from USCA to study. I glanced at the clock on my desk. Ugh! Thanks to waking up as confused as Rip Van Winkle, I'd barely have time to make breakfast and eat before needing to head out. If I didn't eat before I left, I'd be as prickly as a porcupine.

I hastily threw on some clothes. As soon as I opened my bedroom door, I smelled the tantalizing aroma of cooking bacon wafting through the house. My mouth watered. They said ambrosia was the food of the gods, but if that was the case, it was only because they had never tried bacon. Good. More for me.

But who was cooking? I was the one who did all the cooking after Mom died. Dad would likely set the house on fire if he tried to boil water. I remembered when he had tried to make an apple pie for me once when I had come home after a rough day at school. He had used white bread slices as a crust, and had put in equal parts sugar and salt. I don't think he even bothered to peel the apples. Out of politeness, I had choked down as much of the revolting concoction as I could stand. It was not something my taste buds or my stomach would ever forget.

As I walked closer to the kitchen, I heard someone singing. It was a woman's voice. Weird. Had Dad finally met someone he was comfortable enough with to bring home? He hadn't dated anyone since Mom died.

I entered the kitchen. Who I saw there made my heart skip a beat.

Mom?

I couldn't believe my eyes. How could this be? And yet, here she was, as large as life.

"Mom!" I shrieked. I flung myself on her. Startled, she stumbled. We both hit the counter and almost fell.

Even so, I didn't let her go. I didn't want to ever let her go again.

"Theo, what in the world has come over you?" she asked as

she unsuccessfully tried to untangle herself from me. She stopped trying when she saw I was bawling. Her tone changed from indignant to concerned. "Why are you crying? What's wrong?"

"You're dead," I blubbered. "Or at least you used to be. You died from cancer when I was twelve."

"I'm very much alive," she said gently as she stroked the back of my head. I was crying on her shoulder like a baby. Even over the smell of bacon, I smelled her slightly floral perfume I always remembered. "And I don't have cancer or anything else for that matter. I had a checkup just last week. I'm as fit as a fiddle."

She certainly looked healthy, though smaller than I remembered. As I calmed down, I realized she wasn't smaller than I remembered. It was just like my room: it wasn't Mom or my room that had gotten smaller. Rather, I had gotten bigger.

Mom was a sight for sore eyes. She was a short woman with dark features. Though she looked as slim and delicate as a flower, she was far stronger than she appeared. She often helped Dad with the farm work in addition to all the work she did around the house. When she wore short sleeves, you could see the smooth muscles rippling just under her tanned skin. She often said she weighed almost exactly what she weighed when she graduated high school. It was the only bit of vanity I had ever seen in her. Even on formal occasions, she wore but a minimal amount of makeup and inexpensive clothes. Her otherwise black hair was flecked with gray.

"I'm not 19-years-old anymore, Theo, and I'd look pretty silly pretending like I am," she often said when I asked her why she didn't dye her hair. Her eyes had twinkled. "Besides, your Dad likes the gray. He says it makes me look like a sexy librarian."

If there was one fault my mother had, it was a tendency to overshare.

My study group completely forgotten, Mom and I sat down

at the kitchen counter and had a long talk. I told her about the bad dream I had in which she and Dad had died and I trained to become a Hero. A lot of people would have laughed out loud at the notion of their grown son dreaming about flying around in tights and a cape, but not Mom. She had told me more times than I could count that I could do anything I put my mind to and worked at. Even now, powerless though I was, I just knew if I told my mother I wanted to be a superhero, she would say, "That's nice, dear. Do you want me to sew a costume for you?"

As we talked, I held her hand like I had when I was a little kid crossing the street. If Mom thought that was weird, she didn't say anything about it. Memories of the earlier conversation about her gray hair and many other times spent with her flooded into my mind as I clung to my mother as if she was going to disappear.

I remembered how Mom had taught me to read before I even started school. I remembered her sitting up with me late into the night, reading aloud to me when I was too sick and miserable to go to sleep. I remembered her patiently teaching me to swing dance when I was fourteen as I stomped all over her feet. I remembered how she had smelled when she tied my bow tie for me the night of my high school senior prom. I remembered her eyes shining with pride when I got my acceptance letter from MIT.

I remembered it all. Those happy memories and many others filled my mind, replacing the ones from my dream like a bright light displacing shadows.

After a while, my father James came in, looking just as I remembered him: a bigger, taller version of me. I have to admit I teared up all over again, even though I now realized all those bad memories I had weren't memories at all, but rather, remnants of a bad dream. In reality, Dad had never been killed by Iceburn in that supervillain's attempt to kill me. In reality, I had never buried him or sold the land he had spent his life slaving over. In reality, he was a prosperous farmer who had dozens of farmhands rather than being the debt-ridden man who lived from hand to mouth the way he had in my bad dreams.

Mom had to start a new batch of bacon. The bacon she had been cooking when I walked into the kitchen was burnt; I had distracted Mom too much with my crazy talk of her and Dad's death. When she finished cooking, we sat and ate bacon and blueberry pancakes. I now remembered that we ate breakfast together as a family almost every morning.

I felt a warm glow as I helped Mom wash and dry the breakfast dishes. Dad sat at the kitchen table and read the morning newspaper, periodically looking up to read aloud in outrage something nutty one of our political leaders had done or was planning to do. As there were a lot of nutty things in the paper, Dad ranted and raved a lot. It was fortunate for my and Mom's entertainment, but unfortunate for the country.

I had never been happier washing dishes and listening to the news.

Come to think of it, I had never been happier, period.

The only thing that remained from my earlier confused state was I still sometimes glimpsed out of the corner of my eye a gray-white shape. The shape nagged at my mind like a barely remembered undone task. I ignored the shape, figuring it was a figment of my imagination and a stubborn remnant of my dismaying dreams and confusion from earlier.

Besides, I was too happy to be with my parents to think of anything else.

Could today get any better? I thought.

As if on cue, the front doorbell rang.

I excused myself and walked through the living room to go answer the door.

"There you are," the girl on our front porch said when I opened the door. "I thought you had been abducted by aliens or something."

As if a button triggering a video had been pressed in my mind, my brain was suddenly flooded by memories of the blonde in front of me. Her name was Amber Kaling. She was one of my fellow engineering students I was supposed to have had a study session with this morning. Like me, she was a sophomore at USCA. Also like me, she was moving to Cambridge, Massachusetts for the rest of her college career, though she was going to Harvard, not MIT. She had been a USCA cheerleader before giving it up to spend more time on her studies. She was on the track and swim teams, she could knit a sweater, sew a dress, build a computer from scratch, and she could tell you more about *Star Trek* than Gene Roddenberry could. She was a year younger than I and lived just a few miles up the road with her parents.

And, she was my girlfriend.

No, let me correct that: She was my hot girlfriend.

Amber had long blonde hair that looked like it had been spun from gold. It framed her heart-shaped face like a rich curtain. Her blue eyes were the color of a crystal-clear lake. Her square, black-framed glasses augmented rather than marred her looks. Maybe having a thing for the sexy librarian look was genetic. Amber had a rosebud mouth that was subtly high-lighted with red gloss. She had on black skinny jeans that clung to her runner's legs like a second skin. She wore an oversized red plaid shirt that hid a curvy torso I was very familiar with.

If Amber wasn't the most beautiful girl I had ever seen, she certainly was a finalist for the distinction. Christopher Marlowe had been wrong about Helen of Troy—Amber was the one with the face that could launch a thousand ships.

Not only was she beautiful, but she was also smart and

funny and good. She volunteered at the county soup kitchen. Every Saturday morning, she drove her disabled grandmother to the beauty salon and then had lunch with her afterward. She would give a needy stranger the shirt off her back if he needed it.

I swallowed hard. I had a sudden vivid memory of what she looked like without her shirt on. And there I stood, completely unprepared, fresh out of needy strangers.

Best of all, Amber loved me as much as I loved her.

This vision was my girlfriend? I fought off the strong impulse to high five myself.

"Are you okay?" Amber said, jarring my mind from lingering over memories of what she looked like naked. "You're staring at me like you've never seen me before."

"Sometimes I just can't believe how beautiful you are," I said, finally chasing down the cat that had stolen my tongue.

Amber looked at me the way my mother often looked at my father, like he had been personally responsible for putting the stars in the night sky. "If you think a little sweet talk is going to get you out of standing the rest of us up," she said, "then I must say you know me very well." She kissed me on the lips before brushing past me to go inside our house. She tasted like peppermint and possibilities. Kissing her felt the way a sunrise looked.

I followed Amber to the kitchen, admiring the amazing view she presented from the back. Mom and Dad greeted Amber like she was a member of the family. She practically was. My parents knew I planned to propose to Amber before we moved to Massachusetts. I had been saving money from my part-time job as a tutor in the university's computer lab to buy an engagement ring. Dad had offered to loan me the money, but I told him I'd rather come up with it on my own. I had taken one of Dad's Jamesisms to heart: "Neither a borrower nor a lender be." Dad had said that more times than I could count. Despite that oft-repeated advice, Dad had no problem borrowing liberally from *Hamlet*'s Polonius.

As I luxuriated in the warm glow of being surrounded by the people I loved, the nagging feeling about an uncompleted task I had experienced before came back. Though I knew I wasn't seeing anyone except Amber, I got the strangest feeling I was being untrue to someone. The fog I could almost-but-not-quite see out of the corner of my eye returned.

The word "fog" reminded me of the woman I had dreamed about being a Hero Apprentice with. What was her name? Mist? Cloud? No, neither was right.

"Your father and I are going to drive to town to pick up some groceries," Mom said, stopping me from further grasping at mental straws. The fog in the corner of my eye got fainter. "Do you need anything while we're out?"

I told her I was fine. In a few minutes, they were gone, leaving me and Amber alone in the kitchen.

"How long do you suppose they'll be gone?" Amber asked.

"An hour and a half to two hours, probably. Why?"

"Since you missed our earlier study group, I figured we could fit in an anatomy study session."

"Neither of us is taking anatomy," I said, confused. Maybe my memory was playing tricks on me again.

Amber started to unbutton her shirt. She smiled at me the way Eve had probably smiled at Adam when she offered him the apple.

Amber said, "Even though you're one of the smartest people I know, you can be awfully obtuse sometimes."

Her shirt fell open, exposing a very sturdy yet very sexy bra. I found myself gaping. When the Bible said "my cup runneth over," it could have been quoting Amber. Amber was very self-conscious about her big chest, which was why she normally dressed in loose tops to de-emphasize it. She often mused about getting a reduction. I had told her she was perfect the way she was. I had jokingly threatened to break up with her if she did anything to alter herself.

The truth of the matter was I would sooner saw off my arms and legs than break up with Amber.

Amber shrugged out of her bra, exposing even more of her perfection. I reached for her. The urgency of our desire for each other kept us from withdrawing to my bedroom. Soon, our two bodies became one. It happened right in the middle of the kitchen's cold tile floor. Amber didn't seem to mind. I knew I didn't. We were too lost in each other to care.

After an exquisite eternity, Amber and I exploded in each other's arms.

I had been wrong earlier when I thought the day couldn't get any better.

Never before had I been so happy to be so wrong.

22

I filled my umpteenth bushel basket, topping it off with a few more peaches. Even though it was early morning, the sun beat down implacably like a red-hot hammer. The high humidity made being outside like walking around in a steam room. My long-sleeved cotton work shirt clung to me like I was in a wet tee shirt contest.

Summers in South Carolina were no joke. Hell might be cool and refreshing by comparison. If the Sunday morning fire-and-brimstone television evangelists were right, I would find out soon enough if I kept doing what I had been doing the past few weeks with Amber.

I was willing to take the risk.

I wiped my wet brow with my shirt sleeve. It was a mistake. The peach fuzz on the fabric now made my forehead itch. My forehead had plenty of company. Hours of picking peaches had managed to get peach fuzz in places I barely knew I had. I wanted to cover myself in catnip and invite every cat in miles to make me their human scratching post.

I was hot, tired, sweaty, thirsty, and itchy.

I had never been happier.

I was in the middle of Dad's peach orchard. The rows of fruit-laden peach trees around me rustled with activity. Most of the people picking peaches along with me were Dad's employees. They were mostly Mexican. People loved to criticize Mexican immigrants to this country, but good luck getting your average native-born American up before the crack of dawn to go pick peaches in the heat of a South Carolina summer. The brown-skinned men whom Dad employed worked tirelessly, showed up when they were supposed to, and were as honest as the priests who presided over them at Mass every Sunday morning. Some of them had been with Dad as long as I had been alive. Most of them were my friends; many were like uncles or brothers to me.

In addition to Dad's employees being out here with me, several of my friends from college were here as well. When I had told them Dad always needed extra hands to get in the summer's harvest, they had jumped at the chance to make some extra money. Amber would be here too if it weren't Saturday. Today was the day she chauffeured her grandmother around. The fact Amber wasn't afraid to get her hands dirty was but one of the many things I loved about her.

Dad and Mom were here picking peaches too. Dad worked on a tree behind me, while Mom was over on my right. Though Dad theoretically was supervising the rest of us, in fact he was picking as many peaches as we were. As for Mom, as she had put it when I had asked her earlier why she was going to pick peaches with us, "Some women go to the gym and do yoga. I help work the farm. Besides," she had said, her eyes twinkling, "your Dad likes it when I get all hot and sweaty."

Eww. Like I said, Mom sometimes overshared.

Though I was working hard, I was surrounded by friends and family. Who could ask for anything more?

Why, then, did something keep nagging at my mind? It had

bothered me off and on ever since I had awaken confused in my room weeks before. It was the same sort of feeling I got when I had something to do, but whatever it was had slipped my mind. It was as if my subconscious was tugging at my shirt, trying to get my attention, and saying, "Hey dummy! You forgot something."

And, the gray fog I kept seeing out of the corner of my eye hadn't gone away. Not completely, at least. Every time I stopped to think about what was nagging at my mind, the fog reappeared at the edge of my vision, like a ghost whose name had been called. In fact, it was back now. The more I struggled to remember what I had forgotten, the fog got darker and darker, like a gathering storm.

"Hey Theo!" Dad called out to me. I jumped, startled out of my reverie. The fog at the edges of my vision thinned. Mom had stopped picking and looked at me with obvious concern. "What're you staring off into space for? We've got work to do."

"I was just thinking," I said.

"It looks more like you were daydreaming. You think these peaches are going to pick themselves? As the Good Book says, 'A hard worker has plenty of food, but a person who chases fantasies has no sense.'"

I winked at Mom and said to Dad, "You should pay God a royalty every time you use one of His quotes."

Dad grinned at me. "Can't. I'm saving money to buy a new son who won't sass me. I'm sure He understands."

"Mom, are you going to let him talk to your beloved only son that way?"

She said, "I sure am. If I try to stop him, he's liable to replace me too."

"No woman could ever replace you," Dad said. He hesitated. "Two or three women might be able to do it, though." Dad ducked, letting the half-rotten peach Mom had thrown sail over his head.

I went to get an empty bushel basket, stacks of which were nearby. I left the basket full of the peaches I'd already picked right where it was. Later some of Dad's men would drive down the rows of widely spaced trees in trucks and load all the peaches we had picked.

As I started picking again, I thought of how much I had missed Mom and Dad and their playful banter with each other.

That thought brought me up short again. Why would I have missed them? I had seen them almost every single day since the day I was born.

A person who chases fantasies has no sense. Dad's Biblically cribbed words ran over and over again in my mind. The nagging feeling that had been bothering me for weeks got stronger as I chewed on those words. *A person who chases fantasies has no sense.* Something about this whole situation wasn't right. Sometimes it felt like I wasn't in the real world and that I was instead in a play where everyone was acting except for me.

The grayness at the edge of my vision got darker and more pronounced. I could almost—but not quite—bring it into focus.

For some reason, I found myself thinking of a story from the *Odyssey*. In it, Odysseus' men, while sailing from the Trojan War back to their home in Ithaca, were blown off course. They landed on an island where the people offered Odysseus' men the fruit of the lotus plant as food. It turned out the fruit contained a narcotic, making Odysseus' men no longer care about going home. They only cared about getting more of the lotus fruit.

Someone shook my shoulder, jarring my thoughts away from the *Odyssey* and breaking my increasing concentration on the gray fog.

"Hey Theo," Dad said. His hand was on my shoulder. I now

stood in the middle of a row of peach trees. Though I didn't remember doing so, I had apparently walked away from the tree I had been picking. "Didn't I ask you to get back to work?"

I shook my head in confusion and frustration.

"S-s-something's wrong," I said, stammering to put what I felt into words. "There's something I'm supposed to be doing. There's something I'm supposed to be seeing. Something about a lotus."

As I spoke, the grayness at the edge of my vision coalesced more, becoming more distinct. Now that I could see it more clearly, it was a large swirling pinwheel of gray gas a bit taller than I was.

"There!" I said, spinning to try to point at the swirling gray mass. However, it moved as I did, always staying at the edge of my vision. It was like chasing a rainbow. The straw hat I had on to protect me from the sun flew off my head. Sweat dripped into my eyes, partially blinding me. I tried to blink it away and see clearly. "Can't you see it?"

"There's nothing to see, Theo," Dad said firmly. His fingers dug into my shoulder. "Now I'm not going to tell you again—get back to work."

"But can't you see it? It's right there!" I spun again, trying to bring the elusive gray mass into full view.

"Theo, you're talking like a crazy person," Mom said. She was now alongside Dad as I spun like a whirling dervish. "You're scaring me."

The thought of me being like a whirling dervish triggered a new thought in my mind. Hadn't I recently dealt with someone named Dervish? Then again, what kind of weirdo name was Dervish? What sadistic parents would saddle their kid with a name like that? It sounded like a name you would find in a comic book.

I was thinking about the *Odyssey* and seeing things and

remembering people I knew couldn't possibly exist. Mom said I sounded like a crazy person. Was she right? Was I going crazy?

"Theo, that's quite enough," Dad said. He grabbed me firmly by the arms, stopping me from continuing to chase the grayness that danced right outside my view like a will-o'-the-wisp. Dad had been a farmer all his life, and his grip was viselike. A bunch of the peach pickers around us had stopped working, staring at me and the scene I caused. "Now get back to work."

"Not until I figure out what the hell is going on," I said.

Almost as if it was happening in slow motion, I saw Dad's right hand lift to slap me. I wasn't sure if it was to punish me for cursing—something Dad couldn't stand—or to slap some sense into me.

I twisted out of the grasp of the hand that still held me. I lifted my left forearm, blocking Dad's slap. I jabbed with my right, hitting Dad hard in the solar plexus. Dad grunted loudly. I took a couple of steps back, out of his reach. Dad sank to his knees, grabbing his stomach as he fell.

Mom ran to Dad's side, bending over to see if he was okay. Though he gasped for breath, he seemed otherwise unhurt. Mom then looked up at me with shock on her face. Some of the other peach pickers were around us now, encircling my family like spectators at a prizefight. Most of them had known me for years and had not seen me swat so much as a fly. They also looked at me with shock, not knowing how to react.

I felt as shocked as Mom and the others looked. For one thing, Dad hadn't tried to lay a hand on me since I had taken a friend's watch in the first grade. He had given me a well-deserved spanking then, but hadn't touched me since. Him raising his hand to me now was completely out of character. It was like seeing a dove attack a hawk.

For another thing, I had defended myself like I was a trained fighter. Dad was bigger and stronger than I. And yet, I had defended myself with ease, automatically, without thinking about it. I had done it on muscle memory, as if I had blocked shots and thrown punches hundreds of times before. I felt like if the guys around us suddenly attacked me, I would know how to handle myself. I found myself thinking that, if I needed to take them down, I would disable José first. José had been a semi-professional boxer in Mexico when he was younger. As far as I knew, he was the only trained fighter in the group around us. He favored his left leg a little, so I would target him there. Then I would take out my friend Glenn, who played college football and posed a threat simply because of his size and strength.

How the whole thing would go down played out in my mind's eye like I was watching a martial arts movie.

The plan of attack unspooling in my mind surprised me. I had never taken so much as a Taekwondo class. Who did I think I was, Batman?

Batshit crazy was more like it.

I smiled at the thought. That sounded like something Myth would say.

Wait, who the hell is Myth? I don't know anybody named Myth.

And yet, I did. I latched onto his name like a drowning man clutching a life preserver. Focusing on Myth's name got me thinking about the *Odyssey* again. Why did that story about the lotus eaters resonate with me so much?

Then it hit me.

Lotus. The Trials. Isaac, also known as Myth. Neha, also known as Smoke. Mom's brain cancer. Iceburn. Dad dying in the fire Iceburn had set.

The dream I had weeks before hadn't been a dream. That was reality. *This* was the dream. It was all some kind of sick test.

"You're dead," I said to my parents. "You're both dead." My voice cracked. My vision blurred, obscured by tears. "None of this is real. I have to go back to where I belong."

Dad got back to his feet. Mom stood up straight. She stepped forward and took my hand.

"You belong here. Don't I look real? Don't I feel real? Don't I sound real?" Her voice was pleading. "Stay here with us. We love you. Me, your Dad, Amber, your friends—we all love you. We're as real as you need us to be."

Dad said, "Yes, please stay with us son. We love you. Don't leave us."

The gray fog was no longer an elusive chimera in the corner of my eye. It took shape as a swirling gray mass to my right. It was now as plain as the peach trees around us. I somehow knew it was the way back to the world I knew.

I also somehow knew that my Mom was telling the truth. I could stay here with her and Dad and Amber and my friends and my perfect life forever. If it was real to me, did it matter that it wasn't real in reality? The only reason why I had gone through superhero training was to earn the right to legally track down the people behind Dad's murder. If Dad was alive here, what did I need a Hero's license for? If I stayed here, I could be with both my parents. I could be surrounded by friends. I could marry Amber. I could be happy.

For the first time in my life, I could be happy.

Would it really be so terrible to continue to eat the lotus?

I shook my head and pulled my hand out of Mom's. She started to cry. It nearly broke my heart.

"I can't stay," I said. "I want to, but I can't. You have to deal with the world the way it is, not the way you want it to be. You both taught me that. There are people in the real world who have been out to get me. They killed a lot of people trying to get to me. People like you, Dad. The people caught in the Oregon wildfire Iceburn set. And, they almost hurt a lot of people in the Guild complex with the bomb they planted. I must find and stop them. If I don't, who will? Besides, what is it you're always saying, Dad? 'To whom much is given, much is required.' I'm an Omega-level Metahuman. They tell me I have the potential to be one of the most powerful Metas in the world. To be honest, I often wonder if there's been a big screwup somewhere. I feel like a confused, scared kid more than I feel like an Omega-level Hero. But if what they say about me is true, then I have the potential to be one of the most powerful forces for good in the world. I can't waste that potential. I won't."

I shook my head ruefully. "I didn't ask to be given superpowers. There was a time I would have happily given them back if I could. But now that I've got them, I need to do some good with them. There are a lot of people I can help, people who often can't help themselves because they're up against forces that are too big for them to cope with. Half the time I feel like they're too big for me to cope with too. But I have to try. I can't let myself get swallowed up in a dream world."

I thought about my recent realization that I was in love with Neha. "Plus, there are people in the real world I care about. Maybe they all don't care about me the way I care about them, but maybe I can change that. The only way I'll know for sure is if I go back."

I turned and walked toward the swirling gray mass. I wanted to look back at my parents one last time and say goodbye. I wanted to ask them to tell Amber I loved her.

I didn't look back, though. Goodbyes didn't matter. Sending my love didn't matter. None of these people were real anyway.

But, to be totally honest, that wasn't the real reason I didn't pause to look back and say goodbye.

The real reason was I knew if I stayed any longer, I'd never leave.

My body merged into the gray mass. My beautiful dream world dissolved.

23

I woke up.

I was back in the Guild testing room with Lotus. He looked down at me with the same faraway look he always had.

Though there was no confusion now about what was real and what was not, I remembered all of what had happened in the dream world Lotus had put me in. I remembered how that dream world had been so much better in so many ways than my real world. I remembered how happy my childhood had been in that dream world. I had lots of friends and I had never been bullied. I remembered how my family had never been poor and how we never had to struggle from day to day to make ends meet.

I remembered Amber. I remembered the love in her big blue eyes when she looked at me. I remembered how it had felt to touch, kiss, and be inside of her. Being with her made me realize why some people wrote flowery poems about the people they loved. I had thought it was all exaggerated nonsense before.

And, I remembered my parents being alive. I especially remembered them. I remembered Dad's hands from when I had shaken them. Calloused, rough, strong, and determined. I remembered Mom. How she smelled. How hugging her felt like home.

But, as I lay there in the chair, all of it started to slip away. The edges of the memories were becoming fainter, like a shaken Etch-A-Sketch.

"Well done, young man. You passed the test," Lotus said.

I stirred, trying to sit up. My body was stiff from disuse.

"How long have I been here?"

"Two days."

"Two days?" I repeated, flabbergasted. "How's that possible? It seemed like weeks."

"Things are not always as they seem."

Lotus started to turn away. I managed to get to my feet. I was equal parts angry and upset. I started to tear up again. All this pain was because of a stupid test. A test of what, though? My resolve? My resistance to temptation? My capacity to see through artifice? My ability to resist the urge to go shoot myself in the head due to heartbreak and loss?

No, it was not merely a test. It was a lie. A beautiful dream of a lie I never wanted to wake from.

"Hey wait a minute, Lotus. I want to say something."

He turned back around. "Yes?"

I punched him hard in the jaw. Despite my arm being stiff, it was a textbook perfect right cross. Lotus staggered backward, then landed heavily on his behind.

I knew I shouldn't have done it. I knew it before I did it, and I knew it after I did it.

Felt good, though.

I SAT ON THE EDGE OF MY BED. AFTER PUNCHING LOTUS, PITBULL

had confined me to my quarters until he met with the other proctors to decide what they would do with me.

Isaac stood on one side of me, and Neha on the other.

"Dude, you sucker-punched a Hero?" Isaac said. His eyes were wide with disbelief. "I don't know whether to high five you or slap you upside the head."

"I didn't sucker-punch him," I said defensively. "I told him to turn around first."

"Hey Lotus, Mr. Licensed Hero and Trials' Proctor Sir, yeah I knocked you on your ass and yeah I loosened your teeth, but in my defense, I had you turn around first." Isaac rolled his eyes. "You know that sounds lame, right?"

"I was mad."

"Oh the 'I was mad' defense. Well that changes everything." Isaac's voice dripped with sarcasm. "Did you go to law school when we weren't paying attention? If so, you should demand your tuition back. The fact you were mad means nothing."

"How about you ease up on him," Neha said. "Can't you see he's upset? The proctors might throw him out of the Trials over this."

As she spoke, I came to the sudden realization Isaac had been right when he blew up at me and Neha before the Trials started: she did tend to defend me. I feared she did it the way you'd intervene on behalf of a defenseless puppy rather than the way you'd defend someone you loved. Though my memories of Amber were already faded like a picture exposed to the bright sun for too long, I still remembered the way she had looked at me. It was not the way Neha looked at me.

Isaac said, "You're right. I shouldn't berate him. The proctors will likely be doing that and more to him soon enough."

"Not helpful," Neha said.

Isaac shook his head in wonder. "I've said it before, but it bears repeating in light of this incident: White people are crazy."

"That's racist," Neha said.

"It's not racist. It's fact-ist. There's nobody here but us chickens. Screw being PC. We can be frank with one another. White people are cray-cray. Who are almost always serial killers? White people. Necrophiliacs? White people. Skydivers? White people. *National Enquirer* readers? White people. Guys who punch their test proctor in the mouth?" Isaac pointed at me. "White people."

I fought off a grin. Isaac was doing what he often did, making jokes to make me feel better. He really was a good friend.

"I've been to jail," I said. "If white people are so crazy, you'd think one hundred percent of the inmates would be white. They're not. There's plenty of you people there."

"You people?" Isaac raised an eyebrow at my word choice. I had chosen those words deliberately, to get a rise out of him. "Now *that's* racist. Besides your 1950s diction proving you can take the boy out of South Carolina but not the South Carolina out of the boy, you're proving my point by reminding us you're a jailbird. There are two people of color in this room and one paleface. Only one of us has been to jail. And who would that be?" Isaac pointed at me again. "The crazy white one. Now that I think about it, it's kinda shocking you didn't flip your lid before now."

Before a race war could break out, the door to my room dilated open. Pitbull stepped in. With four people now in the tiny room, it was like being in a clown car.

My apprehension about what the Guild would do with me had eased a little thanks to bantering with Isaac. With Pitbull here, my fears now came back with a vengeance. It was hard to read Pitbull's expression. It was tough to believe he had stopped by to pat me on the back, though.

Pitbull trained his eyes on Isaac and Neha. He said, "Don't you two have somewhere else to be?"

"No," Neha said. There was a note of defiance in her tone. I knew she wanted to hang around to stick up for me.

"Well, find somewhere else to be," Pitbull said flatly. "Now."

Neha looked like she was about to argue with him. Isaac saved her from stepping into as much hot water as I was in by grabbing her arm.

"Come on, let's go," Isaac said to her. "Maybe there's a documentary about skydiving serial killers we can watch through Overlord." He pushed her toward the door. Fortunately, Neha chose to go willingly. I doubted he could have made her leave if she decided to stay.

Isaac shot me a look that said *Don't do anything stupid* before the door dilated behind them, leaving me alone with Pitbull.

I still sat on the bed. Pitbull leaned against the wall, his arms folded. He looked down at me. His black eyes were expressionless.

After a few moments, the silence got to be more than I could stand.

I said, "You've gotta stop coming to my bedroom like this. People will start to talk."

Silence.

Finally Pitbull said, "Is that supposed to be a joke?"

"Yes sir. I was trying to lighten the tension."

"Do you think you accomplished your objective?"

"No sir. In fact, I think I made it worse."

That actually got a slight smile out of him. Then he let out a long breath.

"Kinetic, I'll tell you the truth: I don't know whether to admire your sand, or try to beat it out of you." My vote was for the former, but I wisely kept that thought to myself.

Pitbull shook his big head at me. "Assaulting a proctor is a very serious matter."

I could have said that I had battered Lotus by hitting him,

not assaulted him. An assault would have been if I had merely threatened to hit him. But I was sure Pitbull already knew that. He must have studied Hero Law just as I had. It seemed a bad time to point out the legal niceties between assault and battery, so I didn't. Perhaps too late I was learning impulse control.

"I had whether you should be expelled from the Trials put up for a vote among the other proctors. All but two of us voted to kick you out." My heart sank. "Interestingly, Lotus was one of the no votes. Though he wouldn't go into details about what he saw in your mind, he said, and I quote 'I'd rather have Kinetic inside the Hero tent pissing out than to have him outside the tent pissing in.'" Pitbull smiled wryly. "Lotus has a real flair for language sometimes.

"The other no vote was mine. Fortunately for you, the Trials aren't a democracy. It is a benevolent dictatorship with yours truly as the dictator. I let the other proctors' opinions guide me, but I'm not ruled by them. I'm going to let you attempt to complete the Trials." A wave of relief washed over me. "Except for this latest incident, I must say I'm rather impressed with how you've conducted yourself so far. And, if it weren't for you, a lot of the complex would have been destroyed by that bomb."

"Thank you, sir. I really appreciate it."

Pitbull stopped leaning against the wall and stood up straight. He clapped his hands together.

"With all that said, I believe it would only be appropriate if you apologized to Lotus." Pitbull smiled grimly. His big canines glinted under the artificial light. "And going forward, you need to save your punches for Rogues and not waste them on Heroes."

I thought about how I had felt when I awoke from Lotus' dream world. How I still felt. I didn't want to apologize to Lotus. If anything, I wanted him to apologize to me.

"Sir, I can't apologize. I won't. I know Lotus was just doing his job. I know it was just his powers. I know it was just a test. But what he gave me, only to have it snatched away again . . . ." I trailed off. I willed myself to not start crying again. I shook my head. "If you try to make me apologize, I'm liable to take a swing at him again. I won't do it."

Pitbull's eyes were disbelieving. "Weren't you listening to what I just told you? The only reason why you're still here is because I'm letting you stay. The least you could do is apologize to Lotus for your behavior."

"I won't do it," I repeated. I knew it was stupid, but I was feeling stubborn. I folded my arms. "And that's final."

"Who do you think you're talking to? Don't you know who I am?"

Anger bubbled up in me like lava. I was royally sick of being pushed around. People had been pushing me around and trying to push me around all my life. I was sick of being tricked, of people trying to kill me, and of watching good people die. Dad, Mom, Hammer. Who'd be next? Yes, I wanted to be a Hero. But the days of people telling me what I could and could not do were over.

I stood. I was taller than Pitbull. It gave me satisfaction to look down at him.

"Yes sir, I know exactly who you are. You're Pitbull, a licensed Hero and the chief proctor of the Hero Trials. You've probably forgotten more about being a Hero than I'll ever know. But you must not know who I am."

I paused for emphasis.

"I'm the guy who's not going to apologize to Lotus."

Pitbull didn't even get mad. His dark eyes simply became flat and cold. The look reminded me of the way a snake looks at a mouse it's about to pounce on. A while ago the look would have scared me. Not anymore. I wasn't the same South Carolina mouse I used to be.

"I said you could stay in the Trials," Pitbull said coldly. "So you can stay. But know this: I don't care what's happened to you in the past. I don't care if you are an Omega-level Metahuman. I don't care if you are the second coming of Omega Man himself. While you are here, you will show me and the other proctors the respect we deserve. Your impudence will have consequences."

He turned on his heel and left my room. It was probably just my imagination, but it seemed like the door snicked shut behind him ominously.

Well that was an incredibly stupid thing to say to someone with power over you, part of me thought. *You've got a real knack for winning friends and influencing people.*

Oh shut up! another part of me retorted irritably.

24

"Thirty-seven Hero candidates began the Trials," Pitbull said from the dais. "Six of your colleagues did not make it past the written phase. Thirteen of them failed various tests in the scenarios phase. And, unfortunately, eight have died. Four of the deceased have been granted their Hero's licenses posthumously. Their names will be remembered with honor and respect as long as there is a Heroes' Guild."

We ten remaining Hero candidates, all dressed in costume, sat in front of Pitbull in the same holographic auditorium he had addressed us in when we first began the scenarios portion of the Trials. An Overlord node floated in the air slightly behind Pitbull. Hopefully this time we would not wind up fighting a bunch of killer robots at the end of Pitbull's presentation. After all we had been through, I would not have been the slightest bit surprised if we had to fight the robots again, but this time while blindfolded and wearing high heels.

It was several days after my fifth test with Lotus. Since then, I had cooled my heels waiting for the remaining Hero candidates to complete their last tests so we could all begin the sixth and final test together. I was glad for the break. I had been through a lot both physically and emotionally. Thanks to the respite, I was now pretty much one hundred percent healthy physically. Emotionally, I wasn't so sure.

I was not at all surprised to see that Isaac and Neha had made it to the final round of testing. They both sat to my right. Also, Hacker was among the remaining ten candidates. As for the other Hero candidates, I had seen them all before, but had had no real interaction with them.

"As I indicated when I first spoke to you in this room, now that you have successfully completed the first five tests of the scenarios phase, you will now face one final challenge," Pitbull said. "In it, you will be pitted in a one-on-one gladiatorial style fight against another randomly selected Hero candidate. The fight will take place here in the Guild complex in one of the holosuites. The holographic environment the fight will take place in will also be randomly selected. Whoever wins that fight will get his or her license; whoever loses will fail out of the Trials. There have been complaints from prior Trials' competitors about the zero-sum game nature of the final challenge. We have kept it that way over the years because being a Hero is often a zero-sum game. In the real world, if you need to defuse a ticking time bomb, either you do it, or you get blown to bits. When you're fighting a supervillain who's intent on killing you, either you subdue him or he kills you. In the real world, there are no do-overs, no 'everyone is a winner.' There's a winner and a loser, a predator and a prey, a killed and a killer. The final Trials challenge is but a reflection of that stark reality."

I did not like the fact there was a chance I would have to go up against either Neha or Isaac for the final test. The thought that I might be the one responsible for thwarting their dream of becoming a Hero almost made me sick to my stomach. The thought one of them might stop me from becoming a Hero didn't make me want to do backflips of joy, either. Fortunately, there was only a twenty-two percent chance I would face them instead of one of the other seven Hero candidates. I liked those odds. I would like them even better if there were a zero percent chance. If there was one thing I had learned, though, it was that the Trials could not have cared less about what I liked.

"As with many of the tests you have undergone," Pitbull said, "Overlord will be the sole judge of who won and who lost this final contest in the interest of eliminating human error and bias. Other than the fact you all should not be trying to kill one another, all other bets are off. As you already know or you wouldn't have gotten this far, the Trials are no place for shrinking violets. You should do whatever you feel you must do to win. Overlord will end the match when a clear winner has been established."

Pitbull paused.

"Does anyone have any questions?" he asked. No one did.

"Very well. The matches will take place two at a time in two separate holosuites. The Round One matches will begin approximately twelve hours from now. Overlord, please show the candidates who their opponents will be."

A beam like the one we saw when Overlord projected its countdowns shone from the bottom of the node. Words and a list of names formed in the air.

The first thing I saw was that my match was in Round One. That suited me just fine. The sooner I started the test, the sooner it would be over.

The second thing I saw made my heart rise to my throat.

"Myth versus Kinetic," the glowing green letters read.

Isaac and I looked at each other in dismay. My odds had gone from twenty-two percent to one hundred percent. My nightmare scenario had come true.

I felt another set of eyes on me. I looked back over to Pitbull on the dais. He stared straight at me. There was a slight, smug smile on his face.

Like a tape replaying in my head, I remembered what Pitbull had said to me when I had mouthed off to him about Lotus. "Your impudence will have consequences," Pitbull had said. Maybe having to go up against one of my friends was that consequence.

But hadn't Pitbull just said our opponents were selected randomly? A twenty-two percent chance of drawing either Neha or Isaac as an opponent wasn't a zero percent chance.

That's what a part of me thought, the small minority of my psyche that still believed, despite a whole lot of evidence to the contrary, that people tended to play fair and follow the rules.

Random my ass! the rest of me thought.

A SHORT WHILE LATER I LAY IN BED IN MY ROOM. I WAS ALONE AND stripped down to my underwear. I stared at the ceiling, thinking about how unfair my predicament was.

If I beat Isaac and won, I'd prevent him from becoming a Hero. Yeah, he could take the Trials again some other year, but there was no guarantee he would get as far in them a second time. And even if he did, I would be the one responsible for delaying his achievement of his dream to become a Hero.

On the other hand, if I lost, the shoe would be on the other foot. I'd have to take the Trials again. Meanwhile, the trail connecting Iceburn and whoever hired him to kill me would get colder than it already was. I didn't want to wait any longer to find the people who were behind killing my Dad and who had been trying to kill me.

It was bad enough that I had to fight Isaac. But, if I had to fight Isaac because Pitbull had set it up to be that way, that was doubly unfair. If only I had kept my big mouth shut and apologized to Lotus the way Pitbull had asked me to.

My mind groped for a solution.

It came up empty. This really was a no-win situation.

Wait! That's it!

I sat up so abruptly that I got lightheaded.

That's exactly what this was: a no-win situation. And I knew someone who had faced a no-win situation before.

I hastily threw on some clothes and left the room.

There was somebody I needed to talk to.

25

I stood about half a block away from Isaac in the middle of a big city's street. Skyscrapers loomed around us like giants. Thanks to them, Isaac and I were shrouded in shadows despite the fact it was the middle of a sunny day.

Parked cars lined the street we were on. We could have been almost anywhere—New York, Chicago, Houston, Los Angeles, or any number of other large cities. The downtowns of big cities all had much the same feel and look to them. The only thing betraying that we were on a holosuite and not standing in the middle of a real big city's street was the fact the city was almost dead quiet. There was no traffic, no people, no hum of conversations, no sound of airplanes overhead, no anything except the slight whistling of the wind. You could literally hear a pin drop.

I found my mind turning yet again to the bombshell I discovered before coming here for my test against Isaac. I tried to shove the thought out of my head. There was nothing I could do about it now. I'd deal with it later. Right now, I needed to focus.

The ever-present Overlord node was overhead, counting down the seconds until our test formally began. I was heartily sick of seeing that countdown. Win or lose, it would probably be awhile before I could bring myself to wear a watch again.

"I'm sorry it's you I'm facing," Isaac called out. Like I was, he wore the costume the Old Man had given him, the black one with the light blue bands around the wrists and ankles. Neither of us had our capes on. Isaac's face was obscured by his cowl. The blood-red dragon on the front of his costume seemed to glow faintly. If you didn't know him, Isaac would look very intimidating all decked out in his costume. Heck, I knew the guy and I still was intimidated.

"Yeah, me too," I said. I grinned, displaying a humor I did not feel. "It's not going to keep me from trying to kick your ass, though."

"Ditto," Isaac said. He grinned back at me. "When I'm a Hero, I'll let you be my sidekick until you can stand for the Trials again. How does Mini-Myth sound as a new code name for you?"

"And here I was thinking Kinetic Kid sounded like a good sidekick name for you."

Isaac shook his head.

"Typical white person's attitude. The funny black guy has always gotta be the white man's sidekick. You trying to turn me into a stereotype?"

Isaac's grin slid off his face as Overlord's countdown approached zero.

"But seriously man, I'm awfully sorry about this," he said.

"Me too."

Overlord's countdown hit zero.

I lifted my hands and brought them together. Two cars on either side of Isaac flew from where they were parked, shooting toward Isaac like they were iron filings and he was a magnet.

The cars smashed together with a terrific crash. Glass and auto parts went flying.

The problem was, I had missed Isaac entirely. Right before the cars could hit him, he had changed into a huge dog and leapt out of the way.

No, not just a dog. A monstrous, lethal-looking, three-headed dog from the gates of Hell itself.

Cerberus.

Isaac raced toward me faster than any normal dog could. I threw debris from the car crash, metal trash bins, manhole covers, and other objects from the street at him. But, thanks to his three-headed form, Isaac could watch out for projectiles from all directions. He easily dodged all the missiles I launched at him.

Thanks to the speed of Isaac's canine form, the distance between the two of us diminished to almost nothing. I could smell him. He stank of brimstone and rot.

If I didn't do something and do it now, Isaac's slavering fangs would be at my throat.

Time to change tactics.

I erected a force field in front of me. Though it shimmered in my eyes like a translucent brick wall, it was invisible to Isaac. Running full tilt, he slammed into it.

One of his Cerberus heads whimpered in pain and surprise. His huge dog form bounced off my force field like a ping-pong ball smacked by a paddle. He landed on the street on his side and skidded a bit.

He twisted back to his four feet. Two of the heads tried to shake off the impact. The third head, the one in the middle that had taken the brunt of the impact, was a bloody mess.

Before Isaac could recover, I erected a dome-shaped force field around him, trapping him like a bug in an upturned glass jar. Isaac must have somehow sensed he was trapped because one of his heads sniffed the air cautiously. He went up to the edge of my force field and pawed at it.

Was the fight really over that quickly and easily?

I guess I should have known better.

Isaac's Cerberus form shimmered and morphed, changing back to a man's form. It wasn't Isaac's normal body, though. The form trapped in my force bubble glowed green and white, and wore tattered clothing. It leapt right through my force field as if it didn't exist.

Isaac's new shape, obviously a ghost, flew toward me like a heat-seeking missile. I wasn't overly worried, though. What was a ghost going to do to me? Yell "Boooo!" and scare me to death?

Isaac's ghostly fist reared back. Before I could react, he changed again. I caught a glimpse of a huge man with the head of a giant horned bull right before Isaac hit me with an uppercut that made me feel like I had been hit by a two-by-four.

Fortunately I was smart enough to have my personal shield up, or else Isaac could have used me as a model if he ever decided to transform into the Headless Horseman. Even with my shield up, though, Isaac's minotaur form hit me so hard, I felt much of the force of the blow despite the shield.

The powerful punch launched me into the air. Before I could exert my will to slow myself, I slammed into and then through the walls of a skyscraper high above where I had started.

I landed hard on a floor in the building. My momentum made me tumble across the floor like a human tumbleweed. I slammed into chairs and desks before finally skidding to a stop against a bookshelf.

The bookshelf teetered. Before I could roll out of the way, to add insult to injury, the bookshelf fell on top of me. I was pelted with a hailstorm of books.

I groaned, buried under a pile of books. I felt like I had been hit by a Mack truck. Though all I wanted was to take a fistful of aspirin and then a nap, I had to get up. The fight wasn't over.

I lifted the bookcase off me with my powers. I threw it across the room in a fit of pique. I was more than just a little disgusted I had let Isaac get close enough to ring my bell. I sat up. Books fell off me like ornaments off a Christmas tree. Maybe I should have taken a moment to skim through some of them. Maybe one of them was entitled *How To Defeat Your Best Friend Who Has More Tricks Up His Sleeve Than Houdini.*

Somehow, I doubted it.

I gingerly stood up and then levitated above all the debris my chaotic entrance had caused. I floated over to the gaping hole in the wall I had punched through. I landed in front of it, then cautiously stuck my head out of the jagged hole. The wind whistled in my ears. I was pretty high up, many stories above ground level. I didn't see Isaac. I was so high up, though, seeing him from here would be like spotting a tiny ant on the floor while standing on top of your bed.

I was about to extend my powers out to scan the area for the feel of flesh and blood when, suddenly, there was no need. Isaac rose up in front of me like something out of a nightmare.

I knew Isaac could turn into a dragon, but I had never seen him in that form before. I wished I wasn't seeing it now.

His massive dragon shape was as big as a house. His blood-red body looked like the monstrosity that would be spawned if a Tyrannosaurus Rex and a giant red snake had a baby. His scales, the size of dinner plates, glistened wetly. His massive red and black batlike wings flapped powerfully in the air, blasting me with heat. It felt like I stood in front of a kiln.

A kiln with rows of needle-sharp fangs, a stench that would gag a skunk, and huge burning eyes that had malevolent slits for pupils.

This monstrosity was my friend. I knew that intellectually. However, the monkey part of my brain, the part of my genetic inheritance that was a holdover from more savage times that was still afraid of heights, the dark, and monsters that went bump in the night, didn't know this dragon was my friend. It thought this huge scary monster was going to eat me.

That monkey part of my brain made me freeze in front of the dragon in irrational fear.

The dragon opened its maw, exposing more sharp teeth as long as my arm. It let out a roar that was like the horn of a thousand approaching freight trains. The sound hit me like a brick wall. It deafened me. I took a couple of steps back from the power of it. The accompanying stench made me want to throw up. The building shook under my feet.

Flames burst out of the dragon's mouth like they had been shot out of a bank of flamethrowers. They engulfed me like I had plunged into Hell.

By now, though I was still afraid, I was no longer paralyzed with fear. I could have dodged the flames. But, I did not. Using them on me was a tactical mistake on Isaac's part. He knew about how I had absorbed and redirected the energy of the mall bomb. He hadn't seen me do it, though. Being told about something and actually seeing that something in action were two very different things. It was the difference between hearing about a concert and being there to listen to it.

I absorbed the energy of Isaac's flames like a thirsty sponge. I was filled with so much strength and energy from Isaac's powerful fiery blast, I felt like a fully charged battery.

The flames coming from Isaac's mouth shut off. Though the building around me was now on fire, I was completely unhurt. In fact, I was better than unhurt. I was so brimful of force and vigor, that I grinned like a madman at the headiness of it.

Maybe it was my imagination, but I thought I now saw fear in Isaac's reptilian eyes. If he was afraid, he had reason to be.

I was about to give him a taste of my new powers.

I shot out of the hole in the building like a launched rocket. Isaac tried to claw me with his sharp talons as I approached him. I dodged the talons easily. The dragon shrieked in frustration. Thanks to the energy I had absorbed, my reaction time and speed had been increased exponentially. It was as if Isaac was moving in slow motion by comparison.

I literally flew circles around Isaac as I moved to position myself behind him. I grabbed his tail, right in front of the triangular black tip that was on the end of it. Isaac's scales burned my hands before I quickly made my force shield impervious to heat.

Feeling as strong as Hercules thanks to all the energy I had absorbed, I held onto Isaac's tail in my tight grip. I started spinning in a circle, faster and faster, until everything was a kaleidoscopic blur around us. Even Isaac's massive roars of pain and confusion were soon muted by the rushing wind.

I picked out a big black blur a bit off in the distance as I spun like a top in mid-air. I aimed. I let go of Isaac's tail.

Isaac shot away from me and toward the rectangular skyscraper I had aimed him at like a big red bat out of hell.

KABOOM!

He hit the side of the building with a sickening smack. The big building shuddered as if an earthquake had hit it.

Isaac's dragon body clung to the side of the building for a moment like a gigantic iguana. Then, he started to fall. His big body peeled off the side of the building like a postage stamp with bad adhesive. His now-tattered wings fluttered around him as he fell.

Seconds later, he hit the ground far below like a sack of bricks. A cloud of dust rose up from the impact. I stayed where I was, floating high above the ground, watching carefully to see if the fight was over.

It wasn't over, though. Once the dust cleared a little, I saw Isaac, still in dragon form, in the middle of a crater. He clawed the air like a beetle turned over on its back. Though his roar was weaker than before, it was not the roar of defeat.

I marveled at his fighting spirit. Despite Isaac's often goofy persona, he really was a tough bastard.

I hadn't even come close to using up all the energy I had absorbed from Isaac. I channeled more of the pent-up energy. My eyes burned. Beams of energy shot out of my eyes. I used the beams to cut through the top of the building I had thrown Isaac into. The powerful beams cut through the building like a hot knife through butter.

I then grabbed the top of the building with my mind. It was probably about the top fourth of the structure. I shifted the massive weight toward where Isaac lay thrashing below. Once the angle was right, I released my hold on the building fragment. Gravity would do the rest.

The top of the building fell like something out of a disaster movie. It smashed into Isaac like a sledgehammer. The crash was so terrific, it sent vibrations through the air. Even floating high up as I was, I felt the vibrations in my bones. Another cloud of dust rose up, this one bigger than the one before.

The surge of adrenaline I had been feeling tapered off a bit. I suddenly got worried. Had I gone too far in the heat of the moment? Though Isaac was my opponent, more importantly, he was my friend. He was the brother I never had. I didn't want to seriously hurt him. Or worse.

I touched down on the street not too far from the pile of rubble I had caused. The still-settling dust burned my nose. I was about to start lifting the rubble to make sure Isaac was okay. Then, I stopped myself. Had I learned nothing from my fight with Hitler's Youth? Just because it seemed like your opponent was beaten, that didn't mean he was.

I cast a mental probe deep into the rubble, probing for flesh and blood.

Nothing. Despite checking thoroughly, I found nothing.

I was about to take flight again to get out of the range of a possible attack when I felt an excruciating pain in my chest. It was what I imagined a severe heart attack felt like.

I looked down to see someone's arm sticking out of my chest.

I slumped forward, partly to get the arm out of my chest, and partly because it was so hard to stand. As I fell to my knees, the arm cut through my body like a dull saw, leaving mind-numbing pain in its wake.

I rolled onto my back, clutching my chest. Isaac was behind me with the arm that had just been in my chest extended. He was back in human form. Well, not quite his human form, actually. His body was darker than usual, as if he were a computer image with the screen brightness turned way down. I could see through him, too. My legs, squirming in pain, kicked right through him as if he were an illusion.

Isaac's costume was in tatters, and much of his skin was exposed. He bled like someone had taken a thousand razors to him. Despite the pain he must have been in, he smiled grimly down at me as I twisted on the hard asphalt. His teeth were stained with blood.

"My wraith's touch sure does sting, doesn't it?" he asked.

I didn't answer. I was too busy clutching my chest and writhing in pain.

"I guess the fight's over. I win," he said.

Again, I didn't respond. I started gasping, like I was hyper-ventilating.

Isaac's face grew from looking grimly satisfied to looking concerned.

"Dude, are you all right? Maybe we should get you to the infirmary. You're having an unusually strong reaction to my wraith's touch." He bent over me. He turned substantial.

As soon as I saw Isaac was solid again, I twisted and swept Isaac's legs from under him. He toppled over with a startled cry, hitting the street hard. Though I was in a heck of a lot of pain from what Isaac had done to me, I had been exaggerating to induce him to turn corporeal again.

I sprang on Isaac like a cat onto a mouse before he could change forms again.

Isaac and I rolled around on the ground, pummeling each other like schoolboys in the playground. Everything happening so fast. Between that and the residual pain caused by Isaac's wraith attack, I couldn't concentrate enough to bring my powers to bear. I suppose Isaac was in the same boat. He was obviously in pain from what I had done to him, plus I wouldn't let up my current attack on him. I was on him like white on rice.

Wrestling, Brazilian jiu-jitsu, judo, and several other martial arts we had both trained in until our minds were numb and our bodies were spent all came into play. Isaac and I proceeded to beat the hell out of one another. Neither of us was willing to give up or give in. We fought like wildcats trapped in a bag for what felt like hours, but what was probably a lot less than that.

At one point, I let go of Isaac's arm, freeing up my hand so I could take advantage of a perceived opening. But before I could do so, Isaac cracked me on the side of the head with his elbow.

I saw stars and then blackness.

When I could focus my eyes again, I was leaning against the glass door of a building next to the street. I had no memory of how I got there. My chest still hurt from Isaac's wraith attack. My lungs burned. I felt like I had been put into a burlap bag and beaten with a stick. A couple of my teeth seemed to be missing. I tasted blood.

Isaac was two feet away, leaning against the same glass door. If I looked as ragged as he did, I was in a sorry state indeed.

Isaac said something. I only knew that because his busted lips were moving, not because I could hear him. There was a dull roar in my ears. I was so tired, I could barely move. My eyes kept trying to close.

A sidewalk is as good a place as any to take a nap, I thought sleepily. *I wonder why I've never napped on concrete before. It looks so comfy.* I started sliding down the door toward the ground.

Isaac was still saying something. Now there were three of him, all saying something. It seemed important, though I couldn't remember for the life of me why. With a herculean effort, I stood up straight again.

I shook my head to clear my ears a little.

"Keep your goddamned eyes open and take a swing at me," Isaac was saying. His voice didn't sound quite right. He seemed to be missing teeth, too. Tooth decay was a real bitch. We both needed to brush more.

"Huh?" I was having a hard time focusing.

"I said hit me, you dolt!"

I wanted to ask him why he wanted me to hit him. We were best friends, after all. Friends didn't hit one another.

Then again, he did just call me a dolt. Plus, if a friend asked you to do something, you really ought to try to do it.

With an effort, I balled my right hand into a fist. I took aim at the third Isaac, the one on my left, because he was the closest. I hit him as hard as I could.

My punch might have been forceful enough to squash a caterpillar, but only if it was a particularly sickly one. My body followed my fist, hitting Isaac like a wad of thrown paper. We both collapsed into a heap on the sidewalk.

I knew it! I thought triumphantly. *Concrete* **is** *comfy! It's the dirty secret mattress manufacturers have been hiding from us.*

That was the last thought I had. The darkness that had been steadily closing in around me swallowed me like I was Jonah and it was the whale.

26

W hen I opened my eyes, I lay in a bed in the infirmary. Neha stood over me. Concern was on her face like it was written there in big fluorescent letters. Her left arm was in a sling.

For a few confused moments, I thought I was in the infirmary in the Old Man's mansion, waking up after that bomb had exploded in my face. When I painfully turned my head and saw Isaac lying in another infirmary bed a few feet away, everything that had happened came flooding back into my mind. Isaac looked like he had been in a barehanded brawl with a grizzly bear. I imagined I looked much the same. God knew I felt the same.

Isaac's bloodshot eyes were open. They met mine.

"Who won?" I asked. My throat hurt. My voice came out in a whisper.

"I have no idea," Isaac said. His eyes flicked over to Neha. "Chatty Cathy over there won't tell me."

"I can't tell you because I don't know," Neha said. Isaac looked like he didn't believe her. "I'm telling the truth. Whichever of you won, though, it's caused quite a stir among the proctors. Everywhere I go I see them whispering urgently to one another like they're Cold War spies who've discovered a nuclear attack is imminent."

"How long have I been out?" I asked.

"A little over two days," Isaac said. "I myself woke up just a few hours ago."

Two days? My eyes shifted back over to Neha. I glanced at her arm in the sling. Her final test had been scheduled to take place the day after ours.

"Did you pass?" I asked.

Neha nodded. Her face split into a gleeful grin.

"Say hello to the world's newest licensed Hero," she said, as happy as I had ever seen her. "Well, technically, I'm not a Hero yet as I haven't been sworn in. But still. I'd have you two bow and kiss my Hero's cape, but I haven't gotten it yet. Besides, neither of you is in a condition to stand, much less bow." Neha's nose wrinkled. "You two really did a number on one another.

"Speaking of which, I promised to fetch Pitbull once both of you were conscious so he could talk to you. I'll go get him now."

Neha hesitated, glancing at Isaac in embarrassment. She bent over and kissed me on the forehead before walking quickly out of the infirmary.

I wished she hadn't kissed me considering how Isaac felt about her. In her defense, she didn't know that.

"When I woke up, all I got was a hug from her," Isaac said. "Which, by the way, caused so much pain I almost called for Doctor Kevorkian. And you get a kiss?" Isaac started to shake his head. He winced, and evidently thought better of it. "There really is no accounting for taste."

"In Neha's defense," I said, "you do look like a plate of vomit right now. I wouldn't want to kiss you either."

"When you have a minute, take a look in a mirror. Talk about the pot calling the kettle black."

"Why do you have to bring race into everything?"

After a short while, Pitbull, Brown Recluse, and Lotus came in, trailed by Neha. The three proctors stood at the foot of my and Isaac's beds. Neha went to stand quietly by the wall, probably hoping Pitbull would forget she was there so she could hear everything.

Lotus and Brown Recluse stood slightly behind Pitbull. Though his face was impassive and his eyes had that faraway look they always did, Lotus looked down and winked at me. In light of the fact I had punched him, I didn't know if that was a good or bad sign as far as me getting my license was concerned.

Pitbull didn't ask us how we were feeling. Maybe he didn't care.

"Gentlemen, you two have presented us with a conundrum. As long as there has been a Trials, the final test has been a contest between two Hero candidates with only one person declared the winner. It has been this way for decades and literally hundreds of Heroes." Pitbull looked at first Isaac, then me. "Why then, with you two, did Overlord declare your match the first one in history to be a tie and that you both passed the Trials?"

Isaac and I looked at each other, and then back at Pitbull. Neither of us spoke.

"Come now, speak up," Pitbull barked. "The doctors tell me there's nothing wrong with your hearing."

"I'm not exactly sure what you're asking us, sir," Isaac said slowly. "Are you suggesting that we cheated?"

"It is the only explanation for this unprecedented result," Pitbull said. "Overlord was programmed to always declare a winner."

"We did not cheat, sir." Isaac sounded offended.

"We sure didn't," I added.

"The evidence does support their contention," Lotus said

mildly to Pitbull. If I could have moved, I would have kissed him. "We have reviewed Overlord's footage of their battle. Our technicians have checked Overlord for glitches in its programming. As you know, we have found nothing untoward."

"Be that as it may," Pitbull said, looking annoyed at Lotus for chiming in, "the results speak for themselves. There are not supposed to be ties, and yet there is a tie. I do not have to understand exactly how a magician is fooling me to know I am being fooled."

Brown Recluse said, "The Guild's bylaws related to the Trials are quite clear. Overlord is the final arbiter of who passes. You know those regulations were put into place to stop the blatant favoritism that existed before we had Overlord. Unless Myth and Kinetic admit they tampered with the results, you have no choice but to accept Overlord's decision." I had the feeling we were witnessing the rehashing of an argument the proctors had been having for days while I was unconscious.

"We didn't tamper with anything," I said.

"That's right," Isaac added. "If we could game the system, we would simply have had Overlord declare each of us the winners, high-fived each other, and then called it a day. Look at us. Instead we beat each other nearly to death. It was a fair fight. If Overlord says we both deserve to win, then we both deserve to win."

Pitbull sighed in frustration.

"My colleagues are right. I have no choice under Guild bylaws but to declare each of you the winner and allow you to take the Hero's oath and get your licenses." Pitbull's dark eyes flashed angrily. "But know this: If I ever find proof that either or both of you cheated, I will make it my new life's mission to see you are stripped of your license. I'll also have you prosecuted criminally. For fraud and anything else I can think of."

Isaac was so angry, he looked like he was about to have a stroke. With a visible effort, he controlled himself.

"Am I correct in believing that, short of being caught cheating, now that we have completed all the tests, you have to give us our licenses?" he asked Pitbull.

"Yes," Pitbull admitted grudgingly.

"Good," Isaac said. "Then I'm at liberty to say what I've always thought: Your name is really stupid. Pitbull? Really? What, was Chihuahua Man already taken? Is biting children your superpower? As soon as I get out of this bed, I'm going to do the world a favor and put a muzzle on you."

Brown Recluse laughed out loud. His laugh trailed off when Pitbull glared at him. Then Pitbull spun and walked out of the infirmary.

Still looking amused, Brown Recluse opened his mouth to say something. He apparently thought better of it as he turned to trail after Pitbull. Lotus left last, winking at me again before the door drew closed behind him.

Neha, who hadn't said a word this whole time, walked up to stand between our beds.

"Alright guys, now that we're alone, fess up. Which one of you did it? Or was it both of you?" she asked.

"What?" I said.

Neha rolled her eyes. "Come on. This is me you're talking to. If you're worried about listening devices, don't. I checked. Plus, Overlord doesn't have access to this room for medical privacy reasons. The only ears in this room are ours. You can tell me how you guys pulled this off. You know I'm not going to blab it to anyone. I just want to give credit where credit is due." Her eyes shone eagerly. "I will say I'm surprised either of you would do something like this. This is more along the lines of something *I* would do."

"Has everyone suddenly gone deaf and stupid?" Isaac said,

almost shouting. "We did not cheat! You want me to say it in Hindi so you can understand it better?"

Neha looked a combination of suspicious and uncertain.

"Maybe you should just leave, Neha," I said. "Both Isaac and I have been through a lot. We need our rest."

"If I'm wrong, I apologize," she said.

"Just get out," Isaac said irritably.

Neha hesitated for a moment. Then, she walked to the door.

"I'll come visit you guys tomorrow," she said before closing the door behind her.

"Can you believe their gall?" Isaac asked. He sounded both outraged and offended. "All the hard work and sacrifice we poured into pursuing a license, and those knuckleheads are questioning the results."

"It's insulting," I agreed.

The room fell silent for a bit.

"I didn't cheat," Isaac finally said, "but just so you know, I did hold back on you a little. Because you're my buddy. In the real world, if we ever did throw down, I'd beat you like a stolen drum."

"Who do you think you're kidding?" I scoffed. "A real fight between us would consist of two hits: I'd hit you, and then you'd hit the ground."

"It's 'whom' not 'who.'"

"I know that. Don't be pedantic."

The room was quiet again for a bit.

"Thanks," I said, thinking of how he had stopped me from passing out and told me to hit him again. If it hadn't been for that, Overlord would have probably judged Isaac the winner by TKO.

"For what?"

"You know what."

There was silence for a few moments.

"Yeah, I know. Don't mention it," Isaac said. "You would have done the same for me. Besides, you're the guy who got Trey bounced from the Trials. I figured I owed you one." Isaac yawned noisily. "Now stop flapping your gums so I can get some shut-eye. Whatever meds they put me on have got me as sleepy as a narcoleptic."

In a very short while, Isaac started snoring. Though I also was tired and in pain despite the haze of meds I too must have been on, I had a lot on my mind.

I had spoken the truth when I told the proctors Isaac and I hadn't tampered with anything. *We* hadn't cheated.

Unbeknownst to Isaac, *I* had though.

When I had lain in my bed hours before my fight against Isaac, it had occurred to me the situation was a no-win scenario. That had triggered in my mind something from *Star Trek*, of all things. In the movie *The Wrath of Khan*, it was revealed that James T. Kirk had been the only Starfleet cadet to prevail in the Kobayashi Maru, a computer simulation designed to test how the cadets would respond to a no-win situation. After flunking the test twice, the third time Kirk reprogrammed the computer so he could prevail. In his mind, there was no such thing as a no-win situation.

I agreed with Kirk. As far as I was concerned, it was a Hero's job to find a way to win, to make a way out of no way. Once I had thought of the Kobayashi Maru, it inspired me to emulate Kirk. I had left my room to go talk to Hacker. As she had said after our test on Hephaestus, she owed me one. When I had asked her if she could hack into Overlord without it being traced back to either me or her, Hacker had looked at me like I should be in a padded room and kept away from sharp objects. I had taken that as a "yes."

Once I explained what I had in mind, she was only too happy to use her Overlord access panel and her powers to break through its security and reprogram it. She looked as happy as a pig in mud while doing it. As she had told me on Hephaestus, breaking the rules was what hackers did.

Hacker had wanted to reprogram Overlord so that it would declare me the winner of my fight with Isaac regardless of who actually won. I told her I didn't want that. I just wanted to give Isaac and me a chance to both be declared the winner if the fight was close. If we both deserved it, we both would win. If one of us was the clear-cut winner, the other would have lost.

As Kirk said, there were no no-win situations. If the cause is just, a Hero finds a way to win. Even if he breaks the rules a little.

Okay, I'll admit it—as much as I tried to justify it, I felt pretty guilty about cheating. I had been raised Catholic, after all. Feeling guilty was kind of our thing. Guilt was baked into Catholicism the way Purgatory and the Immaculate Conception were. I didn't think my parents would approve of what I had done. What they would approve or disapprove of was my touchstone for what was moral or immoral.

Then again, I was convinced Pitbull had bent the rules himself by making sure I went up against one of my friends instead of my opponent being chosen at random. Also, I would never forget how Isaac had encouraged me to keep fighting when he could have just let me pass out and taken the win for himself.

When I thought about those things, I felt a lot less guilty.

My level of guilt shrank to almost non-existent when I thought about what Hacker had discovered when she dove into Overlord's system.

Hacker had discovered who had gotten into Overlord's system to plant the nanites that had attacked me. That same person had programmed Overlord to allow one of the Hero proctors to plant the bomb in the holosuite that had nearly killed me, Neha, the other test-takers, and God knew how many other people in the Guild complex. Hacker said that person had left almost no trace of their activity. Only a Meta as adept at dealing with intelligent machines as she was would have been able to discover who had done it, she had said without a trace of embarrassment over her lack of modesty.

The person who had accessed Overlord and who had tried to kill me was none other than the creator of Overlord himself:

Mechano of the Sentinels.

Me knowing who had been targeting me during the Trials was the thought that had distracted me when I first faced Isaac during our final test.

I didn't know what my newfound knowledge meant yet. Was Mechano also the one who had hired Iceburn to try to kill me, leading to Dad's death? Neha had told me long ago that a big-time Metahuman assassin like Iceburn only worked for Metahuman big leaguers. As a member of one of the most powerful group of Heroes in the world—if not *the* most powerful—Mechano certainly qualified as a big leaguer.

Was Mechano also behind the blonde woman who had planted the small bomb in my pocket after the bank robbery? Maybe. That bomb was pretty much identical to the one I'd found in the holographic mall, only it had been smaller.

Were the other Sentinels in cahoots with Mechano? And why come after me? What in the heck did I ever do to Mechano or the Sentinels? They were Heroes. To a lot of people, they were *the* Heroes. Avatar himself had been a member of the Sentinels when he had been murdered. They weren't supposed to do things like hiring assassins and trying to kill people. They were the good guys. Or at least they were supposed to be.

I didn't know what was going on. I had more questions than answers.

Here's what I did know: I had finally earned a license and the right to wear a Hero's cape. As soon as I got out of this infirmary bed and was sworn in as a Hero, I was going to go after Mechano. I'd go up against every single one of the Sentinels if it turned out they were behind my father's death. I didn't care how powerful they were.

I had proven to myself I was powerful too.

The End

If you enjoyed this book, please leave a review on Amazon. Even a simple two word review such as "Loved it" helps so much. Reviews are a big aid in helping readers like you find books they might like.

ABOUT THE AUTHOR

Darius Brasher has a lifelong fascination with superheroes and a love of fantasy and science fiction. He has a Bachelor of Arts degree in English, a Juris Doctor degree in law, and a PhD from the School of Hard Knocks. He lives in South Carolina.

Email: darius@dbrasher.com
Patreon: www.patreon.com/dariusbrasher

facebook.com/dariusbrasher

twitter.com/dariusbrasher

amazon.com/author/dariusbrasher

Made in the USA
Monee, IL
01 March 2020